DEADLY RENDEZVOUS

The werewolf shook its head and roused itself, starting across the room with the slow confidence of a predator who has his prey cornered.

Angela raised the gun.

The werewolf stopped.

Both of them held very still. I can't do it, Angela thought, how can I do it, knowing who it is? Then she realized that it was *because* of who it was that she had to do it.

She heard soft sobbing from somewhere, and didn't even recognize her own voice...

HORROR AND DARK FANTASY
Published by ibooks, inc.:

THE VOODOO MOON TRILOGY
by Cheri Scotch
The Werewolf's Kiss
The Werewolf's Touch
The Werewolf's Sin
[coming January 2004]

The Ultimate Halloween
Marvin Kaye, Editor

The Ultimate Dracula
The Ultimate Frankenstein
The Ultimate Dragon
The Ultimate Alien
Byron Preiss, Editor

THE TWILIGHT ZONE
Book 1: Shades of Night, Falling
by John J. Miller
Book 2: A Gathering of Darkness
by Russell Davis

Psycho • Psycho II
by Robert Bloch

THE WEREWOLF'S TOUCH

THE VOODOO MOON TRILOGY
Book 2

CHERI SCOTCH

ibooks

new york
www.ibooks.net
DISTRIBUTED BY SIMON & SCHUSTER, INC.

To my worst nightmares and my most treasured dreams: those who transformed me, healed me, forced me through the fire so that I might be changed, and made me face my most primal fears so that I could be free of fear. To my two Dark Goddesses.

ACKNOWLEDGMENTS

To my mother, both fathers, and my two brothers: one here and one in the Land of Summer.

To Donna Norton Key, Father George Moore Acker, and Ray Garton for teaching me about the loving, comforting aspects of Christianity (although there's still no written apology from Vatican City for the Inquisition).

As always, to the Temple of Diana and our patron deities and guardian spirits.

And to the loups-garous of Bayou Goula, still keeping the faith. *Laissez les bon temps rouler*, and have a dance for me at the spring reunion.

THE
WEREWOLF'S
TOUCH

PART
ONE

†

Acquainted With Grief

1

I close my eyes and wait for the pain, not wanting to open them and catch sight of the moon. That's something I miss terribly: looking at the moon. I used to think it was the most beautiful thing, floating there placidly, glossed with silver or sometimes tinted with a mystic amber.

I was an imaginative kid with a classical education, and I'd read all about the Moon Goddess before I was ten. I used to imagine that the color indicated the Goddess's mood.

Yes, well. I know it makes me sound like a weird little boy, but I wasn't. On the contrary, I was a straight-arrow kid from a conservative family, and those nighttime forays into imagination made my life more interesting.

The dark never held the terrors for me that it did for other children. Even as a very young child, I loved the night, loved the magical darkness in which all things were possible and all dreams were made real. After I had been tucked into bed and the light put out, I'd creep quietly toward the window to look into the sky and feel that crisp air on my face, air that seemed more invigorating without the sunlight in it.

I was convinced that there were wonderful secrets to be mastered, daring deeds to be done. I was sure that the world changed under moonlight, the mundane daylight shapes becoming alive and fantastic. Moonlight made my imagination wander, bewitched me into strange, heroic fancies.

People changed under the moon. They became more mysterious, stronger, more beautiful.

God, how naive I was! Though time has proven me right,

I suppose. Still, being right is no comfort.

Now, even on my normal nights, I can't bear to look at the moon, as if a beloved Judas has betrayed me with a silvery kiss. It seduced me once, and it tortures me now.

But I *will* concede that not every werewolf feels this way. There are other werewolves in Louisiana—they're called loups-garous here—but none of them, so far as I can tell, lives under a curse. They don't see it as a curse at all, but a rare gift, and they've developed a complicated system of ethics for themselves.

I've never been able to accept that.

Looking at the moon, at the source of his strength, is supposed to be something a werewolf loves, even craves. But I can't do it. I go out on the bayou, I wait for the pain, and I never look up. I don't need to; my body tells me what's happening in the sky.

The moon. Ah, yes, I can feel her. There she is, my deceitful lover, hanging there as virginal as the Goddess herself, calling me again. And I'll go, damn her, I'll go . . . I'll do all the things she asks and more besides, until my bruised body aches with exhaustion and my soul shrivels with guilt.

And when the sun rises, then what? What am I supposed to do? Go back to my church and say a Mass for the dead? Make my confession and blurt out my own perverted passion as the blood of Christ spills from my shaking hands?

I was sitting in the pastor's study last night, trying to write my sermon as the choir rehearsed in the sanctuary, when the poignant strains of Handel distracted me. A contralto, her lush voice wrought with equal parts of artistry and emotion, sang in the dark tones of a bronze bell,

> *He was despised,*
> *rejected of men,*
> *a Man of Sorrows*
> *and acquainted with grief.*

And, setting aside my pen and prayer book, I gave in to a cleansing purge of self-pity.

If my congregation knew, I wonder what they'd do. Stone me? Burn me at the stake? Blast me with silver bullets?

But my tragedy is that I can't *stop* being a priest, it's all that holds me together. And I keep thinking that it will save me, in the end, that faith will give me a way out of this when everything else has failed.

So when the moon is finished with me for tonight and I stagger home, blinded by blood, I'll begin the story of the Marley werewolves, a nasty little tale of a good family gone bad. There's just so much *of* it: research papers, journals, letters, personal memories—amazing that with all this documentation, so little about the Marley curse was known. No one wanted to talk about it, you see? It was like some mad aunt locked in the attic. Only one in every generation of Marleys knew anything about it at all, and they certainly weren't going to tell. Then there are the things I found out for myself, through the most profound kind of pain. I want to try and make sense of it, put all the pieces here on the paper and fit them together so that I can see some kind of pattern, find some common pathway that leads this whole nightmare to an end.

This is for the next loup-garou to read in case I don't make it, to give him a place to start where I left off. I want him—or her—to know exactly what's happening to him and why, to know what's been tried and hasn't worked, perhaps to take a perverse comfort in the fact that he's not the first. Hell, he isn't even alone. I want him to understand what it is to be a child of God with a broken heart, and I want to give him the opportunity, in some small manner, to salvage his own soul.

—Andrew Marley
New Orleans

2

Beauty and the Beast
Georgiana Marley von Eisenbach, 1910

It was often said that Stephen Marley had the face of a suffering medieval saint and the soul of a grasping black spider. One would have thought that something dreadful had happened to him, some tragedy so deep that it left a physical mark. Certain devastating events *did* change him, but those came later. In his early thirties, however, the sharp planes of his face and his turquoise eyes set in the frame of his prematurely gray hair and short, silvery beard gave him a look of aesthetic monkishness. But his instincts in business were unfailingly predatory.

Gentlemen doing business with Stephen for the first time invariably mistook his distracted, unworldly attitude for weakness. They treated him with condescension right up to the moment he plunged his knife into their hearts and added their businesses to his own. More experienced men could have told them some grim tales, but in the presence of Stephen's quiet demeanor, they would never have believed them.

Stephen was an unerring observer. He missed nothing, and he always calculated the exact moment to strike with a swift ferocity that seemed demonic. He had arrived in New Orleans with nothing. A year later he had acquired his first ship. Four years later he was master of his own fleet, and the Marley Lines were famous all up and down the lucrative Mississippi routes.

But if he was ramrod steel in business, he was jelly in the hands of his wife and children. He had waited late to marry, being occupied with building his fortune, and he missed the comforts of a family. Now that he had them, he was going to enjoy his four children to the fullest. If they were happy, he was happy.

And now Georgiana, his oldest child, was getting married and there wasn't a young man in New Orleans who wasn't desolate about it.

It wasn't that Georgiana was blindingly beautiful. Although she had inherited her father's startling turquoise eyes, she was pretty but not extraordinary. In fact, nobody could quite put his finger on what it was that made people love Georgiana. Her father came closest to it when he remarked, "Geo has spirit." It was that energy, that unashamed joy of living, that attracted people to her, and in the gathering darkness that would soon be a devastating world war, they moved closer to Georgiana, as if her level-headed optimism could recharge their lagging spirits. To Georgiana, the mere act of day-to-day living was a wonder. She always seemed to be having a good time, even doing the simplest things.

It was no accident that she was having twelve brides-maids. She privately told her mother that she thought twelve was way too showy, but she just couldn't cut the list down: the girls were all close friends of hers.

Georgiana was a prime example of the kind of girl the South turns out so well, the southern princess. So nobody was really surprised when Geo decided to marry an authentic prince.

She had met him when she and two other girls had taken the grand tour after graduation. The girls had been strictly chaperoned against just that sort of thing, but Geo, never

shy about talking to strangers, had fallen into conversation
with the young man at the opera in Vienna. The prince's
father had done quite a bit of shipping on the Marley Lines
over the years and knew Stephen quite well. Stephen took
the news of the engagement as well as could be expected
for an overprotective father.

Stephen and Georgiana stood now in the foyer of St. Louis
Cathedral, surrounded by a dozen young girls in floating
blue silk, Stephen a fidgeting wreck, and Georgiana still as
a clear harbor on a quiet afternoon. She seemed weightless
as air to Stephen, buoyed by clouds of white satin, pearls,
and pink roses, trailing a fountain of lace behind her. She
looked as perfect as he had ever seen her, and so young as
to break his heart.

She glanced through the doors, then back at her father,
and caught the stricken look in his eyes.

"Papa, don't be so upset!" she said with a laugh. "It's
only marriage!"

"And I thought I looked properly happy."

"You look perfectly ghastly. In fact, you look every bit
as bad as Kiril." She peeked through the doors to glance
at her prince, just emerging shakily from the side door with
his best man, Georgiana's eighteen-year-old brother, Robert.
"You don't think he'll be this nervous tonight, do you? He
doesn't look like he'll survive the wedding night."

Six of the bridesmaids had already started down the
aisle. The six remaining gave shocked little giggles. Trust
Georgiana to say something daring at a time like this.

"Good God, Geo!" Stephen said, "I thought I'd raised you
vith more modesty than that!"

She smiled wickedly. "I'm going to give you all those
grandchildren you're forever talking about."

"I don't want to think about it."

The last bridesmaid stepped through the doors.

"Papa!" Geo said in a voice that was suddenly small and fearful. "Kiss me before we go."

Stephen felt his eyes burn as he did.

"I love you, Papa. Try not to miss me."

"Not miss you! You're my firstborn, Geo. I don't even know how to begin to tell you what that means."

"I guess I'll find out for myself. I'm going to be a wife and mother, Papa! It's all I ever wanted. My life is beginning now."

Stephen knew that was true. Georgiana had never wanted anything other than a husband and children, unlike her younger sister Melissa, who—God help us all!—was talking about women's suffrage and making every indication that she was going to help her two brothers run the Marley Lines someday instead of getting respectably married. Stephen had no doubt at all that Melissa would do it too, and embarrassingly well.

"Well, I guess it's our turn, Papa," Geo said. Her sudden nervousness was gone and with it every trace of her childhood. To Stephen, she looked already married; it was as if he could see his daughter as she would be, a confident wife, a superb mother; still his child, of course, but someone else as well.

Stephen brought his daughter down the aisle of the cathedral and entrusted her into the care of another man. Oddly enough, he felt much happier about it than he thought he would.

Georgiana and Kiril were spending their wedding night at the Marley summer house on Lake Ponchartrain.

At two in the morning, Stephen's wife, Cyrie, was awakened by a single, strangled word spoken in the darkness. The voice was so eerie that Cyrie clutched her pillow in sudden fright. Then she saw Stephen sitting up next to her, shaking, his nightclothes soaked with sweat.

"Stephen?" Cyrie asked. "Who is Blanche?"

His head jerked and his eyes widened in terror. "Where did you hear that name?"

"You said it in your sleep. It was the strangest sound I ever heard. You said 'Blanche' in this eerie voice."

Stephen tried to remember if he had been having another nightmare: nothing else had ever produced this kind of terror. He wiped his sleeve across his forehead and rested his head on his knees. Blanche, he thought, after all these years, she still comes after me. Just when I think I've forgotten, she sends another nightmare.

Cyrie turned up the bedside lamp and pulled on her robe. "I'm going to get you a wet cloth for your head," she said, "and a nice cup of tea. I think you may be starting a cold."

His fear started to congeal into something real, and he knew that the center of it lay in the summer house on the lake.

He tried to be quiet as he pulled on his clothes but he was shaking so badly that he kept dropping things and bumping into furniture. He knocked over a small table just as Cyrie came back.

"Stephen, you shouldn't be up," Cyrie said, "you're white as a sheet!" She touched his arm. "And you're freezing! Get back into bed immediately and I'll call—"

"There's something wrong at the lake house," he said tightly, pulling on his shoes. "I've got to get out there."

"Are you insane? It's their wedding night!"

"I tell you, there's something awful happening there. I can't tell you how I know, Cyrie, but I *do know*!"

She took his arm. "Don't do this. You'll hate yourself forever for it. You're just upset at losing your baby, you had a bad dream, and you're probably still a little drunk from the reception. Really, Stephen, Georgiana's fine."

He kissed her quickly. "If she isn't, you'll hate me for not doing anything. I promise you I'll use discretion. Geo and Kiril will think of me as simply a doddering old fool; on their anniversary they'll laugh about this and I'll become a family anecdote."

"Stephen!"

He was already gone.

As he got closer to the lake house the sense of a cataclysmic horror grew stronger. It was so bad that by the time he knocked on the front door a blanket of weakness smothered him. He leaned against the door to keep from falling, and it swung wide open against his hands.

Suddenly he was confused. It struck him that he had created an indelicate situation, and most probably for nothing. Cyrie was right; his panic was simply nothing more than a middle-aged man's refusal to admit that his children were growing away from him. He hesitated to go in, standing immobile in the doorway trying to decide what to do.

He had just decided to turn around and salvage his dignity when an ugly sound distracted him.

It was a savage, repulsive noise, a ripping and sucking sound, as if an enormous starving animal were feeding.

A faint light showed down the hall, through the half-open bedroom door upstairs. Stephen pulled himself up stair by stair, having to overcome a fresh fear with each one, as the sound became louder, more greedy, mixed with soft animal grunts and the thud of a heavy body shifting position.

Stephen couldn't help it: a half-muffled scream came rolling uncontrollably out of him.

The sound from the bedroom stopped instantly.

He pushed open the bedroom door, and the smell of blood in the room was so overpowering that, at first, he didn't see the body.

Kiril had most likely been trying to get out of the opened window, as if his way to the door had been blocked and the window was his only escape. He had been caught by the window, then dragged back across the room, leaving a huge, smeared track of blood across the floor. His throat was torn out and his body mutilated, a red gorge ripped through the left side, broken white ribs pushing through the torn tissues. Two of the ribs lay beside the body, as if whoever had killed him had discarded them like useless paper packing in a box.

Stephen would have fainted right there if it weren't for his panic about Georgiana. She was nowhere in sight. The need to get out of that room, away from the sight and stench of violent death, overwhelmed him. He made a quick, frantic search of the house, terrified of what he might see if he found her, but she was gone.

The beach was a long blank stretch lit by moonlight. Was she there? In the water? Had she been carried off by the murderer or had she wandered away in shock? Stephen could see nothing there, and the only sound was the lapping water breaking on the shore.

Something hit him hard from behind, pushing into him so powerfully that it almost knocked him off his feet. With his old instincts, he jabbed backward with his elbows, catching the attacker just below the ribs. There was an explosion of foul, carrion breath behind him as he spun around.

He couldn't believe what had attacked him.

It was half-beast, half-human, easily seven or eight feet tall, crouched on the ground like a cowed dog, curled up and whimpering in pain. It wasn't his backward blow that had stopped it; nothing that he could have done would have made a dent in a monster that big. Something was happening to it.

It let out a nerve-shattering howl of pain, raising its arms to cover its head as it shook from side to side in a fear that it couldn't express in words. It raised its head briefly, extending an arm to Stephen as if to plead for help, and he caught a glimpse of its eyes, not the eyes of a dumb beast as he had expected, but the eyes of a soul overwhelmed by sorrow.

The pity in him was so unexpected that it was a moment before he recognized those eyes.

Stephen was unable to move, watching the monster in its metamorphosis. Its pain must have been excruciating: he could see the muscles stretch beneath the skin, pulling and knotting under the shaggy, blood-matted coat, the body bending into fantastic shapes as if it were paper being crumpled and smoothed out again. There was no more howling— the agony must have been too intense for that—but the panting and the long intervals between breath and silence were more unnerving than the cries had been.

And when the transformation was over, and his daughter lay shuddering and vomiting in the summer night, Stephen knew that not even God would save him.

"What have you done?" Georgiana said. Her voice, rasping and rough, hurt him. Her words ripped him like a knife through silk.

He put out his hand to her, but she sliced at it reflexively with her claws. "Don't touch me," she said. "It's not finished."

They both watched in repelled fascination as the claws shortened, changed color, and became human fingernails.

He took off his jacket, intending to wrap it around her, but she flinched as he came near and he stopped, frozen in humiliation. She put out her hand and took the jacket, not looking at him as she covered herself, still shivering with exhaustion.

"I killed Kiril." She spoke slowly and precisely, as if she were trying to retain control over at least this much of her own body. "I became this monster and I murdered him. Every night of every full moon, for as long as I live, someone will die exactly like that."

Stephen moaned. Blanche, he thought again. And he knew as clearly as he had ever known anything that she would never leave him. She was his most constant lover, the fixed, dark star that would eclipse his life.

But Georgiana had to tell it, and he had to listen. "I was in the bedroom, undressing. Kiril had gone out for a walk on the beach. Then something was wrong, a pain so terrible that I couldn't stand up. I was afraid I was dying! I felt someone touch me, very lightly, and there was a woman, just about my age, with the most fantastic hair. There were yards of it, clouds of it, catching the moonlight, just like silver. It was so fascinating that even the pain seemed to stop for a minute.

"I kept looking at that hair and my eyes couldn't focus. It was so strange—as if her hair had become a mirror. I was looking *into* it, where I could see movement, madness; I could hear a distant, insane laughter. She told me that I was about to make a payment on an old debt. Yours. That because of what you did to her, the firstborn of every Marley generation will suffer, and always on the most wonderful night of our lives, when we've gotten what we've always wanted. I asked her—I *begged* her—to tell me what you had done, why this was happening, but she only laughed.

"And then she said, 'Tell your father that Blanche has not forgotten him.'

"I remember fainting—I remember that clearly. And when I woke up, I was changed."

Georgiana's voice broke off and her eyes looked blank. The silence of the night seemed to be speaking to her in sounds that only she could hear.

"What was it?" she pleaded with Stephen. "Who is Blanche and what did you do to her that she had to destroy me?"

Stephen was struck dumb.

"Every night," she whispered, "every night of every full moon."

As Georgiana rocked back and forth on the ground, nestling in despair, Stephen's screams echoed across the water.

A single name, repeated under the full moon, that had now become an instrument of revenge.

After what they had been through that night, the next few days were not as difficult for Stephen and Georgiana as they were for everyone else. They clung together, a father and his shattered daughter, away from the workings of the police and the grief of the family. The relatives would discover them sitting in close chairs, their heads together, engaged in long, intense conversations conducted in muted voices that stopped when someone else entered the room.

No one even suspected Georgiana. The very idea of a frail little woman committing a murder so malignant was unthinkable. When the police were summoned to the lake house, Georgiana was understandably incoherent from the shock of having come in from a lakeside stroll to find the body. The police, who knew Stephen as the owner of the powerful Marley Steamship Lines, were respectfully cautious of the lady's emotional state.

Because Kiril had been a prince, and because Europe was in turmoil and untrustworthy foreigners stalked the streets of New Orleans, the police decided that the murder had been the work of an "anarchist."

At the next full moon, Georgiana disappeared. When she didn't join the family for dinner, they all panicked.

"She could be anywhere! She could be wandering the streets!" Cyrie wailed. "I tell you, that girl is just unhinged by grief. I never should have left her alone!"

Stephen was about to call the police when Melissa put her hand on his arm. He looked at his youngest child, whose twelve-year-old eyes looked much older.

"She'll be back in a day or two," Melissa said quietly.

"What do you know, Melissa?" Stephen said. He could feel the hairs on his neck standing up.

"She left the house about three this afternoon. I saw her, and she saw me but she didn't say anything, just smiled and put her finger over her lips. She was carrying a little overnight bag; it couldn't have had more than one change of clothes in it. I think," Melissa said, her brows furrowing, "that Geo just needs to be alone for a while. Everybody deserves to be alone sometimes. So they can do what they want and not have to explain to other people."

Out of the whole family, Stephen thought, Melissa may just be the wisest. He decided to give Georgiana the time she needed.

And Georgiana did return in a day or two, with no explanation of where she'd been other than she'd been "visiting friends." She wouldn't say who these mysterious friends were.

"I can't stay here," Geo told Stephen when they were alone.

"Geo, please," Stephen pleaded, "just give me time to think of something to do."

"What is there to be done?" she said. "My whole life is being reduced to a choice: do I kill innocent people, or do I do the honorable thing and kill myself? You understand about honor, don't you, Papa?"

Those moments of bitter blame from Georgiana made him wonder why any other curse was necessary.

"I'm sorry, Papa." Her voice sounded tired. "I just can't seem to stop myself from hurting you. Sometimes I look at you and I feel such hatred. I know it's not reasonable, but if I stay, it will get worse. Eventually there'll be nothing but that resentment between us. If I go, perhaps I'll get over it in time. And I can't face the family and friends anymore, knowing how I'm deceiving them—and maybe even putting them in danger." She sighed and spoke hesitantly. "Besides, I've been . . . given to understand that there might be some help for me . . . elsewhere."

"Elsewhere?" he said. "Where? What kind of help? From whom?"

She held up her hand to halt the questions. "I was told . . . well, I just can't go into it. At any rate, I want to go away. No one will question that. A grief-stricken widow always needs a change of scene."

She did leave, the next week, supposedly to friends of her mother's in Biloxi. But after a few days, the friends wrote to ask when she was coming, and Stephen knew that Georgiana had followed her own path.

After another year there was a telegram from a woman who claimed to have been Georgiana's traveling companion in Europe. It said only that Georgiana had died there, and that, according to her wishes, her body had been cremated and the ashes scattered over the channel. A small package came a week after that; a gleaming lock of Georgiana's hair tied up in a turquoise ribbon just the color of her eyes, and her wedding ring.

Haunted by his daughter and his knowledge, Stephen became only an observer of his own family. He watched without participation as his children grew up and married, his work and his fortune given over into their hands. He stopped going to Mass because as he knelt before God's sacrifice for man's sins, it was too sharp a reminder that his own child had suffered for his.

In time, he convinced himself that Georgiana had been misled, and that the curse had expended its force on her.

He never spoke of what happened to her, never even wrote it in his most personal diaries, certain that the family, if it suspected, would be afraid to breed and would die out.

But some years later, when his oldest son married and had Stephen's first grandchild, Walter, he refused to look at the baby, terrified that he would see Georgiana's eyes still accusing him. That year, in a paroxysm of strangling grief, he died, his spirit defeated by too much pain and too little hope.

Of all the guilt that weighed on him, one transgression stood out more sharply: that despite her pleas and her perfect right to know, he had never been able to tell Georgiana what he had done to Blanche Pitre.

PART TWO

†

The Mark of the Beast

3

Walter Devaux Marley, 1961

It was curious that Captain Stephen Marley's great love for the sea was passed intact to his grandson, Walter. But where Stephen's sea was all wild wind and swirling water, Walter's was shimmering heat and unstable sand, or dark Sargassos of African vegetation that vibrated with an unseen, secret life. The sight of the land stretching away to the horizon gave Walter the same calm that the sea gave the old captain, and evoked the same mystery.

It was always a little too much for Walter. He would find himself staring out over the landscape with awe, thinking, What's *under* there? What's it hiding?

For most of his life, he'd prodded the thick skin of the earth until it got used to him and began to trust him, yielding up its treasures one at a time, in tiny precious bits.

Finally, it rewarded him for the years of backbreaking work, the long stretches of time spent coaxing ancient stories from unwilling sand. Others had found lost cities, gilded tombs and treasure stores, but Walter was given something more important. He found the original hand that had shaped them all. The gentleman he dug out of the womb of the earth, predating anything yet discovered and changing the ideas of evolution, was as real to Walter as the men he worked with. Touching the old bones with awestruck respect, he had insisted that the fragile remains be treated with dignity. He saw his work as a means of becoming reacquainted with the dead, giving them another chance to tell their stories.

Walter Marley's wife, Johanna, and his twenty-two-year-old son, Andrew, were giving him the noisiest, rowdiest party ever thrown for a Nobel Laureate.

In the years Walter had been with Tulane University, he had never been sure that some of his older colleagues were capable of moving from behind a lectern, but here they all were, smiling and laughing and sucking up the champagne, generally enjoying themselves. Walter loved it all. He caught old Dean Robinson dancing an arthritic but game Lindy Hop. Every movement was just a little behind the music, but by God, the old boy was having a good time!

Stephen Marley's venerable house was certainly shaking its foundations tonight. Too bad the old captain wasn't alive to join in, but everyone else in New Orleans seemed to be invited. Anyone who had ever known Walter in a professional or civilian capacity was there.

People dropped in and out; the tide of guests ebbed and flowed around the house. Noisy, laughing guests of every age filled the house and overflowed onto the verandas and the lawn. People took bottles of champagne and glasses, and formed small individual parties on the stairs and in the garden: some for serious discussions, some for uncontrollable laughter, some for reunions of old friends who had been separated by time and academic fortune. Several parties of two formed in inconspicuous corners.

Walter felt contented, wrapped in a raucous, energetic cocoon of laughter, music, and voices.

He saw one of the faculty relics slap Andrew chummily on the back.

"Well, boy," the man said, "I guess you're proud of your old man tonight, eh?"

Walter figured that Andrew had heard that one at least fifty times already, but he marveled at the boy's ability to make each response sound fresh. Andrew had unusual patience (which he had inherited from him) and wonderful tact (which could only have come from Johanna).

A creamy redhead with conspicuous cleavage, holding a glass of champagne in each hand, kissed Walter on the cheek. "Hey, *laissez le bon temps rouler*, sweetie. This is the best party I've been to since Mardi Gras."

Walter laughed. "My, my . . . you *are* letting the good times roll. Are you drinking for two now, Angela?"

"I wish. This other one here's for Dr. Campbell. He's too drunk to stand up and get his own."

"Angela, you've got to say hello to somebody," he said, motioning Andrew over.

Andrew made his way over to his father. "Andrew, you remember Dr. Winfield? She's joined the department . . . well, rejoined, rather."

"Goddamn!" Angela said in surprise. "Andrew! Jesus, you were eighteen when I saw you last, and that was . . . what?"

"Four years ago. You were finished with your dissertation and you were going back home to the University of Texas. Now, I see, you're the most beautiful full professor Tulane's got."

"Honey, that is just the most sexist and the most appreciated remark I've heard all year. I'd hug ya, but I don't want to spill Dr. Campbell's champagne. So what have you been doing with your handsome self? Did you graduate or what?"

Walter couldn't help breaking in. "He's studying for the priesthood, is that terrific? He's already been accepted to a seminary in Wisconsin. Accepted this morning, in fact, so this party's a double celebration."

Angela took a step back and looked at Andrew—all over—which made him blush. "Well, all I can say, toots," she said slowly, raising one eyebrow, "is that it's a good thing you're an Episcopalian. All that Catholic celibacy is just not healthy, as your daddy would be the first to tell you. Episcopalian priests can fool around, right?"

Andrew looked confused. "Well . . . they can *marry,* but . . ."

"Marriage!" Angela said with a slight gasp, as if she'd just said "syphilis." "But, honey, why make one woman miserable when you can make lots of them so happy?"

Andrew blushed again and his father laughed.

"*I'm* still a Catholic," Walter said, "and the Marleys in England are. Do you have any idea how hard it is to be an English Catholic? Everywhere you look, the damned Anglicans are there with their confessionals and their holy water and their incense. Many a confused Catholic wanders into Canterbury thinking he's in the sheltering arms of Rome. By then, of course, they've got you by the spiritual short hairs."

Sighing, Andrew put his arm around Walter's shoulder and looked sympathetically at Angela. "You see what I'm up against. I tried to get him to convert, but he's terrified that someday he'll be making his confession and I'll be on the other side of the box."

"He has a memory like an elephant," Walter declared. "I keep thinking of all those times I forced him to finish his Brussels sprouts."

Dr. Winfield sipped some champagne and thought it over. "Aw, go on, Walter. What's he gonna do? Make you say six Hail Marys, take away your car keys, and ground you? Come on, sweet thing," she said, dragging Andrew away by the arm, "just let me pour this down ol' Dr. Campbell's throat, then we can dance and maybe you'll convert me."

He allowed himself to be led away, and Walter noticed that he didn't even blush this time.

An hour later, Walter watched Angela undulate against Andrew as they danced. For a while, they were doing more laughing and talking than dancing, then the talking turned to whispering and the dancing to barely moving. Eventually, when Angela looked up at Andrew and licked her lips, his hand slowly slid down her back to her buttocks and pulled her closer.

Walter laughed. Andrew might be inexperienced, but he was certainly willing to learn.

A half hour later, Walter was able to slip away and into the kitchen for a few minutes of relative privacy. He expected to find four or five people there, but found only Johanna, frantically filling more platters.

"Where are the rent-a-maids?" he asked, picking up a carrot stick.

"Circulating," she laughed. "They're probably having a better time than I am. The caterer's people are taking a break on the porch."

"Speaking of a good time, I think Angela Winfield's about to seduce our son. Or maybe," he said, considering, "it's the other way around."

"What! Oh, Walter, you've got to stop her. She's ten years older than he is!"

"What do you want me to do? Hose them down?" He laughed and nearly choked on his carrot stick. "He's grown now, honey; he can do as he likes. Besides, Angela's considerate. She won't bite him."

"I've always been too embarrassed to ask him if he was . . . still . . ." She gestured helplessly. "Oh, you know."

"If you're worried about his virginity, I think it's about to become a moot point."

She laughed and wiped her hands on a towel. "The worried mom. I should be worried about you. I haven't seen you for an hour." She put her arms around his neck and pressed close to him. "Some party! Are you enjoying it?"

"Well, I'm certainly enjoying *this*," he said, feeling her body against his chest.

"I'm so excited," she said in a husky whisper. "I've always wanted to sleep with a Nobel Laureate. They're so distinguished. Let's go upstairs, so I can see if you do it any differently now."

"You're kidding, right? Oh, Jo . . . don't do that," he said as she started to move against him. "A hundred people out there and why are you doing this to me?"

He knew the answer to that one. She did it because she could. Twenty-three years of marriage and nobody had ever moved him like Johanna could.

"Honey, please," he said seriously, "I feel kind of strange. Can you go out there and be charming while I get some fresh air?"

She pulled back and put an analytical hand on his forehead. "Oh my, you do feel a little feverish. Maybe you should lie down?"

"Still trying to talk me into it, eh? Sweetheart, it's just excitement and exhaustion. Ever since I got the notification from Stockholm things have been going nuts. I'm trying to remember when I last sat down, and I've done plenty of boozing here. If you can just keep everybody happy for a while, I'll be fine."

"Don't worry about it. Nobody's any soberer than you; they won't notice. Besides, it's late and the party's breaking up. I'll ask Andrew to cover for you. He knows how to play host."

"I wouldn't count on him," he laughed, starting out the back door.

"Hey, wait a minute!" she said, catching his arm. "Just don't stay out past bedtime. Remember, to the victor go the spoils."

"It'll be a short walk," he assured her, giving her a quick kiss.

She doubted it. Walter's walks sometimes turned out to be interminable nature hikes. He couldn't pass a patch of weeds without telling Johanna about the medicinal uses of each one. He came home with his clothes stretched out of shape because he'd overfilled his pockets with unusual rocks he might want to study later. (He never got around to it, though. She always ended up putting the prettiest of them into the fish tanks.)

Once, he'd completely forgotten that he was on his way to the dentist's because he'd seen a street excavation and, glancing down, saw old seventeenth-century house timber that had been built over when New Orleans was still digging its way out of the swamp. He'd eased right down into the gluey mud with the workmen.

When he took these walks, Johanna was never sure when he'd show up at home, loaded down with artifacts valuable only to him, usually filthy dirty, sometimes with ripped pocket seams.

All of this could have been mildly annoying, but she found it endearing. That curiosity about everything around him was what attracted her to him in the first place.

Well . . . that was only partly true. The first time she saw him it was an overwhelming physical attraction. Nothing like that had ever happened to her before.

She'd been a Sophie Newcomb College journalism major on a summer internship with the New Orleans States-Item, covering a dig that the Tulane anthropology department was involved with in Texas. She'd asked the supervisor, Dr. Foss, if she could interview some of the students.

"Over there," Dr. Foss had said, pointing to the dig area. "Talk to Walter Marley. He's the best we've got."

Johanna squinted into the sun. "Which one *is* he?"

Foss laughed. "The big one. About six foot three. Black hair. He just started to grow a beard and he looks like Bigfoot. You'll know him when you see him, don't worry."

He was lying on his stomach, patiently brushing dirt away from a foot-square area, wearing tiny track shorts that had hitched way up on one side, exposing an absolutely sensational ass. Johanna tried to look away, but it was like a rabbit staring at a python. When Walter finally noticed she was there and smiled up at her, she got the full effect of those turquoise eyes. She was suddenly, terribly confused. She had always preferred brainy, bookish men, the kind of intellectuals that varied from the slightly neurotic to the frankly eccentric. This tall, tanned anthropologist with his self-confident attitude and his athlete's body didn't look like any Phi Beta Kappa she'd ever met.

She wasn't confused enough not to realize that Walter Marley was going to change her life and her ideas about men, in one way or another.

Later, she asked around and found out that Walter was a Sophie Newcomb legend. Girls who had dated him tended to get blurry around the eyes when they talked about him, but they all had the same advice: Don't expect anything permanent, just relax, lie back, and enjoy the ride while it lasts. It'll be sensational.

After all these years, it still was.

Johanna was pretty sure she'd fall asleep alone tonight, and tomorrow she'd feel Walter warm and solid beside her, his nature-walk treasures spread out over newspapers on the kitchen table.

Outside, in the faintly smoky October air, Walter took a deep breath to clear the slight ringing in his ears. He looked up at the moon, a full, gold-touched witch's moon, thinking that he would remember this night, this moment, until he was very, very old. He fixed it firmly in his memory: A rare moment of contentment when his life was complete and everything was good.

The celebratory sounds from the house grew fainter as he crossed St. Charles and faded into the quiet of Audubon Park. After a while he was alone in the night-shaded woods, so deep that no sound could make its way out. Only the zoo animals, floating their cries across the air, heard Walter's first startled screams.

The party was, by that time, rolling along of its own momentum. That the guest of honor was absent was hardly noticed.

"So tell me about your decision to become a priest," Angela said to Andrew, "and don't tell me you've just always wanted to help people."

He shrugged and smiled. "I want to help myself, I think. I've always thought that a priest learns more about life and faith from his parishioners than they learn from him."

"Sounds very humbling," she told him.

"It is if you do it right," he said. "A priest has to remember that he's no messiah: he's only a guide, a teacher, and the day your students surpass you is the greatest day of your life."

"And what's your position on sin?"

"Missionary," he said without thinking and she laughed.

"I was looking for a serious answer, but I guess that's serious enough."

He grew quiet for a minute, thinking. "I'm probably going to come to a misunderstanding with the church about this, but what most people think of as sin, I just can't find terribly sinful. Oh, I guess you could say that sin is anything you feel guilty about, but that's too facile. Guilt is something you're taught, not something you're born with. I suppose that sin is anything that haunts you, that cripples you, keeps you from being happy and content with your life. The church has trivialized sin: we assign different weights to it: mortal, cardinal, venial, as if it were something you could categorize. But committing a sin isn't fatal; *living* with it is, if you let it destroy you. And I think that a good priest is one who can teach the difference between real sin and those petty mortal failings we all have, and show people that nothing is ever unforgivable—even by yourself."

He shrugged, a little abashed at his own fervor. "At least, that's the kind of priest I hope I'll be."

Angela looked frankly into his face and seemed to be reevaluating him.

"I think you have a lot of your father about you," she told Andrew.

"I suppose I don't have a problem with that, but I'd like to feel like my own man, judged on my own merits. That maybe why I turned to religion and not science. Freudian enough for you?"

"That's not what I meant. Walter is a seeker after truth, one of the last of the idealists. Even in his work. It isn't perfection he looks for, it's that absolute reality, no matter how gritty or unpleasant it may turn out to be. He doesn't care what it looks like or smells like or acts like so long as it's true. You know, I think that even the Nobel Prize doesn't mean much to him in terms of the honor or the recognition— or the money: I think it's the validation of his beliefs that delights him. His only passion is for truth."

Andrew considered this. "You're right, but you're also wrong. I'll tell you something I'll bet you never knew about him. Dad is the last romantic. And I mean in the Shelley and Byron tradition. Women were crazy for him, they flocked around him, still do. But he was looking for that one great love, that grand passion, and when he found my mother, that was it. He stopped looking and there was never anyone else for him. He'd found that passion—I suppose if you want to call it the ultimate truth, that's accurate. He knew that Johanna could truly understand and accept him, the way he understood and accepted truth. I think that women wanted my father for a lot of reasons: because he was handsome and intelligent, because he was rich, because he was socially acceptable. But Mother wanted him because she could talk to him, and she didn't seem to care about the rest."

"A wonderful thing," Angela said, "and rare. To meet on that common ground where intelligence and passion balance. And what about you? What are you looking for?"

He thought about it, and Angela watched his face change from thoughtful, to wistful, then back to mischievous.

"Me?" he said lightly. "I'm off to the seminary. So I suppose that all I have time to look for is a good fuck."

She seemed like she would say more, but thought better of it.

"Well, then," she said in that black-satin voice, "how very fortunate that we ran into each other."

"Probably time to dance," he said, pulling her to her feet as a slow, sexy song began.

"I just remembered what it was about you that I liked so much," Andrew told Angela as they danced.

"The fact that I don't wear underwear?" Angela whispered in his ear.

He let out a brief burst of laughter. "That's nice to know, but no. It's your unashamed courage. You say exactly what's on your mind, don't you?"

She drew away only slightly and looked up at him, her eyes not so confident as before, and this mystified him.

"Not always," she said softly. "Sometimes, to let people know what you're thinking is to make yourself vulnerable."

Then, with her familiar seductive brashness: "Anyway, pious cleric or not, it shouldn't be too hard for you to guess what's on my mind."

"Oh, *lady*," he said, and pulled her closer.

"Since you think I'm so honest, I'm going to tell you a secret," she said, looking straight into his eyes. "When I first met you, even though you were only eighteen, I wanted you. I didn't want to love you, didn't want to hold you forever, didn't want to have your children and a house in the Garden District; I just wanted to fuck you until we both dropped from exhaustion, until we'd done everything imaginable between a man and a woman. I'd never felt such a rush of pure lust before. It was almost overwhelming."

He looked delighted. "Why didn't you say something?"

She shrugged. "Because you were eighteen," she said with perfect logic.

"And now? Did the feeling pass?"

She held still for a moment, then took his hand and guided it between her legs. Even through her dress, he felt the heat.

He was suddenly as overcome as she was. It was if his mind had become blank except for just this one rampage of lust, rising instantaneously as if from nowhere. He realized that he had been attracted to Angela before, but now it all melded together in a blinding, red rush.

He was later absolutely astounded at the audacity of what he did next, but at the moment he was unable to stop himself. He looked down at Angela, first at her eyes to confirm what he already knew, then at her parted lips, following the line of her translucent skin down her throat to her slightly exposed breasts. Her black dress was fastened with what looked to him like hundreds of tiny rhinestone buttons down the front.

He touched one finger, very gently, to the first button.

Angela gasped slightly and closed her eyes.

His finger continued, down the buttons, not undoing them, just sliding past them slowly until his hand cupped her gently at her cleft. Then, he undid the four buttons covering just that spot, just that center of her where her heat and her scent stirred him almost to insanity.

She had told the truth, he discovered. She *didn't* wear underwear.

Not believing he was doing it, he pulled her closer, so no one could see, and slid his hand between her legs, plunging his middle finger partially inside her. The tightness, the warmth of her, the sudden images, almost blinded him.

She gasped again and her eyes opened wide, then closed as she moaned almost inaudibly and dropped her head against his chest. She moved slightly to open herself wider for him.

He moved his thumb instinctively against her clitoris, and felt her response. She tightened her arms around him, her fingers gripping his back as if she had to hold on to keep from falling.

Then, "Enough," she said sternly.

He froze, startled and slightly dizzy with a quick rush of embarrassment. He had never done anything so brash before and was amazed that he could do it now, and enjoy it so much.

She pulled back, only a hair's breadth. "We're leaving," she said. "Right now. Four years is long enough to wait."

He nodded, not able to speak. He managed to close the buttons, whether correctly or not, he couldn't tell.

"One second," he said, and moved away so quickly that she was left standing in that same spot, that same position, confused.

When he returned only a few moments later, he was carrying a bottle of champagne, the cold condensing into frosted droplets on the dark green glass. He put his arm around her shoulders and guided her out of the room, through the French doors to the veranda, and into the now-magical October night.

Much later, when they were at the point of physical exhaustion but too driven to let go, a strange sound from outside in the night filtered through the open window.

The far-off howling of a wolf.

"From the zoo," Angela murmured sleepily.

But the solitary sound, as desolate as anything Andrew had ever heard, touched some fearful place inside him and caused him such confusion and such a strange illogical sense of grief that he pulled Angela closer to him, covering her body with his own and, still in his erotic half sleep, plunged himself into her again, drowning his unnameable apprehension beneath the wild waters of sensuality.

It could have been minutes, it could have been hours that Walter twisted on the ground with his knees jammed to his chest, pain like liquid fire seeping through every inch of his skin, through the muscle, down to the bone. It had come upon him so suddenly that the surprise and the agony had been simultaneous.

After the first few screams, the pain was so intense that he lost the power of speech. It hurt his throat to make sounds, it hurt his ears to hear them.

His body was burning, but the sweat washing him was like a film of ice.

A hand grazed his shoulder, a tiny tap, light as the flutter of a night moth, but his skin was so raw that the gentle touch made him gasp.

A woman stepped into his line of vision, her face clouded with concern as she bent to look at him. She was as beautiful as the pain was ugly, her silvery hair against the moon making a halo of light around her perfect face.

He almost laughed in relief. His delivering angel come to wrest him from death!

"Thank God!" Walter wept. "Thank God somebody's come along!" He made a terrific effort to sound rational and calm, so as not to scare her into running away. "Please . . . I think I'm having a heart attack. Get help!"

"But I always come," she said in a voice like a pretty bird. "When the pain begins, when it happens the first time, I'm always there."

The absurdity of what she'd said didn't even register with him. "Please. Go get someone! Don't let me die here!"

She had the most charming smile. "You're not going to die," she said, as if she were scolding a slightly silly child. "Did you think that's what was happening to you? No, no . . . let me show you what's going to happen. You're about to be reborn, Walter!"

She bent closer, and her hair formed a silver curtain, brushing his skin with pain where it touched. It seemed to solidify, turning into a mirror lined with moving mercury.

The hallucinations of fever made pictures in the mirror. He saw his reflection in the polished face, or what he took to be his reflection. As he looked deeper, he saw himself writhing on the ground, then rising, running, howling. . . .

"It's your time, Walter," she told him. "Your payment is due on your grandfather's debt. The firstborn of every generation of Marleys will know me, on the greatest night of their lives, at their greatest moment of triumph." She leaned a little closer and Walter could smell death on the wind of her breath. "You believed that after this night your life would change. And so it will, but not as you wanted it. Your life now will be bound up with the changes of the moon, and you'll never think of one without the other."

An old, primal fear from childhood and beyond stirred

in Walter, and he asked without regard to rational thought, "Are you the Devil?"

She threw back her head and laughed, the sound scraping his nerves. Then she leaned in close again, the madness in her eyes glowing. "Sweet Walter, I'm the nightmare the Devil has when he dreams of damnation."

Walter understood everything that was happening to him, and would happen for the rest of his life. He did scream then, not from the pain but from the soul.

And when he did, she laughed.

Ah, God, how wonderful it felt! He arched his back off the ground, stretching his limbs in pleasure, just to feel their strength. He flexed his fingers, now extended a good three inches by slightly curved, bearlike claws. He held one hand up before his face to consider those claws. How odd, he thought, marveling at them, they were black and strong as wrought iron, like those deceptively delicate swirls of balconies in the French Quarter.

He took a deep, self-satisfied breath and stood up. The familiar landscape of Audubon Park looked a little strange, out of kilter, just ever so slightly different. Then he realized that, for one thing, he was looking at it from a new height, perhaps eight feet. And the light was different. His night vision was as good as his daytime vision, the lenses of his eyes magnifying the moonlight to pick up nuances and throw silver-sheened light into shadows.

He heard an indistinct whisper behind him and spun around, but there was no one there. Gradually, the whisper became clear. He stood a moment, following the thread of sound, and realized it came from one of the houses across the way, a man murmuring to his wife in the night.

His nose tingled and he picked up the unforgettable scent of satisfied sex.

The werewolf laughed and started to run, loping at first, getting the feel of it, then with the supernatural speed that renders a werewolf almost invisible. A human being would catch a glimpse of him, then before the human could realize what he saw, the werewolf would be in another place, elusive as a dream recalled upon waking.

Another sensation crowded his body now, momentarily washing out all the others. Hunger, but a hunger so deep and primordial that all his new senses were shifted to the task of satisfying it. Until that was done, he couldn't restrain himself.

He understood at that moment what his strength was for, what his claws could do, what his entire transformed body was meant to accomplish. Once he understood that, the next steps were clear and true.

From far back in his mind, he could hear someone screaming, fighting to be heard through the beginning haze of fury and determination, begging him to stop, to turn back, to throw himself into the river—anything so that he wouldn't go on with this. This isn't you, it told him, this isn't anything you want to do. If you go on, you're lost. You won't be able to stop, ever. And how can you live with it? How can you face your family, your son, after what you're going to do?

The voice brought the werewolf up short, but only for a minute, only for the time it took for the overwhelming, sensual hunger to take him completely and blind him to the fact that he had ever been human, and that he would never be completely human again.

Then he spotted a man walking all alone, innocently unafraid of the dark, and with a howl of triumph and a flash of claws, the werewolf took his first life. And relinquished his own.

The sound of the shower woke Johanna. She rolled over to look at the clock, but the violet light of the sky, brightening by the minute, told her it was just dawn. The bed felt oddly empty and it took her a minute to register that Walter wasn't in it. His side of the bed was still smooth, the pillow fluffed and undented.

Had Walter been up all night? True, he never seemed to need much sleep, but he always got at least a few hours.

She stretched and decided to join him in the shower. She smiled with a delicious little shiver of sin: they hadn't done that in a while. She slipped off her nightgown and opened the bathroom door.

The clouds of steam almost choked her. "Walter? Honey, how can you stand it this hot?"

She slid back the glass door.

Walter was sitting at the end of the tub, his elbows propped on his knees and his face buried in his hands as the water poured over him. The sounds of his sobbing almost drowned out the sounds of the water.

Johanna had never heard anyone cry like that. It was as if each breath was torn bleeding from his lungs. It terrified her.

"Walter . . ." She reached over and turned off the water, but he didn't notice. "Please, honey, what is it? What's happened? Are you hurt?"

She stroked his streaming hair, but he didn't notice this, either. "Oh, Walter, just *please* tell me what's wrong!"

They remained like that for several minutes, Johanna at a complete loss.

"Baby, come on," she said, trying to take his hand and pull him up. "Come out of there and let me dry you off. You get in bed and I'll make you some hot soup."

But the only move he made was to grasp her hand, so hard that he hurt her. He held the hand against his cheek and she felt the hot water and warm tears.

"Sweetheart, come *on*. You're scaring me. Please."

He took a deep, wracking breath and stood up, not looking at her. He had stopped crying, but he still didn't speak.

Johanna turned her back for a second, to reach for a towel and Walter's bathrobe, and in that second she heard him step out of the shower and out of the bathroom.

"Oh, Christ!" she said softly, quickly pulling on her own robe and grabbing Walter's off the hook.

Walter was halfway down the hall to Andrew's room.

Andrew was sleeping off the evening's champagne, lying fully clothed on top of the rumpled bedcovers, exactly where he'd dropped when he came in from Angela's.

Walter leaned against the doorframe, just looking at Andrew, his eyes wild and apprehensive. Johanna watched several expressions cross his face, as if he were deciding exactly what to say and discarding everything.

Andrew sat up slowly in confusion. He caught sight of his father standing in the door, a silent, naked giant, and Johanna standing frozen right behind him.

"Okay, what is this?" Andrew said in a voice still thick with sleep.

Walter made an awful sound, halfway between a sob and a scream, and began to cry again, sliding down against the doorframe as if the weight of his sorrow was more than his body could bear.

"What's happening?" Andrew said, dropping to his knees beside Walter. "Dad, what's going on?"

"I can't get him to talk," Johanna said. "I found him crying in the shower and he can't seem to tell me why."

Andrew touched his father's shoulder. "Dad? I'm right here. What can I do? How can I help you?"

Walter was trying to speak.

"Just take a couple of deep breaths and try to relax," Andrew told him.

Walter struggled to bring himself under control. He was breathing heavily, gasping for air. After a few minutes, he could breathe, but the tears didn't stop running.

"You'll hate me forever," he told Andrew, his eyes haunted.

"That's very unlikely," Andrew said, trying to sound reasonable and calm. "Why would I hate you?"

"My father never told me. How could he have? How could he have ever made me believe anything like this? That bastard! If he was here, I'd kill him!"

"Walter, what are you saying?" Johanna said, horrified. "How could you think such a thing?"

Walter stared into Andrew's eyes, so much like his own, as if he were searching for something there. "No," he said decisively, "nothing will happen to you. You're so strong in your faith. That will save you."

"Dad, I'm not sure what you're talking about, but . . ."

Walter looked as if he were about to panic. He grabbed Andrew by the shoulders. "Promise me you'll forgive me when the time comes!"

"I'll forgive you and stand by you through anything, you know that. Never worry about that."

Walter dropped his head in his hands and began to cry again, this time very quietly.

"Let's try to get him to bed," Andrew told his mother. "Dad, can you stand up?"

Walter nodded, but when he tried to stand, he was too weak. Andrew caught him as he stumbled, and half carried him down the hall. Walter collapsed into bed and Johanna pulled the covers over him.

"Johanna?" Walter said plaintively. The note in his voice reminded her of Andrew when he was six and had his tonsils out, when he was frightened of being left alone.

She looked up at Andrew. "Go back to bed, sweetheart,"

she said. She knew he wanted an explanation, but she had nothing to give him.

When Andrew had closed the door, she lay down and put her arms around Walter, his head brushing her shoulder and moving slowly with her breathing.

It was only after she was sure he was asleep that she gave in to her own stinging tears.

4

Walter was awake and sitting up in bed when Andrew brought him his breakfast on a tray. Andrew had promised his mother that he'd be cheerful, act normally, and wouldn't ask too many questions. Just give your father a chance to collect himself, she'd said.

"Mother says that she's doing this only because you're a big-shot scientist now. I hope bacon and an omelet are okay; we didn't know what you feed a captive Nobel Laureate."

Cheerful? Hey, he sounded like a cross between Mary Poppins and the village idiot.

"You know, Dad, if you're going to sauce it up, you should stick to the cheap stuff. That was vintage Cristal and I bet you went right outside and barfed it."

"Just set the tray on the table, will you?" Walter said. "And you don't have to act for me. I know what you're thinking." His eyes, set in deep black circles, had a mournful, lost look that made Andrew want to take him in his arms and comfort him, like a hurt child.

In that sobering, illuminating split second, Andrew grew up. His childhood and the last shreds of his adolescence were irrevocably over. For the first time, he saw Walter as fallible and human, not as a Great White Father who'd take care of everything, solve every problem, soothe every hurt. He and his father were on an equal footing now, two men facing common problems, and both of them knew it.

"I'm really sorry," Walter said. "I know I scared you and your mother."

"Come on," Andrew said lightly, "it takes stronger men than either of us to scare Mom." He sat on the bed and spoke more seriously. "What happened to you? *Were* you drunk? Did something happen to you out there in the park?"

"It's so complicated," Walter said, looking away. "I just have to adjust my life for the way things are going to be now." He had that blank look in his eyes again, but it passed.

"Was it the prize? Is that it?"

"Prize?" Walter looked at Andrew like he'd never heard of it.

"Look, I know it's a big change," Andrew said, "the responsibility, the pressure. All that work you did in relative anonymity is now going to be done in a fishbowl. But, Dad, a Nobel Prize isn't the end of a project; it just signifies the beginning of a new phase. You'll have plenty of heights to scale after this."

Walter got the same look on his face that Andrew had seen a hundred times; he was trying to make a decision and his mind was indexing through a dozen choices. He had that concentrated, distant look that meant that he wasn't communicating with the real world.

Then he smiled. "I don't handle success very well, do I?"

Andrew laughed, more out of relief than anything else. "Or your liquor, either, it seems. God, Mother's never going to let you hear the end of this."

Andrew got up and started to leave the bedroom.

"Hey, wait a minute," Walter said. "Where did you disappear to last night, kid?"

It seemed that, no matter what was unspoken between them, they were going to make a stab at normalcy. Andrew had no problem with that.

"Unlike my father," Andrew explained patiently, "I know how to make the most of a bottle of Cristal."

Andrew could hear Walter's short laugh as he left the room. Walter seemed fine, but there was something slightly off about the whole thing. Perhaps it was the effect of his father's smile beneath those hollow, heartbroken eyes. His laughter sounded to Andrew not as if it was something he felt, but something he only remembered.

On an impulse, Andrew stepped silently backward and glanced into Walter's room. Walter wasn't laughing now; he was lying on his back, his hands absently twisting the blanket. He was staring at the ceiling while quiet tears streamed down to wet the fresh pillow.

What hurt Andrew the most wasn't so much that his father still had some painful problem, but that he had obviously decided not to trust his own family with it.

By the end of the week, Andrew and Johanna were relieved to see that Walter was the same again. True, he was quieter, given to sudden silences and long periods of introspection, but he was still Walter.

He announced that he was taking on a new project. A small college upstate was trying to expand their anthropology department and had asked for his help as a consultant. He told Johanna that he was only sorry that it would take him out of town for a couple of nights a month, but he just couldn't see driving two hours up there and back every time.

Johanna wasn't sorry. She regarded this new interest as a godsend. Men who were having nervous breakdowns didn't start new projects.

At first, Andrew was worried about Walter. This new spate of activity didn't feel exactly right to him. There was nothing he could put his finger on, but he sensed that Walter was holding himself together tenuously, building a facade of normalcy. Still, there wasn't anything noticeably wrong with

Walter, and some days Andrew was convinced that he was just overreacting.

Besides, his own life had taken a distracting turn. For one thing, he was finishing up his last term at Tulane before graduating and going to the seminary.

For another, he'd started a discreet affair with Angela Winfield.

He was spending weekends at her apartment on Chestnut Street as often as she'd let him. They were trying to be quiet about it since Angela was on the Tulane faculty with his father, but Andrew was determined to take full advantage of Angela's generous nature. He figured that, with the ten-year difference in their ages and the vast gulf that separated their temperaments, it wouldn't be too long before she got bored with him and it would be over.

But it was exactly that difference in outlooks that kept him interested in Angela. It was almost laughable. He was the cautious, dependable, conservative one and Angela was as uninhibited and as open to adventure as a kid. Angela splashed right into life in the deep water; Andrew always advised careful preparation and easing into it in stages.

Angela was also teaching him everything she knew about sex, and the woman was a walking *Kama Sutra*. Not that he was any slouch himself; sex had always been a passion for him, he'd started thinking about it before most kids knew what it was, but because of his cautious nature, he'd struggled to control himself. All through his teens, his looks had gotten him any girl he wanted, but his ardor had frightened them off. He hated playing those games with their elaborate rules: on the second date he could put his hand on her breast briefly; on the third date he could touch her pubic area but only through her clothes and she might touch his; later on, if they were "serious" she just might jerk him off, but he couldn't take his pants off, only unzip them. The whole thing was too stupid for Andrew and he said so on several occasions. He sensed early that he was in danger of being classified as a "sex maniac" by the hypocritical young ladies of his social set, so he managed, by a great reserve of will, to purge himself of all external show of desire. And once his judgment was no longer clouded with the effort of trying to get them into bed, he became aware of how shallow those girls really were. He realized that any of them would love to marry him—he was going to be a "good catch"—but not one of them would interest him for very long.

Angela interested him. She *more* than interested him, she fascinated him. She was smart, she was funny, she could and did fuck his brains out.

One particular Monday morning, after a weekend marathon of talking, joking, and sex that left both of them energized rather than exhausted, Andrew was still in bed when Angela emerged from the bathroom showered and dressed for work.

Andrew couldn't believe what he was seeing.

There she was, red hair tied back, conservative navy suit, subdued makeup. "Good God," he said, amazed, "you look like a Fundamentalist Sunday school teacher."

"My working uniform," she said, screwing in a pair of discreet pearl earrings.

"Just when I thought I knew you," he said. "But come over here and let me kiss you anyway before you leave."

She smiled and walked over to the bed, bent over, and kissed him. He ran his hands slowly up her legs, over the silky stockings and the bare thighs, reaching further up her skirt. Suddenly, he gave a triumphant little shout.

"Aha! Damn! I thought so." He lifted her skirt.

Underneath that prim uniform she wore a black lace garter belt and no panties.

"This is your idea of conservative?" he asked.

"I can deny my true nature only so far"—she shrugged—"it was enough that I wore a bra."

"You look like the Marquis de Sade Chapter of the Junior League."

She ran her hands down his chest and over his stirring penis. "And don't you just love it, you little pervert?" She gave him a long kiss that didn't help his chances of getting up and walking anytime soon. "When I get back, we'll do it with our clothes on. I won't bother to take any of this off and you can play out your nastiest fantasies, okay?"

He looked at her for a moment. "Sorry. Not soon enough." He quickly lifted her skirt again and pressed his open mouth over her tantalizingly fragrant pubic mound, his hand against her warm buttocks. She didn't even pretend to object that she'd be late for class.

Life was running as smoothly as could be expected, until Walter changed directions again.

Walter was spending more hours in his study, writing some long work that demanded a lot of time. He wouldn't talk about it, which was odd: Walter was normally so enthusiastic about his work that you got tired of listening long before he got tired of explaining.

He developed a sudden interest in folklore, peripherally in his field, but certainly not his specialty.

"It's kind of strange," Andrew remarked to Angela one night. "Dad's branching out into another specialty when he's so well established in his own. I'm not sure I like this."

They were sitting on the floor in Angela's living room, watching *The Treasure of Sierra Madre*, eating fast-food tacos and swigging Dr. Pepper and Barq's Root Beer out of frosted liter bottles. Angela's passion for junk food in a town renowned for its cuisine was one of her most shameful secret vices.

"You're just looking for problems where there are none," she advised, licking hot sauce off her fingers. "You know your father, he loves a challenge. We all want to break new ground sometimes."

But it wasn't new ground Walter was breaking; it was old. Walter had been collecting some very odd books lately. While he was out, Andrew had looked into one of the massive volumes on Walter's desk. It was ancient, so old that the leather bindings were crumbling and the gold lettering was splotched with dark spots. The heavy paper cracked tremulously under his hands, threatening to disintegrate.

It was a book on lycanthropy. His father, the most rational of scientists, was studying werewolves.

Also on the table were more modern works including Robert Tallant's *Voodoo in New Orleans*.

Why would Walter be interested in voodoo and lycanthropy?

"Are you familiar with something called Arthur and . . . uh . . . Grendel?" Andrew asked Angela.

"Grendel? Are you talking about Beowulf or John Gardner?"

He made a frustrated little sound. "Not Grendel . . . something that sounds like it. Gargle . . . Gorgon . . ."

"Oh! *Arthur and Gorlagon*. Yes. Why?"

"Dad has an old copy of it, in Latin, covered with clipped-on notes and cryptic scribbles. And I could only translate part of it; the end is missing. What's the story?"

"King Arthur tells of his meeting with King Gorlagon, a kind and patient man who was transformed into a werewolf through the sneaky machinations of a faithless wife. Gorlagon went through ten kinds of hell before justice was served and the wife and her lover got what they deserved.

Gorlagon was permanently restored to human shape and got his kingdom back." She took a long draught of Dr. Pepper and gave a ladylike little belch. "What an esoteric thing for Walter to want to know."

"That's what I thought, too. He's studying some very spooky stuff."

"I know," she said, "he borrowed some books from me. I was mildly astounded. A paleoanthropologist like Walter doesn't have any professional dealings with the likes of me. What does he need with a folklorist? But there he was, asking if I had any books on local folk superstitions."

"Did you?"

"Honey, assorted horror-story types are my speciality. I can tell you the difference between five types of vampires, and I've got a sampler embroidered with a formula for calling demons. However, my specialty is eastern European cultures. I'm not as heavy into local stuff. But I did have some answers for him. He asked me all sorts of questions about werewolves, including: was it really true about silver bullets?"

"About using them to kill werewolves? Is it supposed to work?"

"Anything silver. Silver bullets, silver daggers, silver baseball bats. Silver is sacred to Diana, the triple moon goddess. Diana has another incarnation as Hecate, the goddess of all things hidden and secret, the giver of justice. The silver supposedly works because anyone wanting to kill a werewolf needs the protection—and the power—of the goddess. Apparently, only the goddess can kill one of her own and, in the execution of justice, the werewolf is the goddess's emissary. You've got this whole complicated connection between silver as Hecate's talisman, the moon, and the werewolf. Especially in southern Louisiana."

She lifted another taco, dripping with oil, sauce, and shredded cheese, and took a messy bite. "You know," she said, considering the taco, "we need soft tortillas with this. You wrap the taco in the tortilla and the stuffing doesn't fall all over the Oriental carpets."

Andrew stared at her in impatience.

She noted his look. "Oh, come on, sweetie! Quit worrying! Look, I was your father's teaching assistant for what? A year. I know him pretty well. He's just interested in so many things that he's bored with the old ones. He wants a change."

"What were you going to say about southern Louisiana?" he said, discounting her advice.

"Well," she said, swallowing the last of the taco, "down here, there's a strong Voodoo community. And where you find that, you find the loup-garou, the old Cajun werewolf. For some reason, they've always been closely allied in Louisiana. The difference we folklorists find in the legends of the werewolf and the stories of the loup-garou is that the loup-garou, more often than not, is motivated to kill by a sense of justice. He's the last arm of the law for the Voodoos; when all else fails, strike up a bargain with the loup-garou to take care of the problem. So there you are again, with another tie to Hecate as the goddess of justice, especially through hidden things and the phases of the moon. Even though Hecate is definitely *not* a Voodoo deity, she *is* the werewolf's patroness, so I think there's a much older tie there, probably from the Greek mythology. Now, are we through with this? Because you made me miss the 'We don't need no stinkin' badges' part."

He had forgotten about the movie. This whole thing of Walter's just mystified him. All these old superstitions and stories were terrific as diversions, and he would concede that there was some value in studying them to understand primitive cultural themes, but for Walter to spend so much energy on this stuff struck him as a waste of time.

"Angela, why in God's name would Dad want to know all that?" he said, still perplexed.

"He's *your* father, dear," she said, "but I'd keep an eye on him at the dark of the moon."

He had grown up among Walter's collection of antiquities: shipments of bones, shards of pottery, and prehistoric tools were forever cluttering the house, burying the priceless old Persian carpets under messy shredded newspaper. Now some very different and very unpleasant things were starting to arrive.

The shipment that disturbed Andrew the most was a small statue of a wolf, carved precisely out of precious black jade and set with ruby eyes. It was undeniably a masterpiece, but it was repulsive. The beast stood like a man, hunched from its grotesque muscular structure. Its face had the uncontrollable look of a compulsive killer. As much as he hated the evil little thing, Andrew found himself drawn to it.

Even Walter had flinched when he took it out of the wrappings.

"What, in the name of all that's holy, *is* that?" Andrew said softly.

Walter held it up, turning it in his hands. "Lycaon," he said. The light bounced off the jade surface. "Lycaon was a king who had the audacity to challenge the gods and even plotted to kill Jupiter."

"Always a bad move in mythology," Andrew observed.

"Jupiter was outraged, and turned Lycaon into a creature half-man, half-wolf. But as to whether it changed Lycaon's homicidal character is doubtful. Lycaon was the first werewolf."

Walter was staring at the figure as if hypnotized.

On some impulse he didn't understand, Andrew took the figure from Walter. As soon as it touched his hand, he gasped and almost dropped it.

"It's warm!" he said.

"Body heat," Walter said. "I've been holding it."

"No, it's almost like it's alive." With a shudder, he put the figure on the table. "Why would you want something like that? God, it's abominable!"

"Abominable," Walter repeated softly. "Yes. It is that. An abomination, a supremely cruel genetic joke. And with all the research, all the work, I haven't learned anything that's of real use."

Andrew could see that his father was close to slipping back into one of his morbid moods. He tried to lighten things up.

"Still," he said, picking up the repulsive figure again, despite himself, "this little guy must be worth a fortune, along with all these other cheerful art objects." He gestured to indicate the artifacts jammed into the study. "And someday, all this will be mine."

He started to laugh, but Walter's sudden look of horror cut him off.

The next week, another box arrived, heavily insured. Walter called Johanna and Andrew in and insisted that Andrew open it.

"Ah! Another priceless artifact from the collection of Gomez and Morticia Addams?" Andrew inquired.

"Very funny," Walter said. "I think you'll be surprised."

Andrew tore off the top of the box. A polished ivory figure, only four inches tall, reclined on a thick bed of cotton. The little man in flowing robes clutched a tiny cross to his chest, his face beatific. He was every bit as well executed as the Lycaon figure had been, but the sight of this lovely little man gave Andrew a feeling of well-being, as if he were sending out a special radiance. As Andrew lifted him out of the box, the creamy ivory warmed in his hands.

"It's Saint Andrew," Walter said.

"He's exquisite," Johanna said. "Whoever made him must have gone blind doing it."

"I wanted him to watch over Andrew while he's at the seminary." Walter took the little saint and held him up to the light. "He's so beautiful. I wanted you both to remember me when you look at this statue, not by . . . the other one."

A wind of melancholy passed over Walter. "I wanted to give you something special," he said. "I have so little to give you that is beautiful and good!"

Andrew sensed a depth of pain in Walter that he could neither understand nor comfort. "That's not true," Andrew said gently, "you've given me everything."

Only Johanna could vaguely comprehend Walter's sadness. She touched him lightly, knowing that whatever was tormenting him was something that, for the first time, they couldn't share.

Three months later, on a clear, sunny afternoon while Johanna was out, Andrew came in from a class to find his father's body lying on the floor of his study. He had shot himself through the heart with an antique pistol. On the desk lay five of six specially cast silver bullets.

Through the days that followed, difficult days of quiet voices and softly closed doors that contrasted with the brilliance of his mother's anguish and his own bitter confusion, Andrew could see only one thing clearly: the calm expression of peace on his father's face as he lay on the study floor.

Years later, when there were things about his father that he couldn't quite remember, details of his appearance and manner that tended to gather a slight haze from distance, only that particular look of serenity shone like carved crystal touched by sunlight.

It was a look he hadn't seen since the night of Walter's party.

5

Johanna knew she was spending too much time alone, locking herself away in the bedroom, but she was helpless. It wasn't a good sign, but it was all that saved her.

If she came out, people started yammering at her, offering platitudes and advice, things that sounded like gibberish to her, all containing the phrases " . . . for your own good . . ." and "Walter would have wanted . . ." and " . . . start living again." She didn't take offense because it was all well meaning and most of the people talking to her were dealing with their own grief. On the other hand, she couldn't listen to it anymore.

What no one could understand was that Johanna had lost half of herself. She and Walter together had made something solid, the two parts bonding into a perfect whole. Now the structure of their lives had disintegrated into nothing more substantial than crumpled paper.

Her daydreams, her memories of Walter, seemed much more real to her than the world outside the bedroom door. She was retreating into time, molding it to fit her pleasure. Johanna could make it travel backward, forward, stretch it out to fill her inconsolable nights, alter what *was* to what should have been. She could even make the future. All it took, she was delighted to discover, was a good memory and a rapidly expanding imagination. If she was willing to be not quite alive, Walter would be not quite dead.

She propped her feet on the needlepoint footstool. She had done the needlework herself, in Kenya, when Walter was still with Leakey. Simply the sight of it triggered a whole series of memories. Everything did, if she worked at it hard enough and fought off any distractions. She was beginning to discover the perverse delights of letting her mind wander.

And people expected her to come downstairs and deal with death! Impossible. It was another kind of reality entirely, one that couldn't coexist with the one she was so painfully, carefully building. Walter's family, at first sympathetic, was getting nervous, but Johanna couldn't help that.

Now, all of sudden, there was this letter to deal with.

When she found it tucked in her bureau drawer under a pile of sweaters, she marveled at Walter's ingenuity. If it had been found with Walter it would have been just a suicide note; police and the press would have had the right to paw over it and speculate on Walter's most intimate thoughts. This way, the contents would remain just as Walter intended: a private communication between the two of them. He had known that Johanna would find it sooner or later, and the time factor hardly mattered now.

Johanna had been in no hurry to open it. At the time, she had been in a period of relative calm. She wanted to wait until the intermittent wave of loss and loneliness came to another crest, when she needed so badly to talk to Walter one more time. Then she would savor the letter slowly and recall a bit of the comfort she had lost.

Now she pried open the envelope as gently as she could, careful not to tear it, and lifted out the many densely written sheets. Taped to one of them was a small safe-deposit-box key.

At first, the letter was an apology for his suicide. Of course he would start with that. She started to cry almost immediately. When he explained why he did it, she stopped crying and stared at the sheets in horror, each one dropping into her lap like a pane of ice.

Only the end of the letter sounded logical to her. *Please, never let Andrew know any of this,* he had written. *It's odd, but I've always believed that as long as someone thinks of you with love, you're never really dead.*

I hate to end it this way, mainly because the people you leave behind always feel that you did it because of something they did, something they didn't do, something they could have done differently. You made me so happy, Jo. I wanted you to know that it wasn't you.

Oh, Jo . . . if only I had known, would I have married you? Would I have had a child, knowing that he would inherit a curse that would shatter his life as completely as it shattered mine? You've been my comfort, Jo, my joy, my safe refuge and my consolation. I always loved you too much to hurt you, and now, without any control over it, I've had to cause you the ultimate pain, and only because my suffering finally outweighed my conscience. It's my own fault, Jo, never yours. If I had been honest with you, if I had been stronger, perhaps I could have told you. But I couldn't bear the thought of the look in your eyes, the terror and disbelief that any normal human being would feel. Or perhaps I underestimated your strength. But believe that I never underestimated your love.

On the same sheet as the little key he had written, *Just keep this someplace safe. It opens the box where I put my research and a few other documents. Andrew will have to ask for it someday, and I think only you will know when that day comes. You're the only one who knows, Jo: the only one. Give it to him, but otherwise don't let him know it exists. Reading these things would only hurt him. Try to be as strong for him as I stubbornly couldn't let you be for me.*

Johanna sat very still. The ghastly phrases, once only part of children's fright games at Halloween, played again in her mind: loup-garou, werewolves, the Marley curse, murder, madness, death. And the inevitability of it: that on the most significant night of their lives, the firstborn Marley of each generation underwent a transformation not only of the body, but of the soul.

She'd had no idea how much Walter had suffered. It was obvious to her now that he had, in fact, had a nervous breakdown that night she found him in the shower. This letter proved it. It was the obsessive outpouring of a genius gone mad. The more she thought about it, the more terrible it became, not only the insane things he had written, but that Walter had struggled through it alone in order to spare his family.

No matter what he wrote, that was why he had fired that gun. Not her fault. Not Andrew's. And, in the end, not even his own. There was no curse. She wouldn't believe that she was going to suffer the same loss of her son that she had suffered with Walter.

Walter had gone insane. It was almost a relief. It was certainly an explanation she could live with.

She sat motionless, turning things over in her mind, gathering bits of information like bits of string gathered into a ball. Each new revelation added to her conclusions about what Walter had written.

All this had to die now. If madness was contagious, she couldn't let it infect her son. She was certain that whatever Walter had locked in the safe-deposit box was something that Andrew had no business knowing, now or later. She tossed the key into a drawer and gathered up the fallen letter pages.

She had to get rid of that letter. Andrew had wonderful memories of his father; there was no point now in letting him look inside Walter's obscured mind.

For the first time in days, she opened her bedroom door and started down the stairs. But when she looked into the living room, she couldn't seem to take another step.

Oh, God. Was the whole family there? Walter's brother and his wife, his sister and her children, Andrew.

Johanna froze on the stairs, terrified that they would expect her to talk. If she did, she was afraid she'd start screaming and she wouldn't be able to stop. What could she say to them? She stood there for a while before they noticed her, things going around in her mind, a thousand things that she wanted to say, but she couldn't find a starting place.

Silence was her best tactic, she decided. She would go right past them like they weren't there. After all, she was downstairs for a purpose. No distractions permitted.

"Mother?" Andrew said gently, and everyone looked up.

They were surprised, of course, and Johanna could see their mouths working, but she couldn't let herself hear them. No distractions. She kept her eyes fixed on the fireplace, with the big yellow fire in the grate. She stood in front of it and tossed the letter in.

As it burned, Johanna shed an enormous weight. Her mind began to untangle itself from the sorrow that had wrapped her like a shroud, the responsibilities that trapped her under cold stone. When the last remnants of the letter sparked up the chimney, Johanna almost floated toward the stairs.

Now she could go back upstairs in peace, and she would never have to come down again.

When she returned to her chair by the window, there were no more memories of the Walter who had written that letter. There was only Walter in his twenties, as she had first met him: exuberant, glorious, in love. She didn't have to hurry: the pictures, the years, would replay as slowly or as quickly as she wanted. She sighed and snuggled into the cushions, pulling the afghan around her. She had closed her door and was sealing it behind her like the entrance to an ancient tomb.

And then came the unbidden thought, the totally unthinkable idea that would forever haunt the dark corners of her lovely dreamworld, intruding even in the midst of her happiest memories: What if it's all true? What if every word that Walter wrote about his family's curse was not madness, not delusion, but the absolute truth?

She knew, with a certainty that froze her blood, that it was.

She experienced a moment of pure, transfixed horror. Then, for the first time but certainly not for the last, she pushed the thought away, buried it under prettier memories.

But its shadow was always there, just slightly visible, waiting.

Andrew went to her room the next morning and was relieved to see her sweet, contented smile. But when he tried to talk to her, he saw that, though she looked straight at him and nodded patiently, she neither heard nor had any desire to respond. Then she lifted her head and looked directly into his eyes, searching for something, fixing him with a look of such appalled dread that it felt as if she had actually slapped him. But it passed like a storm cloud over a summer sky, and her face was as serene—and as lost—as when he had first come in.

6

Andrew started having dreams about his father shortly after he died. Nightmares were more accurate a term. In one particularly unsettling scene, he saw Walter standing a few feet away, almost, but not quite able to touch him. He was in horrible pain, screaming for Andrew to save him. Over and over he pleaded in the most gut-wrenching voice imaginable, "Help me, save me! Only you can save me . . . oh, God! *Make it stop!*" And then he stretched out his hand, but it wasn't his hand. It was grotesque, deformed, like a badly born animal. With the panic of dreams, Andrew knew that if he could only reach Walter, take that terrible hand and pull him out of the dream, that everything would be all right.

So he stretched toward Walter in the fever of visions, feeling his entire body strain with the effort, and all the time Walter kept up that ghastly screaming. Just when Andrew could almost close his hand around his fingers, he heard laughter coming from somewhere; not sane laughter, but with the hysterical edge of a maniac. It chilled his blood, and scared him so badly that he woke up.

The bed was always soaked with sweat.

Andrew could not understand what had happened to his father. The actuality of Walter's suicide was clear, but the internal breakdown of reasoning that made suicide possible was beyond Andrew's grasp. There was a simple, logical explanation, there *had* to be, for Walter to have killed himself the way he did. He had used that particular pistol loaded with those particular bullets just because they were *there*. And they were there because Walter was into this horror-movie stuff so deeply that it had driven him crazy.

Our minds will construct and accept as perfectly plausible any explanation that helps us make peace with suicide, no matter how lame that explanation is. Andrew knew that, but it was no comfort.

The nightmares were even easier to analyze. They were so frightening because he had associated his father's death with the things that scared him most deeply.

He only half believed these Psych 101 theories, patting himself on the back for being such a brave, wise son. But inside, he knew that was easier to think that his father had lost his mind than to come to grips with the fact that the selfish bastard had deserted him, a thought that was beginning to surface with alarming frequency.

He realized that if he'd had Angela Winfield to talk to during those days that he would have had an easier time of it. But Angela had left two months before for a six-month sabbatical in Romania and Eastern Europe, hot on the trail of Dracula or Frankenstein or the Yeti or some such nonsense. Just before she left, she had become a little cool toward him. The sex was still sensational—God knows, they would have both come back from the dead for that—but Andrew couldn't get over the feeling that Angela was pulling her emotions back in. Or maybe, as he had suspected she would from the beginning, she had gotten bored.

With his father gone and his mother trying her damnedest to go with him, Andrew acquired a bizarre calm. The worst that could happen *had* happened and he never had to worry about anything ever again.

He was just about to graduate from Tulane and was due at the seminary in Wisconsin right after that. He didn't want to go. Rather, he wanted to, but felt too guilty leaving Johanna.

That was irrationality on his part. It wasn't like he couldn't have afforded full-time care for her, and it wasn't like he was just walking off and leaving her with impersonal paid help. Walter's family was always around, Johanna's family lived in New Orleans. Someone would be there.

But if she was going to suffer, by God, so was Andrew! Two could play at this penance game, and his conscience was just as guilty about having failed Walter as hers was.

The fallacy in this, of course, was that Johanna wasn't suffering. Not anymore. Andrew became convinced that this was Johanna's salvation—and her downfall.

Some of the best psychiatrists in the South paraded in and out of the house on St. Charles, and they all agreed that Johanna probably wouldn't get better, but she wouldn't get worse. None of them thought that she would become violent or do herself any harm, but Andrew wasn't so sure about that. How could they know what she was thinking?

He grew disgusted with the noncommittal attitudes of the consulting physicians. Some suggested hospitalization, some said it was better to leave her at home. One, obviously a relic of the Third Reich School of Experimental Medicine, suggested electroshock and plenty of it. Later, Andrew found that electroshock was a perfectly valid and valuable treatment for extreme depression, but at the time he had been appalled. One doctor had a whole list of drugs he was just dying to try out. Andrew could decide on none of these doctors. What he wasn't acknowledging was that he didn't want to give her up, that as long as she was in the house, in that room, there was hope that his family would be magically restored. He hired around-the-clock nurses and a reliable housekeeper. Walter's brother, James, arranged for a doctor to see her at regular intervals.

When Andrew finally had to leave, he went in to talk to her. Talking *with* her was out of the question. He looked for a response, something other than her usual gentle smile, but it was useless. She let him kiss her, and hold her for a moment as he tried to explain where he was going, but she squirmed away slightly, anxious to be back in that pretty world where she had made her own peace. Andrew wished that, for just one minute, he could join her in it, that he could finish with responsibilities and grief and guilt, and live in Johanna's head, where everyone was beautiful and no one ever died.

The tremendous seminary work load surprised him, but he was grateful for it. His mind was so occupied with theology that the pain of his troubles faded farther away. He tried to come home as often as he could, spending time with his mother, hoping she could remember something, say something, show some gentle shadow of emotion. She never did. She stayed as she was, mute, motionless, her mind spinning back into itself.

Holidays were bad in general, but that first Christmas was a particular kind of hell. Christmas had always been important to the entire Marley clan, but this year Andrew felt like an orphan. He knew it was stupid and irrational: if he wanted, he could be surrounded by aunts, uncles, and cousins from both sides of the family, but for some perverse reason he just wanted to go into hiding. With that attitude, he thought, I don't know why I even bother going home. He supposed that it was part instinct, part hope springing eternal that Johanna would suddenly jump up from her chair, cry "Surprise!" and begin to dish up the turkey and urge him to leave room for the pecan pie.

He foresaw a dutiful, but uncomfortable, two weeks.

He arrived at the house around ten that night, in a surly mood, exhausted from the flight, a missed connection, and the nerve-wracking ride from the airport. He was so tired that he just dropped his bags in the foyer and went upstairs to see if Johanna was awake. According to the nurses, she had taken to sleeping all day and staying up all night.

She was awake, but not alone. The small frosted-glass bedside lamp provided just enough light for him to make out Johanna sitting in her usual blue wing chair, and the man seated opposite her on the footstool. He was childishly annoyed: that was *his* spot.

The man was older than Andrew, but still young, in his mid-thirties. He was one of those ugly-handsome men whose confidence and bearing make them attractive. His whole attitude was contradictory: He wore a perfectly tailored suit, obviously handmade, but his hair looked as if he hadn't combed it. Andrew almost snorted. One of those elegantly rumpled types, the absentminded professor who inspires women to apply just a few finishing touches.

There was no conversation. The man merely smiled at Johanna and she smiled back. But it was odd that, although she didn't speak, she did acknowledge that he was there and she seemed pleased. The nurses always reported that she never noticed them.

The man became aware of Andrew and turned, putting a finger to his lips. He leaned closer to Johanna, speaking in a quiet whisper that only she could hear.

He straightened up, sighed, and took her hand as he rose.

"Tomorrow," he told her positively, "I think you're going to have to talk to me. It's cruel to keep me waiting like this, even though I'd heard what teases you southern women are."

Oh, *please,* Andrew thought, not an English accent, too? At least old Stephen Marley would have approved of him.

The accent was not only real, but right out of the top drawer.

Johanna turned back to the window, but Andrew could see her reflection in the dark panes. She was smiling; not that vacant, indistinct smile, but a little, teasing smile as if she understood perfectly what she was doing.

"Now don't be obstinate, Johanna," he said to her. "Here's a nice young man come to visit. Say hello, dear."

He said it in such a positive tone that Andrew almost expected her to do it. For a second, it even looked as if she was trying. He took her hand and waited, but after a few minutes, she was gone again and he felt like a fool.

Andrew had crazy, frustrated moments when he was convinced that she was only doing this because she wanted to, out of some whim that she could cast off in a second just by changing her mind. He didn't see that Johanna might have wanted to talk, wanted it desperately at times, but she had either forgotten how or was terrified that talking would force her to reènter a world with which she couldn't cope, and in which she felt she no longer belonged. Who needed her there? Walter was gone, Andrew was grown and starting his own life, independent of her. And Johanna had always been a woman who needed to be *needed*.

The man shrugged, sighed again, and said, "All right. Spite me. But tomorrow *for sure*."

Andrew followed the man out of the room, still feeling surly.

"You want to tell me where my mother's nurse is and who you are?" he said, rather curtly.

"Nurse Jackson is having a short nap. The afternoon nurse had a nasty cold and Nurse Jackson has had to work a double shift, poor thing." He didn't sound as if he noticed Andrew's tone of voice.

"I don't like this. Mother isn't supposed to be alone."

"She isn't alone. I'm with her."

"Yes," he said, as if explaining things to an idiot, "but who are *you*?"

He raised his eyebrows in surprise. "Oh, good Lord! Sorry. I thought your uncle wrote you. I'm her doctor, Simon Spencer. Been treating her for two months, actually."

"I thought Dr. Justin was her doctor. He's the family doctor, Uncle James arranged it."

Spencer looked reflective. "Well, Justin wasn't doing much for your mother. Oh, he's a nice enough old boy and all that, but he's too satisfied with the status quo. As long as your mother is physically healthy, he thinks he's doing a bang-up job. Your uncle contacted me because he wasn't convinced that nothing could be done for her, and I agreed to see her."

"At this hour?"

"She does keep awful hours, doesn't she? But then, so do I. I like to see her every day; I'm still building her trust. And I'm trying to wean her off this terrible habit of staying up all night and sleeping all day. I have the feeling that Johanna is awake at night because she's *watching* for something, or someone. But she needs to go outside, she needs more light and exercise."

"Why wouldn't Uncle James have told me this?"

"I'm a psychiatrist. If you want mind reading, it costs extra. Ah . . . here's our Nurse Jackson!"

"Am I late?" the nurse said, a little out of breath. "You did say I could have an hour, didn't you, Dr. Spencer?" Her plain little face brightened. It was obvious that she had a crush on this aristocratic doctor, something that he was probably used to.

"You're fine, dear," he assured her, "but you can brew Mrs. Marley some hot tea, if you will. Chamomile. I'd like her to sleep and she'll stay up all night if I let her."

"Of course," the nurse said. "Any medication?"

"Let's just try the hot tea first."

"Hot tea?" Andrew said in a nasty, condescending tone that sounded boorish even to himself. "You certainly use all the state-of-the-art medical miracles, don't you?"

The little nurse regarded him with indignant scorn, but Spencer seemed unaffected, maybe even amused.

"If you'll just do that for me right now, Nurse Jackson?" he said.

She scurried downstairs, happy to be of service.

"Shall we talk now, Mr. Marley, or would you prefer to come to my office tomorrow?"

"Right now is fine with me," he said tightly, leading him to Walter's study.

"Mr. Marley," he said, settling into one of Walter's deep leather chairs, "I've had no trouble diagnosing your mother's problems. Would you care to tell me yours?"

This frankness took Andrew so by surprise that he suddenly realized that he didn't know what his problems really were. So he just said the first things that popped into his head. "Very well. You're too young. You're too arrogant. I don't think I like you and I'm not sure you're good for Mother." He knew he sounded superficial and spiteful, like a defensive child, but he was unable to stop it.

"Hmm," he said, considering, "You left out the part about your uncle engaging me without your consent."

"You can add that. Thank you."

"Let's see if I can put your mind at ease. I'm a qualified psychiatrist, graduated at the top of my class at Johns Hopkins"—he ticked off each point on his fingers—"I was on the Tulane Medical School faculty and now I have a select private practice, though I still lecture infrequently. It's true that I probably hold too high an opinion of myself, and whether you like me or not means absolutely nothing.

I'd rather you did, but it won't keep me up nights. As for your mother, what do you want for her?"

That left Andrew at a loss. He wanted his mother to be normal again, but he was afraid to hope that that would even be realistic. Still, medical miracles happened just often enough to delude him into thinking his mother's case was special.

"Let me tell you what I want for her," Spencer said. "I think that mere maintenance is the worst thing for her. It amounts to letting her give up. My patients are never allowed to give up. I don't."

"Dr. Justin said she'd never get better. *Everybody* said it, and believe me, I've asked every doctor in the field."

"I think she can."

"Why are you getting involved with this? Why would you want to take a hopeless case?"

Spencer smiled. "Why are you a priest? If you saw someone in spiritual pain, wouldn't you try to help? I don't like to see people in pain, either, and the mind's pain is the worst of all. It's insidious. It poisons the soul and the body.

"When your uncle started looking for another doctor, someone on the staff at New Orleans Psychiatric recommended me. I had heard about the lady: some of my colleagues knew your father. I was challenged and I started treating her. That's about it, I suppose."

"Can you cure her?"

He shrugged. "Who knows? Psychiatry is like marriage; you're never certain how it will turn out until the two of you have been at it a while. I will tell you that I think she has a much better chance with me than she had with Justin."

"Because you're a better doctor?" He was beginning to lose his angry edge. The man was a sincere charmer.

Spencer knew when he'd won Andrew over, he could spot it in a minute and he was a man who knew how to expand on an advantage. "Well, there's that, of course. And I really want to help her. I can't stand to see the waste of a person like your mother. From everything I've been told, she's a witty, bright, loving woman."

The memory of Johanna as she had been—and so very recently—still hadn't been dulled by distance. It's odd how time can do that, Andrew thought, wear away at the sharp blade of pain until it's so blunt you feel it only vaguely.

"She was that," he said.

"She still is. All we have to do is restore her. It's like restoring a painting: get rid of all the dull layers of dust and cloudy varnish so that the original beauty gleams again. It isn't impossible, but it takes a delicate touch. You have to know what you're doing."

He had definitely restored *Andrew*. In that moment, Simon Spencer had worn away his sulky veneer and bad manners. This was a very honest man: he played no games and he'd let you play yours up until the moment you realized how silly they were. "You love your work, don't you, Dr. Spencer?" Andrew asked him, smiling.

"You're damned right. Nobody stays with this specialty unless they do, it's too difficult. If I'd wanted to be rich and fulfilled, I'd have been a gynecologist."

"Too bad you're not a proctologist because I feel like a perfect asshole. Listen, please forgive me. I'm tired and grouchy and I had a really rotten flight. And I guess I'm too touchy on the subject of Mother's illness."

"Don't give it another thought. I have a very thick skin; it's one of my little survival tricks."

"Look, I'd really like to prove that I'm not a total jerk. Can you stay for a drink? I can give you whatever background you didn't get from Dr. Justin or Uncle James. It might help."

"Sounds good. Thanks."

"I'll just go check on her and say good night, okay?"

He'd started up the stairs, feeling foolishly optimistic, when he heard Spencer call softly after him.

"Make sure she drinks that hot tea!"

Time proved Andrew right about Simon Spencer. He did love his work. More than that, he took it all very personally. Simon was a mental-health commando, driven to seek and destroy madness before it destroyed his patients. Ironically, it was his obsession. The only problem with psychiatry, he complained loudly and often, was that he rarely saw patients when they were in the early stages and something simple could be done.

"They're too ashamed to see a doctor," he said, "or their families are embarrassed. The worst are the kids whose families just think they're bad kids being purposefully difficult, so they hit them to cure them."

Despite their bad beginning, Simon and Andrew became close friends. They saw each other when Andrew was home from the seminary, and once Simon stopped in Wisconsin on his way to a seminar that he called the Spring Schizophrenia Festival.

Their mutual interest in Johanna's case drew them together, of course, and as time went on, Andrew suspected that Simon's interest was getting more personal. Johanna was a very beautiful woman, and Andrew thought that Simon could hardly wait to find out what her entire personality was like. Six months after he started working with her, she began talking to him. Little dibs and drabs of conversation, at first, then whole sentences, then answers to innocuous questions.

Andrew had to know all this secondhand. She wouldn't talk to anyone *except* Simon, which lit a flare of jealousy when Simon told him. Andrew was at the same time elated because she was responding, and disturbed because he thought that if she'd have talked to anyone, it would have been to her own son.

To Johanna, Simon was an impersonal observer and that made him perfectly trustworthy. He was her *tabula rasa,* simply listening and reserving judgment. She had no fear that she would offend or hurt him with anything she said. So she began to speak. She was no fount of oratory, of course, but it was a beginning, and unbelievably encouraging.

Simon's friendship provided Andrew much the same balm. He too could talk to Simon without reservation. Andrew began to see that friendship is based not so much on what you have in common, but how well the friend fills in the gaps in your own life. There were pieces of Simon's personality that drew Andrew, things about Simon that Andrew admired and wished he could develop in himself. Simon had a wonderful, free sensuality, not just about sex, but in the way the term relates to anything that stirs any of the five senses. Like Walter, he was never afraid of new things, of exploring for answers.

Andrew's friendship with Simon ended a growing, restless isolation. Of course he *knew* a lot of people; he had grown up in New Orleans, after all, and New Orleans is a relentlessly social city. But his old friends treated him differently now. New Orleans is a relentlessly *Catholic* city; even if you're Jewish, you can't escape the Catholic influence. And all of a sudden, Andrew was a priest, and the brand of Protestantism made no difference. A priest is a priest. To his friends, even the non-religious ones, he was no longer a man who could appreciate a dirty joke or an all-night session of rhythm and blues at the old spots. They still liked him, but he felt a restraint when they were all together.

Simon never let anything or anyone intimidate him like that. He thought what he thought and he did what he did.

Repression, he frequently said, was the root of all madness.

He and Andrew had several discussions about that. Andrew felt that a little repression was good for the soul; Simon felt that it was a social convention that the world was better off without.

"Okay, let's consider total honesty. Would you tell your best friend that his tie was garish, in bad taste, and made him look like a fool?" Andrew asked him once.

He looked directly and penetratingly at Andrew's own tie. "You don't hear me saying a word, do you? Really, Andrew, sparing someone's feelings is not the same as repression, as you very well know. The only reason you're arguing for repression is not that you believe in it, but that you think you *ought* to, given the strict sanctity of the High Anglican Church."

"I'm not arguing for repression; I'm arguing for morality." He knew the minute that he said it that he shouldn't have. He could almost hear the gong sound in Simon's brain.

And Simon sprung from his corner like a champ. "Aha! And you're now professionally qualified to know what constitutes morality?"

"Not at all. But we have to set some standards, put up some guideposts. Why do you think we have the Ten Commandments?"

"Because people are too terrified of accepting the notion that there are very few natural boundaries to human behavior and so we must set our own individual standards. The responsibility is overwhelming. We're always looking for someone else to give us the rules, and whatever rules fit in with our way of thinking, we make up our minds to obey them. Some people keep looking for the philosophies that fit. They go from religion to religion, from Catholicism to Fundamentalism to Paganism, from group to group, trying desperately to find some moral guide that they can live with. They try Zen, they try spiritualism, they delve into therapy with a vengeance and *that*, of course, opens up a whole new maze of paths to wander."

"There's nothing wrong with *seeking*, Simon. Some of the church's most devout communicants have found peace with us after years of searching. And they become excellent Anglicans; they've made an informed choice, out of many."

"But most people never find what they're looking for," Simon said with a touch of resignation. "They end up feeling as if something is missing, and that they can have no peace, no completeness until they've found it. They might not even have a name for it, but they feel that if they could only try one more religion or one more club or one more cause— or even one more person to love or to fuck or *whatever*— they'd find that elusive part of the puzzle. They never realize that all they need to do is set their own code of standards and live within it. It can be as simple or as elaborate as they like. But trying to live within someone else's idea of morality is a self-defeating battle. What you want to do is try to be a good person—*your own idea* of a good person, anyway. Half my job is spent trying to make people see that one simple fact. And the frustration is that even when they understand it, they can't accept it. No one can believe that life is so simple. They still want to look to other people to gauge their own lives. The struggle to be 'normal' is the very thing that drives people mad."

The discussion on responsibility flowed right over Andrew. He and Simon had had it before. But this time, something he'd said struck Andrew, something that was only a throwaway remark. *The feeling that something is missing*, Simon had said, *and until we find it, we have no peace*.

It was an idea that had already gained a foothold in Andrew's imagination. That feeling that there was something he was *supposed* to be doing with his life but he wasn't doing it, didn't even know what it was.

From an early age he had felt that emptiness, a gaping hole in the psyche, waiting to be filled, and he had thought at first that time and experience would pave it over. Later, after he began to think seriously about the priesthood, he became convinced that his vocation was what was missing. *That* was what he was supposed to do. And for some years, the feeling did go away. He was smugly convinced that he was doing exactly what was required of his life, that everything was moving along apace toward completion.

And then, as he worked in the seminary, that incomplete feeling came back, stronger than ever. It had a vicious edge to it this time, a bleak frustration. Something was still missing in his life, something important. All of a sudden it seemed that he had wasted years on the wrong path, and all his study was only preparation to waste more. The notion that his being a priest was not at all what he was meant to do with his life was something he couldn't, wouldn't, acknowledge. Andrew had pushed it so far back into his mind that it only cast the lightest shadow.

The conversations between Andrew and Simon weren't always that weighty. Many of them centered on women. To Simon, women were all slightly mystical creatures, and his admiration for them was a constant distraction. There were always several women coming in and going out of his life, and it was impossible to classify his preferences. There were sweet young things with enormous eyes and boyish hair, and beautifully maintained older women. Ethereal fashion types, and earth goddesses right out of a Rubens painting. There were statuesque Junos and fluttery, fairylike girls with hair like sunset clouds. For the longest time, there was a mysterious, smoky-eyed brunette that seemed to come and go at strange intervals, and Andrew could only assume that she was a married woman.

Simon was never indiscreet about his love affairs, but Andrew knew. He was Simon's best friend; he *had* to know.

One afternoon, when Andrew was home for the summer, he and Simon were relaxing at an outdoor cafe in the French Quarter, sipping gin and tonic with extra lime under a blue umbrella that cast a cool shade over their faces.

"I love this place," Simon said. "When I first moved to New Orleans, I lived right over there across the street, on the corner of Dumaine and Decatur. Sunday mornings, the first thing I'd hear when I woke up would be the calliope playing on the riverboat, and the first smell on the air would be pralines cooking in the candy factory across the street. I'd burrow a little into the sheets and feel contented, as if everything was going on exactly as it should be and I was occupying my place in the universe."

Andrew sipped his gin and smiled. "That's very philosophical for so early in the afternoon."

"And I'm not even drunk. As I *get* drunk, however, and since I'm feeling introspective, I'll probably tell you all about the women in my life. I've known some wonderful women."

"So I've gathered. You know, Simon, with your attitude, you could have been a Marley. You remind me a lot of my father."

He sighed deeply. "It's remarks like that that make me wish I was a Freudian."

"Before he met Mother, Dad was a great one with the ladies, I heard. And my great-grandfather was supposedly a wild one."

"Too bad you don't take advantage of your heritage, then," he said, raising his eyebrows.

"Which means what?"

"I've watched the way women look at you, my friend, and I've watched the way you don't look back. I don't like the implications of that, professionally speaking."

"I look," Andrew said, sensing trouble.

"But you don't touch. If you're going to be celibate, why didn't you keep up the family Catholicism?"

"I've been in school. I'm not celibate, I'm *busy!*"

"Rubbish. You've got a week of vacation left, you're in one of the world's most romantic cities, the town's full of lonely tourist ladies looking for adventure, and you just sit here with the likes of me." He shook his head at the waste. "Don't you believe in love?"

"I was in love," Andrew said defensively.

Simon arched his eyebrows. Andrew hated it when he did that and he was the subject.

"I was sixteen, she was eighteen, and it came to nothing," Andrew told him.

"Oh. You prefer older women? That's interesting."

"Would you rather I made an appointment for this, Doctor?"

"Oh my, no. This isn't work, it's entertainment. Go on, what happened?"

"Nothing."

He put down his gin in astonishment. "Nothing? You can't mean that you're a virgin!"

Two slightly startled tourists looked over in amusement.

"Good grief! Will you lower your voice?" Andrew hissed at him. "No, I'm *not* a virgin, for God's sake! I lost my virginity at twenty-two to a thirty-three-year-old colleague of my father's. Angela was the sexiest woman I've ever met, it was great, and I haven't had a conversation like this since the high-school locker room. Now, are we through with this subject?"

"I love older women myself," Simon confided. "They're more intelligent and, of course, practice makes perfect. So," he said, biting into a lime, "how long did you stay with this corrupter of youth, and if you tell me it was just a one-night thing I'll never think as well of you again."

"Oh . . . let's see . . . ten months, I guess. Until she went on sabbatical to Europe and we kind of faded out. I suppose I'd had all the education she cared to give me." Andrew laughed as memories of Angela suddenly appeared as freshly colored as if they had just been painted. "She was quite wonderful, really. In a staid community of academics, she went out of her way to be shocking. I was surprised that she kept me a secret, but I think that was because my father was the only person on the faculty that she respected.

"She certainly knew what she wanted, though," Andrew recalled, the thought of it making him smile. "It was one of those instant attractions: the minute I saw that red hair and all that creamy cleavage I was hot all over. You have absolutely no restraint at that age, and don't think she didn't know it! In those few months, she made the most of it, too."

Simon put down his glass, fascinated. "I must say, I'm shocked, Father; really shocked." He said it loudly enough that the tourist couple leaned a little closer, but Andrew was beyond noticing.

"Yeah? Wait'll you hear how it happened. This is great! I met her at my parents' house and she practically seduced me with my father standing right *there*. It was the night Mother and I gave this big party for Dad . . ."

He stopped cold, other memories crowding out the good ones. All he could see, for what may have been several minutes, was his father's face as he lay on the floor, his body floating in a halo of blood.

"Andrew?" Simon said. "Are you still here?"

"That was the night my father died," Andrew said, the words coming out like slow, thick molasses.

"He killed himself *that* night?" Simon said quietly. "On the same night that you had your first sexual experience?"

"No . . . not exactly, but he . . ." All of a sudden, the memories cleared and he was in control again. "No way, Dr. Freud. I can see where this is leading and you can forget it. I think sex is great, women are marvelous, and every man should have one. All right?"

"Andrew, this is serious. Your father's death . . ."

"I was thinking in the abstract. He didn't kill himself until much later. But something strange happened to him that night and he was never really himself again. I always felt that that night was somehow linked to his death."

" 'Something strange,' you said? What happened?"

He didn't want to go into it. When he had told Simon the things he needed to know to treat Johanna, he had left out the part about Walter's weird behavior the night of the party. In fact, he had managed to block that right out of his mind, Scarlett O'Hara–like, by telling himself that he could put off thinking about it until he had more distance. How *much* distance, he avoided specifying.

To distract Simon, Andrew eyed a particularly succulent tourist lady at another table and gave Simon a nudge. "Come on, Casanova. Are you going to teach me your foolproof technique or what?"

"I'm not letting you off the hook," he said. "Why did you bring your father up now? You never talk about him."

"There's nothing to talk about. I loved him, he died, and I never understood why he did it. But analyzing his reasons now could hardly make any difference, so I don't want to talk about it."

"Andrew . . ."

"I *don't* want to *talk about it*!" His tone came off harsher than he meant, but Simon did turn back to his gin and tonic, though not without a slight scowl.

Many times since that summer's conversation, Andrew wished he could tell Simon about the visceral fear that the very thought of his father's death aroused in him. It wasn't the fear of death, it was a terror that had no basis that he could understand. But he could hardly tell Simon about it; he was too busy denying it himself.

But what Simon had said about completion leading to peace bothered Andrew constantly. That look of peace on Walter's face as he lay on the study floor had never left Andrew. What was it? What had Walter been looking for, what had he gained? Did he feel that his life was complete, or had he found the missing piece of the puzzle only when he pulled the trigger?

Either way, the answer was something he didn't want to contemplate.

PART THREE

†

7

De Profundis
Andrew Stephen Marley, 1965

The evening of Andrew's ordination as a priest was the greatest night of his life. Later, when he had the time and emotional distance to speculate on it, he supposed that's why all the details came back with such perfect, painful clarity. Painful, because when we look back on turning points in our lives, what stands out is the touching trust that we placed in the future, and what darkens the memory is our present knowledge that nothing as pure as that trust lasts for very long.

But that night, at the moment when he peeked surreptitiously through the sacristy doors, that innocent trust was still intact, glowing like a bright coal about to burst into a dazzling flame. He had never been happier.

The old Episcopal cathedral was packed with family, friends, and several ancient parishioners who had known his mother's family for years. He was amused to see Simon, sitting through a fortuitous quirk of fate only a pew away from Angela Winfield.

Andrew hadn't seen Angela for the three years he'd been in the seminary, but they'd been good years for her, obviously. She was burnished with that dignity that sat so well on women, the kind that comes with accomplishment. The sight of her had the same effect as it did the night she dragged him away from that party. It was probably the most inappropriate feeling he could have, under the circumstances, and the incongruity of it made him laugh.

As he waited for the ceremony to begin, a rush of excitement pumped through him, making him feel as if he had been stretched five feet taller. The only thing that brought him back to reality was his mother's absence. He kept trying not to think about it. Rationally, he understood how impossible it was for her to be here, but emotionally he missed her. He still couldn't completely come to grips with her illness; her inability to cope sometimes frustrated him to the point where he was half-convinced that it wasn't inability—it was refusal. That was something that he could understand, at least.

He had asked Simon if Johanna was well enough to attend.

"Ask her yourself," he'd told Andrew. "It might force her to make a decision."

But Johanna was never one to be coerced. She had shaken her head and looked at him in that distant, Madonna-like way she had, looking ethereally fragile, her skin almost translucent from so much time away from the sun.

He was amazed to see that she was more beautiful than ever. Johanna was at that age when women reached a glorious peak that excited any man who truly understood women. Walter had understood them, and Johanna in particular, and he would have hated to see her sitting here, living only in her mind. His ghost would have rejoiced to see her, blooming and brilliant, on the arm of someone who appreciated her.

"Mother, do you understand what I'm asking you?" Andrew had said to her. "It would mean everything to me for you to be there."

She studied him for a minute, touching his hands, smoothing her fingers lightly over his face like a blind woman trying to reconstruct a memory. Andrew had no doubt that whatever Simon was doing for her, it was working, but slowly. So maddeningly slow. Every day she showed a little more animation, a little more awareness. She still wouldn't talk to anyone else, as if speech would shatter the thin shell of her memories. Sometimes Andrew was able to take it, sometimes it almost drove him crazy with frustration. He wanted to pull her out of her isolation, physically snatch her up from that chair and shake her. He had this fantasy that she would blink, look around like a woman coming out of a faint, and say, "What's going on? Where am I?" and they'd laugh and everything would be fine.

Faced with what we don't understand, we always hope for simple answers.

"I know you understand what ordination means to me," Andrew said to her, "and I hope you'll be happy. This will be the turning point in my life, Mother; after tonight, I can fulfill my purpose. I can begin to do God's work."

The strangest shadow crossed her face, a desperate anguish in her eyes that didn't belong there, not in the light of the happy occasion he'd come about. Instead, she looked at him almost in horror. Then her face calmed as if a curtain had dropped and she turned back toward the window and her dreams.

Now, in the glowing cathedral, Andrew's life was beginning. After the formal procession, he knelt in the sanctuary, lit by dim electric light and a profusion of candles. The rich, resiny scent of frankincense and myrrh calmed him with familiar memories.

"Good people," Bishop Acker said to the congregation, "this is him whom we purpose, God willing, to receive this day into the holy office of priesthood . . . if there be any of you who knoweth any impediment in him, let him come forth in the name of God."

Andrew had never heard the old words of the Order of Service with so much understanding. He had read them of course, over and over, thinking about the day when he'd hear them spoken on his behalf, and had heard them applied to other candidates, but now they carried a somber weight that brought every insecurity to the surface. Was he truly meant for this? Was he good enough? Were his motives good enough? The thought of people placing their spiritual welfare in his hands was a terrifying—and fulfilling—one.

The most inexplicable thing happened then. A spasm of nausea rose in him, causing him to grip the altar rail to steady himself. He could feel his face flush.

The bishop noticed Andrew's discomfort, giving him a quick, reassuring smile. Nerves. Nothing unusual. The bishop began his address to the candidate.

"Have always printed in your remembrance how great a treasure is committed to your charge," the bishop said directly to Andrew, "and if it should happen that the same church or any member thereof do take hurt by reason of your negligence, ye know the greatness of the fault and the punishment that will ensue."

It seemed that the atmosphere of the cathedral was growing more oppressive by the minute. The incense, so reassuring just a moment before, smothered him like a thick blanket, making every breath a conscious act.

He suddenly had a vision of his mother, a sight so clear and startling in its detail that it might have been projected against the white altar cloth. He saw her bolt straight up from her chair and clutch at her throat as she started to scream. It was so awful that he couldn't see anything else for a minute. He shook his head and the vision cleared, but it left him rattled.

"Do you think in your heart that you are truly called to the Order and Ministry of the Priesthood?"

He opened his mouth to give the reply but he couldn't go on. The incense clogged his throat. He swallowed hard, trying to breathe. Come on, he thought, this is the most important moment of your life!

"I do think it," he replied. It came out clear and strong, somehow cutting through the nausea and the choked breath.

He finished the examination and kneeled in relief as the Veni Creator Spiritus began. At last, he felt Bishop Acker's hands on his head as he knelt, bringing back the peace he had felt in the beginning. Almost at once, the nausea and the dizziness subsided and he felt stronger and more alive than ever before. This was what he wanted, had worked all his life to fulfill.

"Receive the Holy Ghost for the office and work of a priest in the Church of God, now committed unto thee by the imposition of our hands. In the name of the Father, and of the Son, and of the Holy Ghost. Amen."

That moment was so beautiful that all the personal sorrows of the last few years were wiped away, and Andrew was more contented, more at peace, than he ever had been. He was changed forever. His real life was about to begin.

The reception in the parish hall was a swarm of congratulations and introductions. He was taking his second glass of champagne when Simon joined him at the long, candlelit table.

"Are you positive you're all right?" Simon said, collecting his own glass of Taittinger and a few hot hors d'oeuvres. "You turned green as a silkworm during the ceremony, and you still look a little ragged."

"Come on. It's only nerves. How many times have you told me what the mind can do to the body?"

"Probably to the point of boredom, I'm sure. Well, if you feel so cheery, perhaps you can manage to make a formal introduction." Simon scanned the crowd, looking for the right face.

"Oh no," Andrew told him, "absolutely not. I swear I can read your mind. Part of my new job is to *prevent* sin, not cause an occasion of it."

Simon looked injured. "You misjudge me. How do you know I'm not in love and plan to be respectable at last? Now, this is your crowd, so tell me: who is the delicious-looking redhead?"

"Oh . . . right. I think I know the one you mean. I believe that is the eminent Dr. Angela Winfield, department of Anthropology, Tulane University. In your dreams, pal; she'd be on to your scam in a minute."

Simon choked on his Swedish meatball. "Angela Winfield? The seductress who took your virginity . . . *that* Angela Winfield? And you let her get away from you? I knew you were chaste but I never thought you were foolish. Never mind, I'll introduce myself. A recommendation from you might not carry much weight, after all. Well," he said, shaking his hand distractedly, "congratulations and good-bye."

"Confession, Thursday nights at seven-thirty, be there or be damned." Andrew couldn't help laughing as a very determined Simon disappeared into the crowd. If he was going to try to seduce Angela, he was going to get more than he bargained for whether she said yes or no. All of a sudden, he felt a stab of jealousy and hoped it was no. He really wanted to see her himself. Three years. Almost four. That should be enough time for him to act rationally around her, to put what he had felt for her into perspective. Looking back on it, he had the uneasy feeling that Angela had been—and would always be—the right woman at the wrong time.

Before this thought could really depress him, he got caught in a swarm of well-wishing ladies, all of whom seemed to remember him when he was four years old and none of whose names he could recall. This was going to be his first test as a priest, he realized: how to make conversation and not have the slightest idea whom you were talking to. As it turned out, the loquacious ladies only required a few charming smiles, some "Oh, reallys?" and a couple of "You don't says!" and they were off on a conversational bender.

By the time he got away, he had lost sight of Simon and Angela. He had no idea if they had connected or not.

"Since when are you pimping for your friends?" The woman's voice came amused and clear behind him. He was too embarrassed to turn around and find out who was speaking and to whom.

The voice came again, closer to his ear this time. "Yes, I mean *you*, Father. Shame on you, sending your shrink over to make a pass. What kind of therapy are you in, anyway?"

How could he have forgotten that warm-honey voice? "God, Angela!" He turned to hug her, careful to make it the kind you give a friend. "I'm so glad you showed up."

"The first woman to seduce you always has a hold over you, they tell me. How you doing, sweet thing?"

"Still with a taste for the slightly shocking? And I heard you were a full professor now, with tenure."

"Tenure? Honey, I'm practically an emeritus, tottering around the campus. I can't believe you went ahead and did it. Became a priest. And after everything I did to talk you out of it."

He shrugged. "I wasn't trained to get a real job."

"Honestly, I'm really proud of you. I thought of calling you a hundred times over the past few years. Especially after Walter died. I was on sabbatical in Romania or I would have been right here for you and Johanna."

"We got your cable, though, and the flowers. And Mother said you'd called her. I appreciated it." In truth, in the aftermath of Walter's death he had been surprised to find that there was no one he wanted to talk to more than Angela. Being with her in times of trouble was like spreading cool ointment on a burn. He had never been sure just why their affair had ended, but it had definitely been Angela's decision. Nothing about it had been said outright between them, just Angela's subtle, gradual withdrawal until her going on sabbatical was like closing a door.

"Well, I respected your father so much," she said. "I was probably the worst teaching assistant in the history of education, but he tolerated my mistakes. Turned an air-headed Texas deb into a fairly decent anthropologist, too."

"He was a good man."

"How's Johanna?"

"She's fine."

The sudden flash of pain didn't escape Angela. "She's not fine. Don't give me any of that polite bullshit. What's wrong with her?"

"I wish there was some simple way to put it," he told her, relieved to let it out to someone who cared. "You met Simon. He's her doctor, not mine. I don't know . . . after Dad died, she just fell apart. She went into the worst depression I've ever seen and nothing seems to touch it. Not drugs, not time, not therapy. The doctor before Simon tried antidepressants. The doctor before that wanted to check her into some trendy, experimental hospital. I told him where he could shove that, and mentioned the name of a good malpractice lawyer."

"Jesus," Angela said, somewhat taken aback, "for a pampered rich kid, you've had a pretty bad time of it. Why didn't you call me? I was probably back by then."

"I'm supposed to call you after all that time just to dump on you?"

"Look, I'm trying hard to be polite, and you know what a strain that is on me," she said. "Now that you're back in town, if you ever want to come around, just to talk or anything, do it. I think about you from time to time, you know. I used to worry how a naive kid like you was ever going to get along in the world."

"Then how come you kicked me out?"

"God! Five minutes with you and you're difficult already. I didn't kick you out. I wasn't getting any younger, kid, and you didn't seem to be getting any older. Besides, I wanted you to remember me as I was before my tits started to sag."

The flip tone didn't fool him for a minute. Whatever she had been holding back years ago was still in reserve. He felt he had even less right to ask her about it now than he did then.

"Angela, the ten months I spent with you aged me twenty years."

She brightened at that. "Yes? Well, that just makes me so happy that I think I'll have some more champagne. But . . . honestly . . . if you'd like to come by . . ."

"You're sure you'd like to have me?"

Her laugh was slightly suggestive, whether she meant it or not. "Interesting choice of words, Father. But call me anyway."

The good-bye kiss she gave him looked innocent enough, but the warm flicker of her tongue across his cheek made him feel twenty-two and hot again. Maybe it *was* true about the first woman who seduced you. He wanted to say more, but she was gone. That seemed to be his pattern with Angela.

He saw Father Moore coming his way. Father Moore had been the priest of his home parish since before Andrew was born. Andrew hadn't really known any other, and Father Moore was such a good priest that Andrew was always in awe of him.

"I haven't had a chance yet to tell you how proud I am of you," Father Moore said to him. "When a priest comes out of my parish, I feel like I've fulfilled God's purpose in a very special way, and you . . . well, I never doubted your vocation for a minute."

Andrew loved the old man. His kindness and strength had helped him through uncertain times, those incidents of growing up that he just couldn't tell his parents, no matter how he trusted and loved them. Father Moore didn't preach and he didn't condemn, he had just helped Andrew understand life a little better.

"You can be sure it was your example, Father."

The sudden dizziness he'd felt in the church caught him totally by surprise. He clutched Father Moore's arm to keep from falling.

"I'm still feeling the aftereffects of everything," Andrew told him, somewhat embarrassed at the loss of dignity.

"Perfectly natural," he said. "The excitement, the nerves . . ."

"Most likely the champagne," Andrew said. "Father, do you think anyone would miss me if I disappeared for a while? I could use a few minutes of fresh air in the cloister garden."

He wandered through the dim corridors of the cathedral and out into the humid night air.

He had come to the cloister garden often. Its seclusion appealed to him, the silence of the high walls covered in concealing vines. The garden was, like so much of New Orleans, timeless, untouched by the changes of the years, so that you could lose yourself in any century you wished. It was a poetic place, especially now, with the flowers and trees frosted by moonlight.

He wandered to the farthest part of the garden, feeling only a little better with the gulps of night air. When another wave of dizziness swirled through him, he sat down heavily on an ornamental iron bench. The nausea returned, too, this time violently, like a fist in the stomach. The sharp, bitter bile in the back of his throat forced him to lean over and vomit into the grass as he held desperately to the arms of the bench to keep from falling. He clung to the old iron as if he'd sink, weighted with chains, to the bottom of a stinking sea if he let go. When he tried to stand, pushing himself up against the bench arms, he realized that he was too sick to walk. His legs, inexplicably, were hurting, a spasmodic pain like a charley horse, but more intense.

The dizziness was getting much worse. A distant echo grow louder and louder, blotting out the night sounds. He put his hands over his ears and discovered that it was his own heart, beating out of all rhythm, being pushed beyond its limits.

He was wild with fear, which only made it worse. He was having a heart attack or a stroke, and no one, *no one*, was going to come out to this garden for a long time, maybe days. He thought of the people inside. How long before they missed him? By the time anyone thought to look for him, it would be all over. How long does it take to have a heart attack? Could he possibly make it back to the corridor? If he yelled for help, it might echo down those long empty halls and someone would come.

He opened his mouth and couldn't scream. He didn't have any breath.

Seized by a massive band of pain around his chest, Andrew fell facedown on the grass, not even noticing the pain for the fear. His body felt so hot, his skin burning! He tore at his clothes, popping buttons, ripping seams, trying to get out of what felt like a flaming envelope of cloth and skin.

All he could think, over and over, was, Oh please, God! Please, not now! I *can't* die now!

He finally became aware of someone standing close to him, and started to sob in relief. His face boiling with fevered sweat, he raised his head.

A woman was standing not four feet from him.

The dizziness had turned into an agonizing pain that tore through his muscles and joints, sending them into spasm. He felt his shoulder dislocate as the muscles pulled out of their natural shape. But the sudden relief of knowing that someone was there, someone was going to bring help, drove the pain to some anesthetized pocket in his brain.

Andrew reached out to her, every movement a new experience in torment. "Please," he pleaded, "help me!"

There was something strange about the way she looked at him: with an intense curiosity, but no sympathy.

He was suddenly terrified of her.

He screamed then, as the agony ripped through him once more in fresh waves. He thought he could see the cells in his body, distended and bursting as they distorted inside him.

The pale beauty, a *fleur du mal* if ever he'd seen one, bent down to look a little closer, so that he could see into her diabolical eyes.

"The greatest night of your life, is it?" she asked, quietly, but with a venomous edge. "You're right, priest; your life will never be the same after tonight."

She bent over him, covering his face with her incredible veil of silver hair, its strange incense inducing hallucinations of a cold flame that burned the very air. That flame, alive and moving, gathered into pictures: A young girl with eyes like his, screaming in the dark; Walter, a monster, running through the woods; a flash of young men and women, future generations of Marleys, all devastated by the blood clinging to their hands and their souls. In that hot silver fire he watched them change, watched them kill, and at last, watched them go mad.

"Do you understand what's happening to you or shall I tell you?" the woman asked.

As soon as she said it, he did understand. The instant the knowledge came to him, the woman burst into the screaming laugh of a maniac, the same laugh he had heard in his dreams of his father.

"Why?" he asked her, his throat burning around the words. "Why is this happening to me? Who are you?"

The pain returned worse than before, the breath crushed out of him by the bones thickening against his lungs.

He saw his hand, clutched to his belly, and watched in horror as the fingers stretched, the nails darkened and grew hard, as black hair covered the skin.

The woman's eyes glittered as she stooped over him. "You're about to make a payment, priest, on an old debt. It won't be enough, but it will do."

Even as she spoke, the woman was fading into the night.

"Bless yourself, Father, for your sin is great!" she sang, her laugh like smoke on the rising wind.

In unbearable pain, he fainted. The last thing he saw was the moon, its placid face changed to the rictus of nightmares.

When Andrew awakened a few minutes later, he was calm and purposeful, renewed, as if he had been forged in fire and remade in another image. The werewolf threw back his massive head, his wolf's teeth gleaming like the scythe of Death, and bayed his pleasure at being alive and released.

He bounded easily over the wall, and the cathedral garden was as silent as before he came.

Jerry Moffatt, defensive lineman for the toughest team in the NFL, was plenty pissed. Here it was, the middle of the night, and he was stranded who knew how many miles from a phone. Hell, he hadn't even passed a house for at least five miles.

That nasty little tramp would pay for this, if he could ever find her, which was doubtful. When Jerry thought of her, he got all hot and bothered again, though not quite in the same way.

It had been partly his own fault. He always went a little wild on these out-of-town games. Well, the old boys on the team liked to do that: They'd all run around, whoop it up, let the yokels know they were in town. The front office didn't approve—bad PR and all that junk—but hell! Didn't hurt nobody. So here he had been, with a winning game behind him and a couple of days of freedom ahead of him, so he had done what you're supposed to do in New Orleans: hit the bars, do a little blow, and find a nice dolly to hang on his arm.

He'd had a lot of nervous energy left. The Saints had given his team a hard time. He remembered when the Saints were a pussy team, and playing them was only a little diversion from the nonstop partying in New Orleans. Now you had to work your butt off to keep them from running your ass into the ground, and like as not, they'd do it anyway. But he and his boys had squeaked by them this afternoon, making it in the last second by a point conversion. Jerry loved playing when it was that closely matched, when he had to work at it, when he felt that what he was doing was really football, the way it should be. No matter how physically beat he was, he was mentally up for hours after he'd recovered from the game.

So he'd jumped nervously from one bar to another until he spotted her. She looked real good sitting on that barstool. She had on one of those shiny, sexy dresses that clung to her body and was cut so low that she was practically falling out of it. The little lady had no secrets, that was sure. She said she was a dancer. Maybe she really was, she sure moved like it. When she got him out of the floor she practically raped him right there. She knew the things he'd wanted to hear, too. He didn't think she was a pro: she was trying too hard.

He bought her drinks, those faggy, lady things made with three or four kinds of booze and dyed pink. She kept slapping them back but he couldn't see any effect.

This place was really boring, she told him, strictly tourist. She knew this *really* great place with a *really* great dance floor and a *really* great R&B band. He didn't want to stay here, did he? Didn't he want to see the real New Orleans?

He'd have agreed to anything; he was so horny that he could barely walk to the car.

The car did it for her. It always did. That was why he preferred to drive to out-of-town games if he could. It was a red Ferrari that the guys on the team had nicknamed the Pussymobile.

The place she wanted to go turned out to be way out in the middle of nowhere with a dark stretch of highway in between, the kind of paved path that passed for a highway in Louisiana. She snuggled up close to him with a little wiggle that didn't make his hard-on any better. Boy, that girl had educated hands! The team's wide receivers should have hands that good.

"Oh, honey," she said, her eyes wide, "can I drive it? Just a little ways? Please?"

He considered it, then decided it was probably best. He was drunk, stoned, and hated these dark roads. If she drove, he could just sit back and do a couple more toots.

They pulled over and got out, switching sides. She slid in behind the wheel, squealing with excitement. As soon as Jerry was about to sit down, she let out a little cry of distress.

"Oh! My earring! I must have dropped it out there! Oh, honey, it was real diamonds! Could you look around on the pavement while I look in here?"

"Shit, baby," Jerry complained, "couldn't you have lost it before the highway lights ran out?" It was dark as hell out there, but Jerry started searching, not bothering to close the door.

She suddenly gunned the motor and took off, the open door grazing him enough to roll him onto the gravel shoulder.

He lay there for a second, stunned, with what felt like a sprained ankle. He couldn't believe he'd fallen for an old trick like that. Shit! The insurance company was going to squeeze out his blood for this one. He felt for his wallet before he remembered he'd left it in the car. Of course.

Well, he was sure the prize asshole. What did he expect? You didn't exactly meet the kind of girl you could take home to Mom sitting on a barstool talking dirty with her boobs hanging out.

Jesus, but this road was dark! If it hadn't been for the moon, he couldn't have seen anything. No cars had come by in a while, so he'd either have to wait or walk.

He decided to walk. He stood up, testing his ankle. It hurt, but he could put his weight on it, so it couldn't be too bad.

Jerry heard the leaves crackle behind him. Raccoon, or most likely a skunk, the way things were going tonight.

He became aware of someone hiding in the bushes, right close behind him. He could hear the breathing. He wasn't too afraid. Who's gonna screw with a defensive end? Usually his sheer size scared off the wiseasses. Still, you had to be careful: lots of nuts out there these days.

He walked a little faster, never hearing actual footsteps; that was what was so weird. Just that dry crackling in the bushes. He stopped, and it stopped. He walked, and it walked. The thought of nutsos crossed his mind again. Jerry knew what was what—he had seen that movie *Deliverance*, so he knew what southerners were like.

Then the breathing started. Real heavy, like those guys with—whatchacallit—asthma. Ragged, wet-sounding breathing. Slobbery.

It began to get to him.

"Okay, asshole!" he yelled. "Quit hiding like a sneaking rabbit. You got anything to say to me, you fucker, come out an' say it!"

Nothing. Just that slow, steady rustling of leaves, coming closer. And that spooky-sounding breathing, a little louder now.

Jerry stood very still, listening, his hands getting cold and wet.

And then all the sound stopped.

He felt a pressure on his back, right in the middle, then kind of a warm, wet feel through his shirt. The pain didn't actually hit his brain for another few minutes. He spun around and gasped.

His panicked mind told him that it was a bear; he couldn't let himself believe what he was really seeing.

Jerry was plenty quick, but not quick enough. He'd never seen anything that big move that fast. He felt a wrenching, then a hot pain as his arm was cracked out of the socket. The thing spun him around to face it, its foul breath gagging him. Jerry punched at the monster with his good arm, kicking out blindly with both legs as the werewolf lifted him into the air.

Its teeth bit through his shoulder. The huge claws ripped at his chest. Blood was already gushing from the claw lacerations in his back and arm, making him progressively weaker. He couldn't hold on any longer. The monster seemed to know that it had won and threw him down like an overused stuffed toy.

As Jerry's eyes misted over, he caught a glimpse of his chest, gaping open on the left side, blood pumping out, red-glazed bones of his rib cage broken, lungs like glistening bellows, the delicate organs starting to tumble toward the opening. It was so shocking that at first he didn't connect it with his own body. Then perfect clarity . . .

Oh, my God! he thought. My heart! It wants my heart!

Then it was over, and the werewolf crouched hungrily over the remains of Jerry Moffatt.

Ripped and bloody as he was, the werewolf still felt an ecstatic joy, the pure passion that comes from doing exactly as he wished. It was animal instinct that drove him into the night, enhanced by human intelligence but unrestrained by human conscience.

He remembered his kill with pleasure. A man, a strong man, a werewolf's favorite prey. He was learning that the fight was everything; yes, the *kill* was important—a werewolf had to feed—but it was the *fight* that exhilarated him. The struggle, the blows on his body, the feel of his muscles pushing his limits gave him physical satisfaction. The blood and adrenaline pumping through his brain gave him a galvanizing mental charge. And finally, there was the addictive taste of human flesh, sweet and succulent, to renew his strength.

The kill this night was more than just a kill. It was teaching him about his nature and his new body. He found that the bitter smell of his victim's fear did something to him. When it flooded into his blunt nostrils the last vestiges of human restraint left him. This loss of humanity seemed necessary to complete the transformation, but the werewolf wasn't sure. He also discovered that they made no difference, these small peculiarities. He simply did what he had to do and reveled in it.

He found that he could cover an enormous distance. He bounded along on powerful legs with a supernatural speed, a fluidity of motion not possible with man and a dexterity not possible with animals.

The werewolf also knew many things that the priest did not—or, at least, that it would take the priest time to learn. The lunar cycle, for instance: 29 days, 12 hours, 44 minutes, and 2.8 seconds, the waxing moon before and the waning moon after, the time that would give him life and set him free no matter how the priest raged against it. He didn't know it intellectually: it was an instinct, something bred in his body, felt with each heartbeat.

He knew what would kill him and how to avoid it. He knew what would lift the curse and destroy his freedom, but the priest would never know the werewolf's mind as well as the werewolf knew his. The werewolf didn't want to know what the priest thought, he didn't care. All he wanted was to live, to run under the moon, to kill over and over until he was sated.

He also knew that this particular night was a bonus, a birth-night gift. Each Marley werewolf's first transformation was on the greatest night of his life, whether it was a full moon or not. The werewolf didn't understand this, but understanding was not important to him. Just knowing was enough: psychological complexities and rational human logic were useless. He was born of instinct, of physical impulse, of the hidden and dark secrets of the moon and the night.

His time was short now. This night was almost gone, but there would be another for him, and very soon.

He ran with his huge, bounding stride back toward the city, taking care to conceal himself when necessary with an animal's stealth. A werewolf knew how to blend with the night.

He had run a short way when his sharpened hearing detected footsteps, when his newly sensitive nostrils caught a scent that was human, yet not human, a scent like his own. The footfalls were heavy, powerful, and the stride perfectly matched his, step by step. Puzzled, but with a growing excitement, he stopped and turned.

Another werewolf stood looking at him, its face almost human in expression. This was a graceful creature, smaller than himself, with an elegant blond pelt whose highlights shone in the moonlight like polished gold. The golden were-wolf's topaz eyes fixed the young werewolf to the spot. The young one was too fascinated to move.

As he watched, the golden one changed, mutated almost effortlessly back to human form, until a woman stood there, absolutely in command and absolutely still. She was tall, majestic, with the inbred hauteur of a queen. Her quiet, wise eyes looked at him with great sympathy.

Warily, the werewolf pulled back a little.

"Can you speak?" the woman asked.

The werewolf hadn't even thought to try. He made a few inarticulate sounds with the cadence of speech, but not the clarity.

"Never mind," the woman said, "it will come in time. You're very young." She stroked the werewolf's pelt. "Only a few hours old. Do you have any idea who I am?"

The werewolf shook his head.

She smiled. "Well. No reason you should. But I've known your family before."

The werewolf stood still in confusion.

"My name is Marie-Thérèse. But my friends call me Zizi. And I hope we'll be friends, Andrew.

"You must learn," Zizi told him, "that there are were-wolves and there are werewolves. Some choose that life, born into it of free will. Some have it given as a wonderful gift. But some come into being like you, because of a curse. And that's a terrible way to live, Andrew. I can offer you the opportunity to make peace with yourself, if you're ready to take it.

"You feel glorious now, don't you? Free and strong, powerful and in control of yourself. But for cursed loups-garous, that lasts only for the night. And your nights will haunt your days, your victims will confront you in visions when the sun rises, your life will become a compromise of conscience in which you constantly weigh the sin of suicide against the sin of murder. A cursed loup-garou has none of the joys and all of the despair. Your life will be lived in solitude; your days will be full of fear for the night and your nights will be endless, with no help nor solace nor justice.

"But for those who willingly *choose* the werewolf's life, it can be an intoxicating one. Their senses are heightened, they have psychic bonds with each other, they have a life span of hundreds of years, and those years will be a dream of sensuality and freedom. The transformation is orgasmic, the kill a righteous act of justice."

She reached up to touch his face. Overcome by an emotion he didn't understand, the werewolf covered her small hand with his and cradled it against his cheek. When he did, he felt a warmth between the two of them, an attraction beyond human ideas of love.

"I can give you that life, Andrew. I can change your curse into a blessing. And when you want it, all you have to do is tell me. I'll never be very far away. You'll remember this only vaguely at first, because you haven't yet integrated your werewolf and human conciousnesses, but what I've told you will mean more to you as time passes."

Looking into his eyes a last time, she pulled her hand away, slowly.

As the werewolf watched, Zizi dissolved into the night as if she had been no more than a golden dream. The werewolf stood stunned for a moment. He didn't understand all of

what was happening to him, but he knew that what Zizi
had just told him was the absolute truth.

He started back to the cathedral garden. That was something else he knew by instinct: that it was best to die his temporary death in the same place he'd been born at moonrise.

The moon was going down now, the animal waning with
it. He had no sooner gotten over the wall when he felt the
first shock of transformation. The pain was as bad for the
werewolf as it had been for the priest, paralyzing his voice
so that he couldn't howl against it. That was for his own
protection, he knew, because in this twilight state he was
vulnerable to anything.

He doubled over, the fur dropping off his body and
vanishing, leaving him stained with blood. Fragments of
human skin, not his own, still clung to him and clotted his
fingernails as the claws receded. His body elongated, then
contracted, his mind changing with his body, getting more
human as the light changed from dark to dawn.

Andrew lay curled up on the wet grass, shivering with
cold and his whole body vibrating with pain. He looked
up and saw a young man standing there, a ghost, white
and accusing, crying for the life he'd lost at the werewolf's
hands.

This was the worst. Out of the whole episode, this was
the cruelest part.

One ghost. What would it be like when there were two,
ten, twenty? How could he stand their accusations? He
thought of earlier Marley loups-garous, of Walter, of the
months, the years of murders and the regiments of the dead
that confronted them all.

And here he was, the latest of a dreadful line, destroyed
by what he knew, and what he had still to learn. He could
remember what the werewolf had done, as if he were a

horrified spectator standing to one side, unable to stop the outrage he plainly saw coming, but forced to look. The clearest memory was of the silver-haired woman, the most confusing was Zizi. Of the murder itself, he remembered very little, only the uncontrollable feeling of being over-whelmed.

Andrew knew that he had been told something very important, but it was like a dream conversation: while you're dreaming it seems to hold the key to your life. When you wake, you try desperately to recall it, but can't.

He gathered his clothes discarded the evening before and tried to stand on legs made unsteady by grief and exhaustion. The cathedral was deserted now. He could kneel in the darkness and try to think what to do.

And to offer prayers to a God who may have stopped listening.

8

The lights came up in the theater, signaling the end of the first act of Bizet's *Carmen*. In one of the boxes, two women sat quietly, their eyes adjusting to the brightness. A matched pair of golden goddesses, their blond heads catching the lights from the crystal sconces.

"Ah, I just love it," the younger one said to her companion. She stretched slightly but satisfyingly, trying not to test the limits of her strapless ebony velvet dress. "All that wonderfully lowlife passion, all those nineteenth-century whores singing right through the cat fights." She sighed. "If life were only as interesting."

Her companion, equally blond, a little more beautiful but graced with an air of ancient experience, cocked an eyebrow at this. "Your life isn't interesting enough?"

The younger woman fanned herself absently with the program. "Well, anything gets stale after a while."

"I think," her companion said with a slight tease, "you're just trying for an effect. No werewolf's life is ever boring, Georgiana."

Georgiana opened her turquoise eyes innocently wide and turned to her. "Now, why did you come all the way up here to Boston to see me, Marie-Thérèse? I hope it's because you still think of me from time to time."

Her companion regarded this flirtatious fluff with the disdain it deserved, but she smiled at the name. Georgiana was almost the only one who ever called her by her real name these days. "I never stop thinking about you," Marie Thérèse

106

said, "I never forget those I love. But that's not enough to bring me all the way to the godless East. I'm here because you have to come home."

Georgiana froze at this. "Forget it. I'll never go back there, not as long as there are Marleys in New Orleans. Besides, the family history says I died in London; I made sure of it. How am I going to explain the fact that I'm back . . . and that I only look about twenty-six or twenty-seven? Remember what you taught me? A werewolf only ages one year to a human's ten?"

"I thought I had taught you something about responsibility, too. And you have a very serious responsibility now."

"Not to anyone in New Orleans, I don't."

"You just haven't been keeping up with things. There's a young man there who needs your help. Badly."

Georgiana's eyes went dark with bitter irony. "I can no more help him than I could help myself all those years ago. And I refuse to rake up the pain that going to New Orleans would inflict on me."

. Marie-Thérèse shifted slightly in her velvet seat to lean closer to Georgiana. "Do you remember, *chérie,* when I found you on Honey Island, crying like you'd dissolve in your tears? And I consoled you, and held you until it was finished, and tried to persuade you that being a loup-garou wasn't as bad as you thought?"

Georgiana pulled away from her. "Well, you *did* persuade me. I was able to accept it, even welcome it, and now I can't imagine living any other life. But that doesn't mean I have to go back to Louisiana."

Marie-Thérèse sighed with resignation. "You're just like the rest of your stubborn family. Bullheaded. I've always admired you, Georgiana; I know what it took for you to hang on after what happened to you. Cursed loups-garous just don't dig in and deal with it the way you did. Most likely, they walk Walter's path. It's easier. This young man is as strong as you, but I tell you, Georgiana: he isn't strong enough to do it alone. No one is. There is no way he can reconcile being a loup-garou with being a priest, not without help. And he needs the kind of help only you can give him. Blood calls to blood, Geo. Family calls to family. Your curse binds the two of you together, even more inevitably than blood. You can fill in the gaps for him, tell him the family history that I can't. I might be able to teach him how to be a loup-garou, if he'd listen—which he won't—but only you can teach him what it means to be a Marley, to tap into that well of strength."

Georgiana looked away, but the anguish in her eyes was the bitterness of seeing the truth, naked and blinding. She had no choice, and Marie-Thérèse knew it.

"This is your responsibility, Geo, and you have to shoulder it. This is *family;* doesn't that stir anything in you at all? You've had a lovely life of freedom all this time, you cut yourself off from any emotional pain."

Geo's voice was choked and low. "How can you *say* that?"

"Because it's true. You remember the pain of the past, but you bury it, you push it away every time it comes up. You haven't done with it, Georgiana. You haven't banished it, and you never will. Not as long as you hide here. Be as strong as you can, Geo. Go back to New Orleans and save this young man. You can save yourself in the bargain."

Georgiana looked as if she meant to speak. Her quick, grieved look changed to anger; whether at herself or not, Marie-Thérèse couldn't tell. Instead of saying another word, she rose rapidly from her chair and swept out of the box, her magnificent, infuriated figure retreating into the shadows of the hallway.

Marie-Thérèse started to follow her, but as the orchestra began the second-act overture, she sighed and poured herself a glass of champagne from the bottle Georgiana had chilling in a silver stand beside her chair.

What the hell, Marie-Thérèse thought, if you've invested this much time in Act One, you might as well stick around for the finale.

9

Johanna knew that her period of grace, her beautifully constructed peace, was coming to an end. She had known it the night before; the horror of it had overwhelmed her at the time, but this morning she was numb, as if her skin had been flayed and all the nerve endings had died and been sealed over.

Everything that had been suppressed, all Walter's last words about the truth of his transformation and the Marley curse came back to obliterate the images she had so carefully cultivated. She had told herself all along that Walter had been wrong, been insane, been duped; anything but that what he wrote was true. Now it was obvious that her lovely invention had failed. That letter of Walter's, so lately fogged over with a deliberate coating of forgetfulness, now stood out polished like a diamond, every sentence shining and clear.

She knew what had to happen to her son, and it had to have happened last night or not at all.

All her life, Johanna had protected the people she loved, but in this she was reduced to an audience, helpless to direct, only able to observe. Well, she refused to watch the rest. She didn't want to hear any more of what had happened to her son, and what was still to come.

When she heard him open the door so quietly and considerately, she felt her body tense, then relax. There was no need to hold things together anymore. He moved in front of her, taking his place on the little needlepointed footstool.

"Mother," he said quietly, "I hate to bother you, but did Dad ever tell you . . . about his research? The work he was doing just before he died?"

My God, he is such a handsome boy, she thought. She looked at him with the pride an artist takes in her most magnificent creation. It had always made her happy that he had always been as good-hearted as he was good-looking. How could he become a murderer? How could he live through the pain and the guilt? Never. He could no more come to terms with it than Walter could. She reached out to touch his face, his hair, very gently. She only wanted to hold her son once more, but when she touched him, she felt the monster beneath the skin and she shuddered.

"I mean . . . ," he was saying, "it seems such a shame to leave his work unfinished. He was such an excellent researcher, and if I had his work published it might help some other researcher along." He was telling a gentle lie to make it easier for her, she knew. Or perhaps to make it easier for himself.

She felt the little silver key burn her palm. She had been holding it tightly since last night, since the minute she knew he'd need it. She opened her hand and held it out to him, without a word. A little tag dangled from it, identifying the Whitney Bank and the box number.

"What is this?" he said, frowning slightly. "Did Dad give you this? What did he say?"

She turned her face back to the window. "You have to go now," she said. Her voice sounded old, so terribly old, a ruined, rusted gate that would never open easily again.

He took her hand and held on as if he could pull the sound out of her. "Talk to me, Mother, please!" he said. "We have so much to say to each other."

But he was wrong. She had nothing else to say, it would all be useless. Johanna had reached a critical mass of pain that allowed her to be cruelly selfish. She sat in grieved obstinancy, staring out the window and seeing nothing but the horror that Walter's life had become, and that would now become her son's life.

As soon as she heard him close the door she could feel it happening: an almost imperceptibly slow relaxation as if she were surrendering to a tub of hot, rose-scented water, lulling her to sleep.

She could feel things happening in her head. An exhausted blood vessel throbbed, swelled, blew itself out. Synapses flashed for the last time and went dark, stopping the automatic functions that fed the life she didn't want.

At the very end she was surprised. Her last thought was of Simon Spencer.

10

Andrew found his way to Angela's apartment by automatic pilot. He hadn't even intended to go there; he just started walking and pretty soon the route looked very familiar.

Her place was on Chestnut Street, the top floor of a house shaded by old trees and scented with wisteria. In the days when he was still seeing Angela, when no one suspected that he was anything more to her than the son of a friend, he often heard his father's colleagues say that Angela lived in a place that was totally unlike her. It was draped in fragile lace and chintz cabbage roses, filled with overstuffed chairs, with portraits of her ancestors hanging over massive rosewood furniture. To find a free spirit like Angela Winfield recreating a period of Victorian reticence was regarded as a contradiction.

Andrew never thought so. The closer he got to Angela, the more he understood that she was a woman who believed in tradition. Not that she let it hold her back from living her life the way she wanted, but Angela had a respect for the past. She believed that to understand the past was to be able to move forward, that times may change but basic human instincts and reactions never do. That was what made her such a good anthropologist, that inborn understanding of behavior.

Andrew was convinced that Angela was an old-fashioned romantic, though she would die rather than admit it; she believed in love and in tender feelings and in protecting the people she loved. But what drove Andrew crazy was

Angela's elaborate distancing mechanisms; every time he got too close, he was driven back by her prickly thorn hedge of cynicism. Even with all that, there was something comforting about Angela, some wonderful spiritual balm that she could spread on hurting wounds.

Andrew rang the downstairs bell. When he saw Angela through the beveled glass door, he felt much better.

"My God!" she said, looking at his bloodshot eyes first. "Where have you been and how much damage did you do there?"

"You said I could come see you if I wanted to talk, even after all this time."

"You look terrible. Come in. This is a fancy neighborhood and I don't want you standing there lowering the property values."

Angela really was shocked by the way Andrew looked. He didn't look like he'd slept in a while, and he certainly hadn't shaved or showered. Angela wasn't sure he'd even changed clothes in the four or five days since Johanna's funeral. He looked weak and exhausted. His only strength seemed spent in holding tightly to a thick parcel wrapped in brown paper.

She settled him in a large chair and made him put his feet up on an ottoman. "Have some brandy," she told him, "you look like you need it." She gathered a glass and a brandy bottle from a mahogany sideboard.

"Everybody's been looking for you, you know," she said, pouring, "from your friend Simon to your uncles and aunts. Simon called and thought you might be here. Where did you disappear to after the funeral?"

"My father had a little cabin on Honey Island. I went there for a few days."

"If you wanted to be alone, I can't think of a more remote place than that swamp."

"Not nearly remote enough, though," he said, gulping the fine old brandy as if it were cheap beer. "Can I have another of these, please?"

Angela frowned and poured. "You sound awfully odd, Andrew. Are you sure you wouldn't rather be home? All your relatives are there and they're worried about you."

"God, no. I'm all right. I just wanted to hear someone else talk. I've been locked up in that cabin, thinking, going crazy—I just couldn't be alone for another minute, but going home and facing the family isn't something I can handle right now." He took another gulp of brandy. "Please. Just talk to me."

"Nobody ever had to ask me twice to talk. What subjects do you want to cover? Religion and politics are safe, but sex is definitely out. You're a holy guy now and I don't want to do any more time in Purgatory than is absolutely necessary." In the past, talk like this had always cheered him up, but she could see that it was doing little good now.

He sighed and leaned back in the chair, his eyes so lost that Angela had to restrain herself from taking him in her arms and smoothing his hair, like a mother reassuring a child.

"What do you know about werewolves?" he said suddenly.

Well, that was certainly out of the blue. "You want me to talk shop?" Angela said. "On a Sunday?" He didn't take the bait, but there was something in his question that frightened her, something sitting in the back shadows of her mind.

And then the memory rose and lumbered forward. "Wait a minute," she told him. "I know it's been a while, but refresh my memory. Aren't you the second Marley to ask me something like that? What is this, the family fetish?"

She had been hoping to make him laugh, but not like this. At first it was a mindless giggle, then a spasmodic laugh, pouring out of him in fantastic, breathless whoops; eddies, swirls, cataracts of laughter that wouldn't stop, rolling him off his chair still doubled over with it.

Angela recognized hysteria. "Oh, Jesus!" she said. She grabbed him by the shoulders and tried to hold him still. "Andrew!" she said firmly. "Listen to me! Are you listening?"

He started to hyperventilate. She pushed him flat on his back and propped his feet on the chair. "Breathe!" she said. "Just breathe very deeply, very slowly. I'm going to start counting, and each time I get to five, you take a breath and relax. All right?"

Andrew tried to say something but couldn't.

"Don't talk, honey. Breathe."

She could see him concentrating on doing just that, keeping his mind on the slow sound of her voice droning numbers. She put her hand on his chest and felt the muscles relax with each deep breath. The hysteria began to pass.

"Feeling better?" she wanted to know.

He nodded.

"Fine. Now, here's what I want you to do. Stay here for a few days. I'll call your house and tell the aunts and uncles where you are, so they don't notify the FBI or something. You just lay there while I run a hot bath for you and put these disgusting clothes in the washer, then I want you to go to bed. Honey, you look like an armadillo that's never made it to the other side of the road. I'll bet you haven't slept in days, have you?"

"Not really. I can't sleep."

"Well, I've got something in the medicine cabinet that'll knock you right out."

He started to bolt up. "No! No drugs!"

She pushed him back down. "Jeez Louise, who do you think I am, the neighborhood pusher? It's just one mild sleeping tablet, Andrew."

"Do something for me," he whispered, his voice ragged and tired. He pushed the paper parcel at Angela. "Read all of this tonight. You may not want me to stay tomorrow."

"What is this?"

"Something my father left me. Some notes, fragments of family history. Please don't make me explain now. Just read it. You're the only person I know who'll understand it."

"I will. As soon as you're asleep and I don't have to worry about you. I'm going to put you up in the guest room, nice and proper. I don't want anyone saying that I compromised a young priest. Now, stay put while I make these phone calls, and try not to think. You'll be much happier that way."

With Andrew bathed, settled in the guest room, and sleeping like a stone, Angela turned to the papers he had given her. She intended to scan through them after she went to bed. She loved reading in bed, couldn't get to sleep without at least a half hour of it.

After reading the first pages of Walter's journals, though, it was uncomfortably obvious that she wasn't going to be able to sleep at all—not that night, and maybe not for the next one.

Angela had always thought she knew Walter Marley. She had first heard about him when she was an undergraduate, and by the time she finally met him she had, like most of his students, already idealized him. Walter was the only one who recognized her as an exceptional student, fiercely serious about her work despite her breezy ways about everything else. She had learned to do her best work with Walter; he wouldn't let her get away with anything else.

The man who wrote these journals couldn't have been the same Walter Marley she knew. This was the work of a full-blown madman.

Almost without thinking about it, she picked up the phone and called Simon Spencer.

11

Andrew went to see Simon on one of those diaphanous days that only seemed to happen in New Orleans. The city was at its most romantic before a late-afternoon rain; the diffused light touched everything with a moody lethargy, the perfect atmosphere to stare out the window and dream.

In his glass-walled office above the Garden District, Simon was doing just that. It was Johanna's kind of weather, he thought. It stirred melancholia and memories. He wondered whatever happened to melancholia; it had gone the way of those tragic, operatic diseases like "the vapors" or "consumption," delicate illnesses redolent of Puccini and Verdi, destined only for beautiful, unstable women.

Johanna's ghost floated just beyond the rain-fogged panes, translucent against the lavender-gray clouds. Simon wondered what grand opera would have made of her. Even the useless way she died was pure Italian drama: there was no good reason for it, but it was a magnificent gesture.

His last patient of the day had canceled and he'd sent his receptionist home early to outrun the storm. Johanna's death had made him upset, guilty, confused; he wanted to wallow in misery. He'd had to put it off for days because of the funeral and his obligation to the family, but now his time was his own and the weather was with him. He had opened a bottle of fabulously old sherry, dark and sweet as liquid raisins. The sherry and the fragile crystal glasses had been a gift from an associate. His only previous experience with sherry had been with the dry variety that tasted to him of new varnish; he hadn't expected the full richness of the Muscat, and his immediate fondness for it was a complete surprise.

He lifted his glass to Johanna, and imagined that she smiled at the incongruity.

He was so entangled in his thoughts that he didn't notice Andrew for a few minutes. When he did, it was only as another reflection on the glass. Johanna's shade moved, danced away, dissolved in the sparkling rain.

"I'm sorry," Simon said, turning his chair slowly from the window, "I'm not terribly responsive today. The weather, I think."

Andrew nodded and sat down. Simon noted his movements: slow and careful, like an old gentleman in pain.

Simon took another glass from his desk. "Try some of this," he told Andrew, "you might like it."

"Not now, thanks."

"I could only stand to see one person right now, and that's you," Simon told him. "I've been sitting here for an hour, thinking about your mother."

"What were you thinking?"

"I don't know. Lots of things I haven't sorted out yet. Frustration. Grief. An impotent feeling that I hadn't done enough, hadn't had enough time with her. I keep doing the most damaging thinking, the 'if only' kind."

"You shouldn't feel like you've failed," Andrew said. "You were doing very well, you know. She *was* improving."

Simon shrugged. "Some days were better than others." He took another sip of sherry and closed his eyes as the jeweled liquid touched his tongue.

"That's only part of it," he said.

"What's the rest?"

"Oh . . . I don't know. I think I was a little in love with her."

"I sometimes thought that," Andrew said kindly. "I wish you could have known her before."

"I didn't have to. I could see. Remember, she talked to me."

"Still. It would have been nice."

"No, it wouldn't." Simon said, suddenly contrary. "I could never have competed with your father for her. I'll tell you something. I never knew Walter, but I felt as if I did. Incredible how the man has become part of my life: I know his colleagues, his son is my best friend, I loved his wife. It's always as if Walter has just stepped out of the room for a few minutes. When Angela called and told me how shattered she'd been by his papers, I knew just how she felt."

Andrew shifted in his chair. "Don't judge him too harshly, Simon. Not by what he left behind."

But it was exactly what Walter had left behind that disturbed Simon. An interesting, intelligent wife; a son who had idolized him; an honorable career; friends who thought well of him and enjoyed his company. Likely that Walter had thought of them, but not enough to spare them. Suicide is always the last selfish act.

He couldn't say that to Andrew, of course. "You know I don't judge," Simon said, only half lying, "I just try to diagnose. Angela sent Walter's papers over by messenger and I spent most of the day trying to decide what was wrong with him. Paranoid schizophrenia? Walter had been too lucid too much of the time. Multiple personality? Didn't fit the pattern. The closest I could come was paranoid psychosis. Walter's actions were pretty much consistent with the paranoid psychotic's behavior. And then . . . the suicide fit right into it. I don't know . . . it's useless to try a diagnosis after the fact."

Both men fell into a long silence, sealed into thoughts they couldn't express.

Finally, Andrew said, "Do you really think Walter was insane? Could it be some kind of genetic thing?"

"It hardly matters about Walter now. And the whole issue of genetics and mental illness is too complicated for me to handle a discussion right now. But if you're worried about heredity, all I can tell you is that, contrary to what a lot of us believe, we are not our parents."

Andrew shook his head. "I'm not quite sure of that. I don't know what's real anymore. All my life I've been so *sure* of the truth. Everything clear-cut, black and white. Life was ordered, logical, intelligently organized. You didn't have to like it, but you could at least decide what was and was not true."

"The truth is elusive sometimes."

"Not for me. Not as long as I had the church and my family. Neither one of them ever lied to me. And now the whole thing's changed."

Simon pulled Walter's papers over to the desk, where they lay between him and Andrew like a stone fence. "When someone we love falls into insanity, it turns our lives over. And Walter's was so unusual. He was able to divide his life into perfect halves. He functioned normally as a family man and as a scientist and teacher; then he had this astonishing secret fantasy life for himself. He carried it off without his family having a glimmer of the truth, too. Paranoid psychotics often do that. Tell me: did he really disappear at the full moon?"

"Yes. He told us he was teaching upstate, but he was at Honey Island. He'd built this little cabin out there in the swamp—apparently the land's been in the family for years and no one's known about it. How he found out is still a mystery to me, but I guess he figured he'd be safe there."

"I wouldn't have expected otherwise. That's part of the behavior pattern. If he chose to believe himself a werewolf, he had to do what a werewolf *would* do: run off at the full moon. Still, there was enough of his rational mind operating to allow him to acknowledge that he had a conscience. He saw himself as a good man; he simply had this evil counterpart that he couldn't control. It wasn't Walter that wanted to do these things, it was the werewolf. Very Judeo-Christian, that idea of some evil entity that makes us do things we'd never do otherwise. Devils and demons have always been an excuse to get around personal responsibility. In his own eyes, this idea of a 'curse' absolved Walter from his baser thoughts and feelings. That's the point Stevenson was making in *Dr. Jekyll and Mr. Hyde*.

"It's a very convenient thing to have these alter egos," Simon continued thoughtfully. "To express violent emotions would mean that we have flaws, and some people find it impossible to admit that. So they create these Hydes who can and will do everything they don't dare. Of course, Stevenson was making a moral point, not a medical one, but he was describing a model paranoid psychotic.

"In the end, I suppose Walter finally knew what was happening to him, that he was losing control over his own mental processes. God! What a bitter blow that must have been for an intelligent man like him! Still, he couldn't admit it, not in any terms except the ones he'd chosen. When things became impossible, he finished it in the only way he could and maintain the fantasy: silver bullets. Even in the end, Walter didn't want to be responsible for the sin of suicide. It was the *werewolf* who pulled the trigger, not Walter."

"That's where you're wrong," Andrew said. "It was Walter. Pulling the trigger was the only thing left that he *could* control."

Simon looked at him, puzzled.

"Do you know what he was doing out there in the swamp?" Andrew said, becoming agitated with each word. "He was locking himself in the cabin every full moon. He thought that if he could only stay in there until dawn, he wouldn't kill anybody. It worked for a while, but the older he got, the stronger he got, until he was ripping the door right off the hinges every time."

He said all this with such conviction that Simon began to be alarmed. But Andrew went on, rising and pacing the room as he talked.

"And then, Honey Island wasn't as remote as it had been. Oil companies were taking samples out there, developers were planning landfills, survivalists were playing war games, environmentalists were camped out there doing studies. Sometimes they went in and never came out.

"I wish you'd seen that cabin, Simon, then you'd believe. I was *out* there, I *saw*. The walls, the door . . . they're scored all over with these awful gougings. Claw marks. The door's been repaired several times. The doorframe's been completely replaced at least once."

This talk was beginning to spook Simon. It was time to insert some rational thinking. "All this reinforces the fact that your father was a very sick man whose imaginings were becoming gradually more real to him. And those are *not* claw marks: there are any number of ways he could have done damage like that."

"I believe he did it in exactly the way he said."

"Be rational, Andrew. Listen to what you're saying."

"At first, I wondered why there'd been no reports of any gory murders, especially all in one place. I had just forgotten how the swamps are, how they can swallow unwanted things, like dead bodies. Between the animals and the climate, there wouldn't be much left. And, I have to tell you, a werewolf doesn't leave a lot behind; it doesn't just kill for sport, it kills to feed.

"What really amazed me was how he'd managed to keep himself in there. He left that part out of his journals." Andrew went on, pacing and talking faster and faster, absorbed in his story and unaware of Simon's growing horror. "Then I figured it out. The door had a two-inch deadbolt but the key was very small. He locked himself in there and stuffed the key into a tiny slot in the wall. When he was himself and had human hands, he could fish the key out, but when the hands were changed . . . the claws may be long, but the hands aren't very dexterous, they're too big; they lack a fine coordination. They can hack and slash, but they couldn't get that key out of that little slot."

Simon felt his skin prickle.

"You'd have to see those claws to believe them, Simon, to realize the power in those transformed hands. They're repulsive, but they have a kind of clumsy grace. What they can do with just one slash is incredible, unspeakable."

Andrew knew he was ranting, but he was unable to stop the rush of words.

"And the blood! Oh, my God! Simon . . . the blood! That's the most ghastly part. I never knew the human body could produce so much of it. It just keeps flowing and flowing and you can watch a man's life draining out with it. No . . . that's *not* the worst part. The worst part is the adrenaline. I think that's what makes a werewolf kill so savagely. The smell of blood must produce it—I haven't figured that out yet— but the enormous swell of it through your body makes you unbelievably powerful, absolutely unstoppable. But it makes you sick afterward, sicker than you can imagine."

The sharp, crystalline splash of Simon's dropped sherry glass stopped him. He looked up, bewildered, just as Simon slammed into him and pinned him against the wall. Simon's face was drained, his eyes enormous.

Astonished at himself, Simon held Andrew pinned there. All he knew was that he had to stop Andrew from saying another word.

He forced himself to regain his composure. He slowly let Andrew go, and slumped back into his chair.

"What happened to my father happened to me," Andrew said calmly. "Exactly as he described it in his papers. I tell you, Simon, I am what my father was."

"He was a madman."

Very calmly, as if he were comforting him, Andrew put his hand on Simon's shoulder. "I wish that were true. And maybe in the end it was closer to the truth than he thought. But you know it isn't. Someplace inside you, you know I'm telling you the truth, because I've never lied to you."

For years, Simon thought, he had counseled the friends and families of mental patients but he never dreamed that he would become one of them, watching in impotent pain as someone he loved slowly fell apart. He felt that Andrew was tottering on the brink of the abyss; if only he could grab him in time and hold on tight enough, he could stop Andrew from going over. And from taking him along.

"How long . . ." Simon's voice wouldn't work right. He tried again. "How long have we been friends? Wouldn't I have noticed your slinking off at the full moon, or maybe that you were just a little strange at times?"

"It only happened a few nights ago."

"I don't think you realize what you're saying," Simon said, his voice rising again. "You're asking me to disregard a lifetime of rational thinking and retreat into the fifteenth century to believe in werewolves. Specifically that my closest friend, who is the kindest man I know and a priest besides, is a werewolf. Can't you hear how that sounds?"

Simon knew he was handling this all wrong. If Andrew was a patient, he'd never be talking like this, but he couldn't stop.

"What can I say to convince you? I can't *show* you."

"No. Go ahead! Do that!" Simon demanded, belligerent with misery. "Walk in here some night, slavering and howling, and I'll believe you. Until then, Andrew, I can't listen to this!"

Defeated, Andrew sat with his head in his hands.

"Listen, my friend," Simon said gently, "you're in a highly susceptible state right now. In a very short time you've had a lot of trauma and this revelation of Walter's came at the worst of it. I want you to see someone, an excellent therapist. . . ."

Andrew looked up, aghast. "I can't do that! I agree that I need someone to keep me from going crazy and blowing my own brains out, but that's why I came to you! How could I trust anyone else?"

"Andrew, it's not just the ethics involved in treating a friend. Do you think that a psychiatrist isn't affected by his patients? That when he shuts the office door in the evening he shuts off his feelings? You're very wrong. I've seen your kind of pain more than I want to remember, and I have no stomach for watching my closest friend suffer through it. I'll be more specific: *I* can't suffer through it. Your family is killing me, Andrew; first Johanna and now you. All that's ever saved me has been my hard-won professional detachment: I have to fight for it through every case and I won't risk it through another Marley insanity! I'll stand by you, but I won't treat you."

"You can't leave me alone in this. If you won't help me, the only way out that I can see is my father's way. I'm trying to stay alive!"

"You're manipulating me, Andrew."

"That's right. I am. But what happens if I tell another doctor what I've told you, what do you think he'd do? He'd hospitalize me, and I'm *not crazy!* If someone put me in an institution, you have no idea how tragic the consequences would be."

"You don't have to be hospitalized . . ."

"I'm asking you to suspend disbelief for just a minute and imagine that there *are* werewolves. And imagine that there was a werewolf whose affliction came upon him without warning, after he had begun to build a life for himself. Imagine that he's capable of a precise, coherent memory that torments him, remembering all the things he's done when he was helpless to stop himself."

"Please don't do this, Andrew."

"You know me better than anyone. Do you think I'd suffer? I've got to find a way out of this, but I have to have time."

"And what if I can't save you? Is that what you're asking me to do? Walter tried everything and he couldn't save himself."

"My father, rest his soul, tried to go it alone. I'm not going to do that, Simon, not if you're there to keep me from madness."

Simon felt himself edge closer to the abyss. "I can't do this on *your* terms, only on my own. I'll treat you like any other patient, as one with a disorder I'm familiar with and that I think I can cure. What I find may be at all odds with what you believe, and I'm going to work to tear those beliefs down. Can you accept that?"

"I accept it, but I know better."

"No. You've been *convinced* that you know better. You're very empathetic, Andrew, and very vulnerable, and you loved your father enough to accept his word without question. What I want you to accept is his madness, his delusions, and see them for what they were."

Simon noticed that his shirt was soaking with sweat. "Look . . . Andrew . . . let's just forget all this for now. Let's talk about other things and other times. We'll drop by my house so I can change clothes and we'll go have a civilized dinner with some good wine. It'll restore our balance."

Andrew shook his head. He looked at his watch: twenty to five. Not great but not catastrophic. "I can't do it, Simon. I have to go back to Honey Island before the sun goes down and the moon rises. I've stayed too long here as it is: I'm just going to make it."

"Andrew! Please!" Simon knew he was in danger of losing his equilibrium again, but he couldn't help it. "Just . . . just don't mention this again. Not tonight."

Andrew looked up. The sorrow in his eyes making Simon wince. "These are hard things, Simon, but they have to be said. I need to start adjusting to the sheer damnable mechanics of this problem."

It seemed as if they'd waited forever for the elevator.

"The damned thing's going to stop at every floor," Simon told Andrew as they stepped through the doors. "The elevators in this building are totally inadequate."

"And at these rents," said a man behind him, "can you believe it?"

Bitching about the elevators was a popular pastime of the residents. This time, it made Simon feel reconnected to the real world, as if what he had just heard was simply a fading dream.

At the fifth floor, the elevator doors opened about four inches wide and two feet above the floor. The lights flickered and the car stopped moving. There were groans and complaints immediately.

"Oh, shit!" another man complained. "Again?"

One of the women waiting in the hallway said, "Hold on. I'll go back to my office and call the elevator people."

"I don't believe it," Simon said, punching the alarm button, "This is the fourth time this month."

"Is there a problem?" a voice said through the speaker. The building superintendent at the lobby desk.

"Nah, no problem," the man behind Simon said in disgust. "We just called to say we love you, you schmuck."

The other passengers cheered and laughed.

"I'll try to get you down from the control board," the voice said.

"Don't worry," Simon told Andrew, "this happens all the time. It won't be more than ten or fifteen minutes."

"Anybody know any good stories?" a woman said.

Andrew was wracked by a sudden shiver. He began to feel clammy all over, dizzy. He could feel his blood pressure drop, as if he were going to faint.

"Andrew?" Simon said with concern. "What is this? I never knew you were claustrophobic."

"I'm not. I just feel really sick . . . it just *happened*." He doubled over.

The passengers all started in with advice.

"Everybody make room!"

"Let him lie down!"

"It'll be okay, pal . . . this elevator's never stuck long. Look, the doors are partly open and the air-conditioning is on, so we can breathe fine. No need to panic, right?"

Andrew dropped to the floor, staggering against the wall. Simon took his arm and eased him down; one of the men took off his own coat and bunched it up under Andrew's head. He was in a fetal position, his arms curled against his chest, his legs pulled up.

Simon crouched beside him. "You're going to be fine. Just calm down."

Andrew couldn't talk, he could only gasp faintly. "What . . . time is it?"

"Six . . . six-fifteen. We won't be much longer."

Andrew's face went even paler. He looked at his own watch. It still said twenty to five: it had stopped. *"Oh, God!* Simon . . . get me *out* of here!

He felt his hand hidden between his chest and knees, shoved inside his shirt. His nails felt longer, harder, sharp as tiny scythes. He screamed as his lungs burned.

Andrew held Simon's arm with his good hand, as if to anchor himself to reality in the tossing sea of pain.

The elevator lights flickered again and the doors closed, but the car didn't move.

Simon gasped as Andrew's fingers closed too tightly on his arm. No one had a grip that strong; Simon's arm was starting to swell, the blood flow stopped. He tried to pry Andrew's arm off but couldn't budge it. "Andrew," he bit out through rigid jaws, "let go! For God's sake!"

The buzzing in Andrew's ears was so loud that he barely heard. He could see, but it was like looking through red-tinted glass. He let go of Simon's arm. The pain was reaching a familiar peak: it was starting to turn into strength. He remembered that just after this point, the change would be fast.

The dizziness cleared. The pain was still there, but so was a near-orgasmic anticipation. He wanted to move savagely, quickly, but there was enough rational mind left to keep him crouched on the floor. He knew he couldn't hold on to that for much longer.

Fangs were beginning to push his teeth back in his jaws.

The elevator made a loud pneumatic sound and started to move, slowly.

Andrew couldn't stop himself; he felt his control begin to leave him.

He started to rise from the floor.

With a noisy *whoosh* the elevator doors suddenly opened wide into the lobby. Andrew leaped through them, still crouched slightly to hide his changing form, and rushed through the building, out into the darkening evening.

He was aware of Simon running behind him and calling his name, but he knew that no human could catch him.

In the next few minutes, he was lost in the night.

Simon called Angela from the lobby pay phone and told her what had happened.

"One minute he was in agony and the next, he was tearing through the lobby like a man possessed. He's in terrible shape, mentally and physically. I'm going to look for him, but I want you to go to his house. There's a key in the mailbox. Would you wait there in case he comes back?"

"Sure, but where are you going to look for him? He could be anywhere."

"I don't know, but his car's still parked in front. How far can he get on foot? I'll just scour the streets around here first. Look, Angela, it's entirely possible that he'll go home, and he's in no condition to be left alone. If you've got any kind of tranquilizer, Valium or something, make him take it. Tie his hands and choke it down him if you have to, and don't let him leave there. I'll phone you every hour or so, and I'll be there as soon as I can."

Then he quickly called the hospital and told them to expect an admission that night.

12

He could feel the moon feeding him as he ran, a silver spill of light that warmed him as much as the sun ever warmed the priest. If he could have laughed, he would have. The priest, with his human self-doubt, would never experience the satisfaction of knowing that he was doing exactly what he'd been put on this earth to do. The werewolf was the instrument of someone else's revenge, and someone else's destiny.

A young man was reeling out of a noisy roadhouse where the music of a Cajun band blared into the night. No one heard the man scream just before the werewolf stunned him with a single blow, then dragged him deep into the backwoods.

The werewolf sat on his haunches as he waited for the man to come around. In a few minutes, the man shook his head and started to his feet. The werewolf was very still.

The man caught sight of the motionless werewolf and, for a few minutes, was afraid to move. Then panic took him and he ran, but the werewolf was faster, blocking him every way he turned.

The werewolf sucked in the scent of fear. That's what he had been waiting for, what he needed before the struggle could really begin. The man fought with wonderful ferocity; he was a big man, tough and muscled, a policeman or a soldier trained in hand-to-hand combat, and the battle was spectacular even if the outcome was preordained. As the man became weaker, the fear scent became stronger and the werewolf was in his element. The man did him some damage—he had a knife—but that was what made the fight so invigorating. The damage would quickly be corrected but the satisfaction of the fight would stay with the werewolf through the night.

The man died, of course. His heart, so savorily consumed, gave the werewolf renewed strength.

His exhilaration pushed him back into the night. He ran a few more miles, as much for the unfettered pleasure of it as for the anticipation of the next kill.

Yvette Gabriel's mother had told her to stay away from Paul Landry. Not only was he too old for Yvette, being twenty-two to her seventeen, but there was nothing special about him. He had no real prospects. He and his father scratched out a living on that little farm, which, in Mrs. Gabriel's opinion, would never bring in enough money to support an exceptional girl like Yvette.

Yvette's looks were going to support her and her mother for the rest of their lives. Mrs. Gabriel had it all planned. Her daughter was a true beauty, a dark-haired Louisiana willow. As soon as Yvette finished high school, Mrs. Gabriel was sending her straight to business school in Baton Rouge. That way, she would learn the skills that would put her in constant contact with young gentlemen who offered the right kind of future. The girl wasn't likely to meet that kind back here on the bayou.

Mrs. Gabriel went to bed early, satisfied that her plans were being well laid.

What she didn't know was that, at that very moment, so was her daughter.

Paul and Yvette often had conversations about their future. Right then, in the warm Landry barn, they were having one about their immediate past.

"I don't feel right about this, no," Yvette complained,

"with your Papa right up there at the house and all."

"Why are you worried?" Paul said, reaching out to stroke her bare thigh. "He goes to sleep early these days. His back is bothering him."

"It's not just that," she said, poking around in the hay for her shirt, "It just seems so cheap. If I wasn't really crazy about you, I'd never let you talk me into these things."

If there was one thing that irritated him about Yvette, it was this obligatory purge of her conscience after every time they made love. Still, there was something charming about it. At least she cared about her reputation, not like some of the wild little tramps running around the parish. And he knew he was the first man she'd had, something that had as powerful a hold on him as it had on her. Yvette was a good girl, the kind who'd been raised to help a man along with his future. She often said how much she wanted a husband and children; Paul thought that not enough girls said that these days. Paul wanted to marry her as soon as possible, before her mother married her off to someone else, the old bitch.

"This isn't forever," he said soothingly. "I know it's not the right place for a girl like you, but it's all we can manage right now. Don't you think I'd like to take you off to the French Quarter? We'd stay in the Monteleone Hotel with those big soft beds and that gold wallpaper, and the sounds of the city going all night. We will, one day, when the farm is going good and paying off. I'll show you the best time you've ever had."

She smiled. "Hey . . . I think I just *had* the best time I ever had."

The idea of king-sized beds in the French Quarter sounded slightly decadent to Paul, and he felt warm, liquid thoughts flowing their way downward. He gently pushed her back down again.

Even as engrossed as they were in making love, the sound

of the metal barn door screeching open made Paul roll off
Yvette in surprise. Yvette sat up and tried to cover herself
before she even looked up.

When she did look, she felt sick.

In the door, illuminated by the weak light in the barn
and the clear light of the full moon behind him, was Papa
Landry.

Yvette wanted to die right there. Better that than have to
face her mother when Papa Landry told her what he had
caught Yvette doing with his son.

Papa was an old-fashioned man with old-fashioned ideas
that definitely did not include the scene he was witnessing.
Old and arthritic he may have been, but he crossed the distance between the barn door and his son like a young sprint-
er.

As Yvette scrambled out of the way, grabbing up whatever
clothes were closest, Papa grabbed Paul by his hair with one
hand. The other arm swung behind him, ready to deliver the
first blow.

It never came. Paul felt the old man pulled away from
him like a small child snatched by strong sea tides.

Confused, he looked around.

Papa was in the grip of an enormous . . . *thing* . . . almost
eight feet tall. If it had been an ape or a wolf or some animal that Paul could recognize, he could have dealt with it.
But *this*! He had never seen *anything* like this! The shock
paralyzed him.

Yvette's screams and his father's roars of pain reconnected
his thinking.

Yvette was halfway up the ladder to the loft, climbing in
pure panic.

"Pull the ladder up after you! Fast!" Paul shouted.

The monster had its back to Paul, wrestling with the old
man. Papa had been toughened by a lifetime of hard work

and was putting up a hell of a fight. Paul threw himself on the monster's back, trying to lock his arms around its massive throat. Shit! It didn't even *have* a neck! It was all solid muscle.

The monster shook Paul off by the simple expediency of slicing open his arm. Paul fell off the thing, rolling onto the barn floor on his good arm.

He ran into the house and grabbed his hunting rifle, always kept ready by the back door. The 300 Winchester Magnum would take down the biggest raging swamp gator; it would deal with this thing.

Papa, stunned, was lying on the barn floor, the monster just starting to bend over him. Paul had a clear shot from a distance of no more than thirty feet.

The beast flinched as the shot connected. Paul knew he had hit it; he was an expert at longer distances than this.

It slowly straightened up and turned to Paul. Oh, *God* . . . it *smiled* . . . not a real smile but a horrible, mad grin drawn back over incredible teeth. It moved slowly, almost casually, as if it had all the time in the world.

He couldn't believe the damned thing was still moving, not with a shot like that in it. Paul's second shot, to the head, should have been the coup de grace. But that grin! That grotesque smile! Paul was so unnerved that the shot went over the beast's shoulder. He wanted to scream and run, but knew that if he lost control, he'd be a dead man.

Paul started to back off, slowly. He felt himself connect with the hayloft ladder. Yvette hadn't pulled it up all the way! He was closer to the ladder than the beast was to him; he might make it, even with one arm.

With a sudden ferocity, he threw the gun at the monster, distracting it for a few seconds. Paul jumped on the ladder, skipping the first two rungs and climbing as fast as he could.

He knew he'd never make it. All that thing had to do was cross the barn, get to the ladder, and pull him off. Still, Paul kept climbing.

Yvette was screaming, holding out her hands to him, trying to pull the ladder with him on it.

The beast, however, looked unconcerned, even amused. It moved with a casual slowness, stepping over Papa's body.

But Papa wasn't through yet. As the monster stepped over him, he wrapped his arms around one of its legs and hung on.

Annoyed, the monster stared down at the old man. It smashed him a blinding blow against the side of the head, but Papa, dying, held tight. The beast couldn't reach the old man easily because of the odd angle, and twisted for several minutes, trying to get a grip on him.

Paul used those minutes to climb higher, his arm making the ladder slippery with blood. He could hear Yvette above him, screaming and crying.

Papa lost his grip on the monster and, with an impatient howl, the beast picked him off as if he were a clinging burr and slammed him against the side of the barn.

Paul heard the sounds of his father's bones breaking. He shut out the sound and the pain, concentrating only on the next rung. Papa had given him the precious time he needed and he wasn't going to waste it.

He reached the loft, and he and Yvette frantically began pulling up the rest of the ladder.

Seeing his prey escape, the monster lost no more time with games. He rushed to the ladder a split second too late as it disappeared into the loft.

Enraged, he bayed furiously at Paul and Yvette. They huddled together against the far loft wall, terrified that any moment they'd see that horrible face roaring and snarling at them.

Yvette was suddenly, inexplicably, calm, her mind acquiring some sort of contrary efficiency as she ripped the sleeves of her shirt to make a tourniquet for Paul's arm. The simple act of concentrating on an immediate need helped both of them keep their wits.

"Yvette," Paul whispered, "do you remember when we were little kids, remember the old stories of the loup-garou?"

She kept wrapping his arm. "No, I don't remember anything like that."

"The old Cajun stories of the werewolf of the bayous. My mama said that if I was bad, the loup-garou would come and get me. And it has. That's what that thing is: the loup-garou."

Almost as soon as he said it, the howls stopped. They could hear a rustling in the straw below, and heavy, quick steps along the barn floor. Much as he dreaded doing it, Paul crept to the edge of the loft and looked down. The loup-garou was not there.

Then where was it? In his terror, he looked wildly around the barn but nothing was there. He pulled himself painfully to the loft window overlooking the farm and the road. The loup-garou was out there, running swiftly toward the bayou as the sky got lighter.

Paul remembered part of the old legends: a loup-garou never kills in the same place twice. Still . . . he decided to take Yvette to the marriage license bureau the next morning, then to the Justice of the Peace, then as far away from Louisiana as possible. One of his cousins could handle the sale of the farm for him.

Paul wasn't going to be anywhere near the bayous at the next full moon.

13

The Marley house was full of ghosts.

Angela found that she was unconsciously roaming the halls, standing and staring into each room, her thoughts wandering. She could almost see Walter and Johanna still here, could see how happy they had been, and how tragically unhappy they were at the end of their lives. She wondered if happiness was worth the pain.

She had been thrust back into Andrew's life too quickly and too deeply. She had made herself vulnerable, something she had hoped to avoid when she let their relationship drift apart years earlier. You couldn't fall in love and expect there to be no wounds, Angela thought; her own parents' tumultuous marriage was proof of that. The resulting injury, she was beginning to see, was in direct proportion to the degree of love.

It had seemed like the most sensible thing to do at the time. The whole thing had started out as a little fling between them, but it was obvious after the first night that there was more substance to it than that. They had only made love once that night; they had intended to do it again—and again—but had been talking so earnestly that they forgot. Nothing had surprised her more. In the next few months, they threw themselves enthusiastically and unreservedly into love, with only enough discretion so that Angela's colleagues, including Walter (or so they thought), were unaware of the relationship.

Out of all they'd shared, one thought kept coming to

Angela: This is really it. She heard it as if it had been spoken clearly into her ear, and after all this time, the memory of it still wouldn't go away.

But she didn't want this to be "it." Too much could go wrong. Andrew was too young; she was too old; he had his life rigidly scheduled for the next few years; he hadn't had enough time to sow his wild oats; he hadn't had enough contact with real life.

It wasn't Andrew that voiced these obstacles. They were the inventions of Angela's own fears. Still, they were enough to turn her away, although it took an act of will on her part to do it.

It hurt for months afterward, and *that* surprised her, too. She'd thought that breaking it off was going to spare her this.

Just day-to-day living was hard. Little things she'd hear on the street or see throughout the day that delighted or dismayed her, and her first thought was that she'd have to remember to tell Andrew. Then she realized that he wasn't going to be around to hear it and the sense of loss was devastating.

She understood now why Johanna might go crazy without Walter, just for self-preservation. It would have been easier if she could have shut down like that.

Only a week after she stopped seeing Andrew, Angela had tried to distract herself with an evening at the opera. She'd planned to let the luxurious music of Richard Strauss spread over her mind like cream over velvet. But the opera turned out to be about a worldly older woman with a young lover. The story opened with their lovemaking: charming, poignant, and oddly intimate, given the audience. But by the last act, the young man had left the woman for a sheltered girl his own age, and the wom- an's heartbreaking music mourned her loss but accepted the way of the world.

Angela had been too stunned to leave during the first act, and by the last one, when the audience was a little weepy anyway, Angela had disgraced herself by sobbing uncontrollably. She'd had to get up and leave.

She had begun to realize that she had sacrificed the good in order to spare herself the possible bad. She should have savored her time with Andrew for however long it lasted and taken her chances. She knew that *now*. But at the time she'd been looking for a guarantee of happiness; she had wanted to be absolutely sure that if she took the risk, she'd reap the rewards. She had no idea how she could have been so naive.

Her stupid sacrifice had been useless anyway. From what she'd heard, Andrew had no other women after her, at least nothing serious.

Once, a week before her sabbatical, she'd asked Walter about how Andrew was getting along, and he'd said that all Andrew did was study and go to school. She tried to be casual when she asked if he'd had any special girlfriend yet. Looking at her a little more curiously than she'd have liked, Walter said that women his own age didn't interest Andrew: he considered them too self-absorbed and superficial. "He takes after me, I suppose," Walter had said. "He likes smart women. To him, a doctoral dissertation is an erotic object."

So here she was again, years later, years older, and perhaps a little wiser. Although he was unaware of it, Andrew had given her another chance and, like the first time, the romance had come equipped with a full set of problems.

This whole werewolf delusion was a real brick wall. She didn't know where to begin to demolish it. Walter had made such a convincing argument for lycanthropy that it almost made sense.

Angela's nerves were being slowly shredded from all this waiting. It had been half the night and Simon had called only once. He had been to Honey Island, had even found Walter's cabin, but there was no sign of Andrew's having been near it.

"I can't think of anywhere else to look," Simon had told her. "If it was me, you'd know to check the bars in the French Quarter . . . but Andrew?"

"How many churches are still unlocked at night?" Angela said. "If I had his problems, that's where I'd be."

"What an asshole I am!" Simon said. "Of course that's where he is! Look, I'll try the cathedral, St. Roch's, the shrine of St. Jude . . . Damn! This town's got almost as many churches as bars. Look, try not to worry. I'll have him home soon enough."

Angela had felt a little less anxious. The amazing thing was that neither of them had thought of the churches right away. However, that conversation had been at four A.M., an hour and forty-six minutes ago, and there had been no word from Simon since then. She kept thinking that the phone would ring or that Andrew would come home exhausted or that Simon would bring him home; she wished that one of those things would happen. Soon.

She couldn't sit still, which accounted for all this prowling around the house. She opened a set of double doors and found herself in Walter's study. So strange to be in here again after all this time! She'd worked here with Walter while she was still his teaching assistant and had always found it a warm, comforting place, especially in winter with the fireplace glowing, Walter's books and artifacts carelessly littered about, everything eminently touchable and reassuring.

It didn't look so reassuring now. The artifacts she'd remembered were all gone: old bones, weapons and stone tools, ancient maps, and everyday items from lost civilizations. Stored away, she supposed. The things that had taken their places were not so comforting; in fact, Angela

had never seen such an unusual collection of arcane objects
and books, not even in museums. Angela had some fairly odd
stuff around her own place: amulets and talismans associated
with the early Witch cultures and fertility religions, magical
objects said to come from the ancient Temple of Diana at
Ephesus, Voodoo charms and tribal ceremonial masks, several original drawings for the Crowley Tarot deck, things she'd
collected and things that had been given to her by students and
colleagues. But this collection of Walter's, put together after
he'd developed his lycanthropic obsession, was both serious
and frightening. He'd gathered these things out of fear, not
out of genuine scholarly interest.

She inspected the books and couldn't believe what she saw.
Some were priceless, including an original manuscript of the
Malleus Maleficarum. She touched the venerable, crumbling
binding with one finger, trying to place the familiar texture.
It came to her and she jerked her hand away: human skin,
cured like leather. God! Where had Walter acquired this disgusting object and at what expense? Based on the fraudulent
information in this treatise, invented by two sadistic religious
psychotics, nine million people had been condemned to die.
She had heard about this particular volume; it had been bound
in the skin of one of the victims.

Walter had certainly been thorough. Nothing was over-
looked. There were respected academic works; clinical studies of rare psychological disorders; penny-dreadful novels
from the Victorian era, cheap thrillers then but valuable
antiques now; magical treatises, spells for power, spells
to call demons, spells to dismiss demons. A rare, but
quite effective work on Native American shape-shifters.
The respected Sabine Baring-Gould and the crackpot, but
entertaining, Montague Summers on werewolves.

She had no idea where Walter had gotten some of this
stuff; she was certain that at least two of the items belonged

to German museums and she had heard that the *Malleus Maleficarum* was owned by a Wiccan high priest in Massachusetts who had acquired it for the express purpose of keeping it under a binding spell so that no such thing could ever happen again.

Walter even had a copy of the pact written and signed in blood, supposedly between the devil and Father Urban Grandier. Grandier was accused of being the evil power behind the possessed nuns at Loudun. This document had assured him of a ghastly death at the stake, more for his worldly charm and his politics than his heresy. Angela looked at it and shuddered. It didn't look like a copy: it looked like the real thing.

One of Walter's desk drawers was partly open. Well, she thought, you've gone this far . . . she pulled the drawer open and immediately wished she hadn't.

Nested in an open box was an antique pistol. Beside it in the black velvet compartment was a set of silver bullets. There were six little indentations for the bullets: only four of them were filled.

The sight of them was like ice down her back.

She knew this was the gun that Walter had used to kill himself, but what she couldn't understand was how Andrew could bear to keep it here—to keep *any* of these things here. Fascinated, repulsed, Angela picked up the gun and saw the single circle of silver shimmering in the chamber. She put the gun back and slammed the drawer shut.

The whole atmosphere made her more nervous. It wasn't the objects themselves: in other circumstances she would have been excited by the scholarly value of Walter's acquisitions. But knowing that this collection was spawned out of the growing, crippling madness of someone she respected clouded everything with horror.

She was suddenly seized with the desperate need to know

what had gone on in Walter's mind, what had driven him to this. She opened one of the books on French lycanthropes and sat down to read.

She had no idea of how long the sound outside had been going on. She only heard it when it became so loud that it made its way into her consciousness. It was a scratching sound, the noise a tree branch makes when it scrapes across a window, but this sound was more regular, as if it were being done deliberately to draw her attention.

Angela lifted the receiver of the desk phone and heard the reassuring buzz of the dial tone. She thought a minute, then set it down again. She wasn't going to explain to some cop how a branch in the wind scared her. She could just hear it: "Whatcha been reading there, lady? Uh, huh . . . maybe you should lay off the scary stuff at night."

She went to the window to see just how bad the wind was: nasty storms could whip up pretty fast in this town.

The trees stood straight and still. There was no wind.

The sound came again, louder, longer, deeper, as if a giant hand scraped its nails across the entire length of the house.

This was deliberate. Bored teenage hoodlums trying to terrorize her just for something to do, or maybe burglars seeing if there was anyone home. She moved slowly back toward the study doors, away from the windows. If they didn't know which room she was in, she wasn't going to advertise it. Just in case someone got in, they were at a disadvantage: they didn't know the house and Angela did.

As quietly as she could, she threw the bolt on the inside of the study doors. It made a solid, protective sound.

She picked up the phone and dialed the police. Okay, let the cops think she was a neurotic spinster or something. That was their job. She heard one ring, then the line went dead. She hung up and tried again. Nothing.

The front door opened and closed. Impossible! She'd

locked it! Nobody could get in unless they broke the heavy lock with lots of noise.

Or had a key.

What a jerk she'd been. Naturally, it was Andrew or Simon.

She had just started over to unlock the study doors when she watched them rattle uncertainly. She held her breath. It was Andrew, of course it was . . . and he'd call out any minute.

But something held her back from opening the doors.

That low, scratching sound began again, this time on the other side of the study doors, then a soft moan, a wet slobbering growl that made her think of an angry, cornered animal made mad by starvation. The cry grew louder, then was almost drowned out by a volley of poundings so loud they made the doors shake. The cry became a bellowing howl as the doors began to quiver on the hinges.

Angela backed toward the windows. Thank God she was on the first floor and the drop wouldn't kill her. The old brass window lock didn't want to open. Angela rattled the frame as she tugged on the lock handle.

She heard the slow splintering of wood behind her. The doors swung open and she felt a rush of wind as something monstrous fanned the air behind her. The only glimpse she had of it was in the wavering reflection of the glass just as the window lock opened.

Fortunately, the window glided up easily in the frame. Angela dived through the window headfirst and was almost through when the monster grabbed her by the calves, the claws scratching deep into her skin. She caught one of the forsythia bushes beneath the window and held on, trying to give herself enough leverage to break away.

She kicked furiously, her legs making swimming motions in the air. The monster tightened its grip. The pain was so awful that she reflexively let go of the forsythia.

She was pulled back inside, her fingernails breaking as she tried to grasp the windowsill, the sash handles, anything for leverage. She landed on her stomach inside the room and felt the claws let go. She took that moment to twist her body and face whatever it was.

It wasn't as brutish as she'd have imagined. In fact, it had a grace that would have been affecting: long, tip-tilted eyes with straight brows that swept back toward the temples; aquiline nose; the face covered with a fine sheen of silken hair that shone blue-black even in the dim light. The forehead rose to a widow's peak hairline with a magnificent mane of long black hair that swept around its shoulders and hung almost to its waist. It was a mesmerizing mixture of man and animal.

But the face was made demonic by the mindless, glittering fire of its eyes. There was no humanity there, no reason or compassion. The monster backed away from her and now sat on its haunches a few feet away, observing her, letting her fear build. Angela knew that it could afford to take its time.

Then, out of the mist of fear, she had a closer look at its eyes.

Its *eyes* . . . my God! Its *turquoise eyes*!

Don't faint, she told herself on the edge of hysteria, just don't faint or scream and you might get out of this alive. Control your breathing . . . oh, God, oh, Jesus! . . . Come on, *breathe* . . . don't faint . . . *think*! You *know* this stuff. . . . What stops a werewolf?

The werewolf started to rise, its murderous claws flexing.

Just when her mind went blank with fear, the answer popped in. An old charm: call a werewolf by its Christian name.

At first, her voice didn't work. She swallowed and tried again.

"Andrew . . . it's Angela, Angela. . . . You know me . . . you couldn't hurt me." Then the panic overcame her. "Oh, *God,* Andrew! Don't kill me! *Please, please* listen to me, Andrew!"

The old folk charm worked. At the sound of its name, the beast hesitated.

Angela moved almost imperceptibly to the desk and silently slid the drawer open.

The monster didn't move.

Her hand closed around the cool reassurance of the pistol, her finger closing lightly on the trigger as she withdrew it from the drawer.

The werewolf shook its head and roused itself, starting across the room with the slow confidence of a predator who has his prey cornered.

Angela raised the gun.

The werewolf stopped.

Both of them held very still. I can't do it, Angela thought. How can I do it, knowing who it is? Then she realized that it was *because* of who it was that she had to do it.

The werewolf stood looking at the gun, the ragged sound of his breathing incredibly loud in the large room. he raised his head slightly and looked at her, his mouth working as if he were trying to make a human sound. All that came out was a moan of animal pain.

Almost imperceptibly, he nodded his massive head.

It was the right thing to do. Angela knew suddenly that it wasn't Walter who had left that gun loaded. She couldn't find any words to say to him; she only wished that, just once, she could have touched him again, even as he was, could have smoothed her hand over his face and told him that everything would work out all right.

She heard soft sobbing from somewhere, and didn't even recognize her own voice.

She took careful aim at his head. There would be only one shot and it had to be true. It had to be painless.

Steadying the gun in both hands, her elbows locked, she slowly squeezed the trigger.

She heard an explosion of sound, not the blast of the gun, but a woman's voice, an unnatural shriek. Then she heard the crack of the gun as her shot went into the wall.

The monster roared and lunged across the room at Angela. They lost their balance as they fought, rolling together on the floor. He had her securely pinned in a moment, her arms under her body as she screamed and kicked, jerking her body back and forth trying to get free. Angela could hear the other woman crying out Andrew's name, but she was only dimly aware of the woman throwing herself on Andrew's back, grabbing his long hair in her fist and yanking his head back.

Never, never, Angela thought, would I have dreamed that death would be like this. If I have to die, I refuse to look it in the face. I want the last thing I see to be something beautiful.

Oddly calm now that she knew she was going to die, she turned her head toward the window to concentrate on her last image: a perfect spring dawn, the clear sky streaked with apricot lights.

She felt a sharp intake of breath as the werewolf stiffened over her body. She could hear the woman's voice growing calmer, cooing soothing sounds. Angela felt the body lifted or pulled or rolled off her. She closed her eyes and let her mind go blank with relief.

She heard her name spoken again, by a familiar voice far away. Simon. She opened her eyes and saw him, frozen against the splintered study doors.

Angela turned to look.

The monster was there, writhing in terrible agony, cradled close to the woman who held it in her strong arms. Its body stretched, contorted, every muscle, every tendon changing shape under the skin. In its agony, the werewolf seemed capable of only the most muted sounds, as if all its strength was melted into that grotesque change. Oddly enough, those wrenching soft moans were more heartrending than screams.

The woman, her own face transformed by another kind of pain, still held the monster close to her as it changed, trying to comfort it as a mother comforts a hysterical child.

And then it was over. The body cradled close to the woman was perfectly Andrew's, his skin glistening with a slick gloss of sweat and blood, the remains of a terrible wound in his shoulder that even then was healing. He was so still that only his too-rapid breathing showed that he was still alive.

He raised his head and they all saw that he was concentrating on a point just beyond them, as if he were watching something or someone. For a few interminable moments they all stood fixed in place, until Andrew dropped his head and burst into tears.

The woman simply smoothed his wet hair.

It was as if he had just noticed that she was there.

"I know you," he said softly, "I've *seen* you. Which . . . which one are you?

The woman looked into his eyes, eyes that were exactly the color of her own. And her face was young, almost as young as his.

He touched a finger lightly to her cheek. "Yes . . . Georgiana," he said in wonder, "you were the first."

He took both her hands in his as they shared an anguish that no one else could understand.

14

He didn't know exactly by what mechanism he knew that it was Georgiana; of course there was the strong family resemblance, but that wasn't it. It was as though the curse had produced some kind of bizarre bond between them, some supernatural link. He hadn't been aware of it, but the minute he realized who she was, it was as if he'd known her forever. He had a nasty flashback—not his, but hers—a terrible instant replay of the gruesome scene of Georgiana's wedding night. He didn't know where it came from; he thought at first that it was an image he picked up on his own.

He soon became certain that it was something much more painful: a psychic transfer between the two of them in which he was allowed to touch the inner core of Georgiana's anguish, the scene that played itself over and over in the back of her mind, pushing its way forward in any instant that she wavered and dropped her guard.

He knew that Georgiana had led a frenetic, nonstop life, compulsively filled with lights, color, movement, action, all in an attempt to divert her mind from that final look in her husband's eyes.

Her coming back to New Orleans, where all her nightmares became real and the past was never far enough away, must have been the last thing she wanted to do, and the only thing that would begin to heal her.

Only Georgiana would understand what went through Andrew's mind when he realized what he'd done to Angela. And how easily it could have been worse.

Afterward, Angela had been hysterical: screaming when he looked at her, crying, cringing. Simon, dealing with his own shock, seemed several beats behind the rest of them. But it was Simon, whose cool professional training had taken over when it was most necessary, who had sedated Angela and cleaned and bandaged her wounds, who had made sure that Andrew had sustained no physical damage from his earlier forays that night. Simon had healed himself by healing others. It put him back into perspective and gave him something solid to do, something real and immediate to deal with.

The explanations, the bewildered questions, the pain came later.

They were all gathered in the kitchen, around an enormous table, gulping coffee as if it would magically grant them the wisdom to understand what had happened. Even Angela, who by all rights should have been as far away from that house as she could get, seemed transfixed by the night's events. The sedation she'd had was very light; it was her own hard-headedness and passion for logical thinking that was keeping her there. That, and something else that she didn't want to think about right then.

"I should have believed you," Simon told Andrew. "I knew you weren't crazy and I knew you weren't lying, but I just didn't believe it."

Andrew made a disparaging gesture. "Don't blame yourself. Who *could* have believed it?"

"The question is," Angela said, "now what are we going to do?" She rose, intending to go to the coffeepot on the kitchen counter, but as she stood, the pain in her leg made her catch her breath.

Andrew winced.

She bent slowly to touch the blue bruise starting to show around the edge of the bandage and her face paled.

"It isn't true, what you're thinking," Georgiana said quietly, "about becoming a werewolf if one injures you. The scratches won't do that. Creating another loup-garou is a conscious act, not an involuntary one."

Red-faced, Angela sat down.

"How do you *know* these things, Georgiana?" Andrew said. "The night it happened to you, you didn't know any more than me, did you? You were just as confused and angry and in pain. So how did you find out? And how come you're alive when every family story says you died in London right after . . ." He couldn't bring himself to finish that particular thought.

Even Simon and Angela had stopped in midmotion, waiting for the answer. Georgiana was acutely aware of it: Angela's sudden fascination with her nails, Simon's concentration on his coffee cup. Only Andrew was frankly staring, waiting for the explanation that was his every right to hear.

Georgiana drew in a deep, calming breath.

"I don't need to explain to you, Andrew, how shattered my life was after that first night. It wasn't only what had happened to me and what I had done, it was that it had altered all concepts of reality. Nothing was true anymore. Everything I had relied on all my life—my future, my family, even the knowledge of my own body—all that was now called into question. If nightmares had just become reality, then where does nightmare end and real life begin? That line was not just blurred, it suddenly became nonexistent.

"Even worse was what had happened to my relationship with my father. We had always been close; there was nothing I couldn't tell him. I adored him."

She suddenly smiled and looked directly at Andrew. "You should have known him. He was wonderful, really. He had our eyes and all this marvelous hair that had gone prematurely gray. He was lovely to look at. And he had such a romantic history, right out of an adventure story! He had left an aristocratic, impoverished English family and took his chances on the sea, determined to make his fortune, landing finally in New Orleans. He bought his first ship here and built the Marley Lines on the strength of it, until he was one of the richest men in the city. He courted and married one of New Orleans's most beautiful women from one of its oldest Creole families.

"But can you imagine what it was like to be the daughter of a man like that? Of course I adored him. And he loved his children, especially me. There were four of us: me, Robert, Timothy, and Melissa—the baby. I was the oldest, and for Father, that seemed to carry special meaning. I was his first, his hope for the future, confirmation that he had indeed made his place in New Orleans by building a family. I grew up with his telling me about his life in England, his adventures on the sea, his tales of the Mississippi River trade.

"What an effect my father's romantic story had on me! And how shattering it was to find that it was true only superficially. Below that pretty surface was a much nastier story.

She glanced around the table. "I'm not going to tell you my entire history. I think Andrew knows most of it, or what of it that he needs to know." She cast him a significant look. She knew that he was finding out about the werewolves' bond, the psychic connection that bound them together. Much of what she knew, Andrew would know eventually, even without words. "But after my first transformation, I was determined not to kill again. I didn't care what I had to do to avoid it, and if that included suicide, then I had resigned myself to it. I couldn't have carried on a life like that, killing innocent people. I might as well have died.

"I devised a delaying tactic. Honey Island is a big swamp; you could get lost there. If I walked deep enough in before sunset, it would take a long time, maybe until dawn, to find my way out. And it was mostly deserted in those days. I wasn't likely to run across anyone.

"Of course, I was only buying time. I was sure that this wouldn't happen again or, if it did, that I could find some catch, some loophole, some way out, if I only had time to find it."

Andrew couldn't restrain a bitter laugh. Georgiana's ironic look echoed it.

"Yes," she said, raising an eyebrow, "the first and last illusion of a cursed werewolf's life: *this can't be permanent.*" She sighed, shook her head sadly, and resumed her story.

"It happened again, of course, just after sundown, when the full moon started to rise. The pain was just as shocking as the first time. Obviously, I wasn't going to get used to *that.* I was cringing on the ground, unable to scream, suffocating, feeling my very blood boil in my body. And all of a sudden, I was aware of someone kneeling beside me.

"I expected the same woman I'd seen the first time, the silver-haired woman. But this one was different. She had the kindest face I'd ever seen, and she was looking at me with real concern. She smoothed my hair. 'Just stay calm, *chérie,* and it will all be over soon.' she said to me in this lovely French accent. French, not Cajun. Even then, I could tell." She shook her head. "Funny what minor details we notice with perfect clarity when our souls are otherwise going mad. She took my hand, and when she did, the pain was much less intense. It seemed to be connected with my body, but not with my mind—a strange sensation, very hard to describe. It was like . . . like nitrous oxide at the dentist's. You know the pain's there and you can feel your body reacting, but you can't actually feel the pain itself.

"And then the wonder: As I watched, she began to transform also, much faster and with seemingly much less pain than I had known. Her blonde hair billowed and spread, flowing like liquid gold over her body. She changed shape; she became like me. And all the time, she kept hold of my hand, now changed. I felt her claws grow out, long and curved, and felt them interlock with mine. There was such strength to her! Not just physical strength, but something from the soul. I wanted to cry, but I had no idea why.

"She took a long breath when her transformation was complete, then spoke to me again, in a voice that was changed, but still beautiful and with that pretty accent. I was astounded. I didn't know a werewolf could speak. I didn't even know there *was* another werewolf!

" 'You mustn't give up,' she said. 'You mustn't think that your life is over. Even though it has changed, and that change seems catastrophic for you, it isn't disaster.'

Georgiana took a long breath. "She was right. My life wasn't over. The lady was Marie-Thérèse de la Rochette." She smiled at something only she would know, a private joke between two women. "The duchesse de Marais, over three hundred years old. But everyone calls her Zizi." Georgiana noted Andrew's raised eyebrows. "Yes. I know you've met her: she told me. Zizi is what you'd call the motherly type, though she doesn't look it. A loup-garou, you'll find, ages only one year to a human's ten. That's why I look like this. But Zizi was the first loup-garou in Louisiana."

Andrew couldn't hide his shock. "The first? You mean there are others?"

"Many others. And not like us. We're cursed, Andrew; we're werewolves because someone wanted to cause us the worst possible anguish. Our days will be lived in terror of our nights. But all werewolves are not like us. Especially, the loups-garous of Louisiana are not like us. You'll learn the difference, like I learned it. And you'll learn to live with it, like I have. Like Walter couldn't."

"I'll never learn to live with it," Andrew said bitterly.

Angela, who had not moved since Georgiana began, slowly stretched out her hand and covered Andrew's with it. He looked up at her with such hesitant hope in his eyes that Angela was close to tears.

"You mustn't say that," Angela said softly. "Ask yourself why Georgiana's here. Why would she come back to a place that obviously hurts her?" Angela looked at Georgiana. "It was Walter, wasn't it?"

Georgiana paled slightly and dropped her eyes. "I could have saved him—*perhaps* I could have. But I was such a selfish coward. I simply wrapped myself in the artificial cocoon I've made of my life and refused to think about him. Walter had no one, you see? He suffered alone. Even Zizi was with me, in Europe, keeping me whole. But I heard him, dimly but distinctly. I heard his cries, muffled with despair. And I shut them off. He was my blood, my favorite brother's son, and I couldn't bring myself to come back here for him. And I let him die. Of all my murders, it was Walter's that has never left me, never will. What I did to my husband was out of my control; what I did to Walter was deliberate."

She turned to Andrew. "Zizi forced me to come back here. She told me about you."

"And why didn't she just tell me all this herself? Why put you through this torture?"

Georgiana looked directly into his eyes. "This time, I think, she wanted me to save myself."

"There are so many things to tell you, Andrew," Georgiana said, "and to tell Simon and Angela, so much that you all have to understand. For instance, why this curse works the way it does, why it happens to the eldest child in each generation, and the first time on the greatest night of his or her life, regardless of whether the moon is full or not.

"But I can't even get into it unless I start at the beginning. It's a ghastly story, and a long one. What I suggest we do is for everyone to go home. Angela, you look dead tired and Simon doesn't look any better. I'll stay with Andrew and see that he gets some sleep."

"I couldn't sleep," Andrew said grimly.

"Of course you can." She looked at Simon. "You can take care of that, can't you, Doctor? For just a few hours?" Simon nodded. "Tomorrow afternoon we'll meet here and I'll tell you everything I know about the Marley history and the Marley curse."

"How do you know all that?" Andrew asked her. "Even Walter wasn't able to put together a coherent family history. There were too many dangling ends."

"I got the information in bits and pieces," she admitted. "There were several people who knew parts of it, but no one had the whole story. Lots of it I found out from Zizi. The only one who knew the entire story was my father, and he never found the courage to tell me." Her eyes darkened and Geo's face turned hard as chill marble. "I despised him for that, for a long, long time. I had idolized him, had trusted him without question, then when my life had been destroyed and he might have held the key to my salvation, he locked himself in the silence of cowardice. You've seen a little of the loup-garou's psychic power, Andrew: I was just learning how to control it. So I used it, shamelessly. I picked my father's mind, I raped his memory, even those tormenting secret thoughts he'd buried in the sealed recesses of his guilty conscience. And I found what I needed to know—what *you* need to know. But be prepared, Andrew. Your most cherished ideas about our family are about to be smashed."

Georgiana glanced at Andrew, and at Angela, who had still not taken her hand away from his.

"Dr. Spencer," Georgiana said, "why don't I walk you to your car?"

Andrew had no idea what to do about his immediate problems. As it stood now, he had two: the obvious one and Angela.

All his life he had been dreaming of a woman who could share with him what his father had shared with Johanna. His parents hadn't been perfect, but their love was. It was so obvious that, even as a child, it affected him.

When Andrew was an altar boy, Father Moore had told him about a theological theory that pretty much described his parents. When God created the world, he was so pleased with it that he made man in order to have someone to share it with. Walter and Johanna's love was like that: they opened it to embrace their child, their friends, the world.

When Andrew and Angela had first been together, he'd been too callow to recognize that what he'd wanted had already come to him. Afterward, when he couldn't stop thinking about her, he began to imagine that after he was through seminary and ordained and was settled into a parish job that perhaps they could start again, this time on a more equal footing.

Now they *had* started again, and everything was all wrong.

Angela could comfort him, stave off the relentless solitude of his horror, give him a safe harbor when the night was over. What could he give her? Only a glimpse into a nightmare that might kill her.

"I apologize," he said quietly. "Not just for last night . . . there aren't words enough to apologize for that. But for . . . everything. For showing up at your house after I *knew* what I was, for involving you in all this. It was irresponsible. Selfish. The most selfish thing I've ever done. I'll never be able to make it right, Angela. If I tried, it would just involve you further."

There was more he wanted to say, but it just seemed so futile.

They both sat there, sealed silently in their own miseries.

"Don't you have anything else to tell me?" Angela demanded, so suddenly that Andrew jumped.

"No," he said with regret. Nothing that wouldn't make things worse, he supposed. The exhaustion had returned again, so completely that he could hardly hold his head up. Everything hurt. There was no muscle in his body that didn't ache. "Please, Angela. Go home. Don't come back. There's really no reason for it."

Angela's dark copper hair caught his eyes, bright streamers that fanned out over her shoulders where the sunlight touched her skin. For a moment he indulged himself in the luxury of watching her, imagining that he was normal, that sitting here across a breakfast table with her was something he was entitled to do because he loved her. He could project farther, seeing himself saying Mass on Sunday mornings, watching Angela in the front pew bribing a couple of kids to keep still.

Children! The thought had never occurred to him! He loved kids, had always wanted them. It was only at that moment that he realized he would never have them: what in God's name would he be passing on? Walter was lucky: he'd had twenty years of fatherhood before the horror, and that was one thing the curse couldn't take away from him.

The vast difference between what he had wanted his life to be and what it was going to become was grotesque. He wasn't any stronger than his father had been, and he had much less to live for. He had no wife, no child, no one to consider besides himself. No one to leave behind in guilty grief over a suicide.

He was so paralyzed by the sudden thought of his future that he hadn't noticed the way Angela was looking at him. When he *did* notice, it brought him up short.

She was furious.

"You're going to give up, aren't you?" she said.

"What?" He was caught completely off guard.

"You're thinking of Walter, and you're thinking of doing what he did."

He couldn't answer.

"Because that's the worst. The absolute worst. I'd be ashamed of you forever."

"Angela. Think about it. Aren't you afraid of me right now, whether you admit it or not?"

"No. Not now. In a few hours, perhaps. That's not a sight you'd get used to. But it isn't you." She grabbed his hand and held it up between them. "*This* is you."

"You can't separate the two."

"Walter did. Look how he carried on his life and his work. For *you,* Andrew, because he loved you and he didn't want to give in until he'd tried to find something to help you. God! When I think of him holding on like that, all by himself, I want to cry!"

She realized that she *was* crying.

"What are you saying, Angela? That I should go back to the church? Hear confessions, administer the Host, preside over little kids' Sunday school classes?" He couldn't stop the sudden tide of bitterness.

"Now that you bring it up, that's exactly what you should do. It's your job."

"It would be sacrilege."

"No. You know as well as I do that intent is everything. Isn't that what sin is based on? Intent? You don't do what you do at the full moon of your own will, but if you give up, you do that of your own choice. And if you walk out on the church, you walk out on your life."

Her anger had risen out of nowhere and surprised her. She got up and started looking for her bag, her car keys, all the while listening to her voice, crying in the wilderness of its own volition, unable to calm itself.

"I'll tell you something else," she said, pulling on her shoes, "I don't understand this passivity of yours. It isn't like you. It isn't like Walter."

At the mention of Walter's name, she started to cry again. She stopped in midmotion, unable to continue, and buried her face in her hands.

Andrew touched her hair softly, knowing he shouldn't. "You loved Walter, didn't you?"

She raised her head. "Loved Walter? Not like you think. I loved *you*."

And now that we know *that*, she thought, what good is it? She rose and found her car keys.

"Don't leave, Angela."

"You just told me to leave."

"You never listened to me before; you're going to start *now*?"

He caught her without thinking and held on like a sea-swept sailor hangs on to a floating mast in a summer squall. All he could say was, "Don't leave, don't leave, don't leave." He had no idea where the words came from, but he suspected they were the first true things he had said all day.

Her reply was inaudible against his chest, but he didn't need to hear it.

Andrew felt his bones and body give in and take the strength she wanted to give. He couldn't fight Angela's decision, didn't want to. He might have inherited his father's curse, but he had found his own comfort.

PART
FOUR

†

15

Origin of Species:
Stephen Marley and Blanche Pitre, 1880

Humid. God, yes. Nobody stays in the city of New Orleans in August. Even the poorest people make pilgrimages out to the lake, bathing in the waters like lepers taking the holy cure. The night breezes blowing off the river can't lift the misery, and when the fog comes in you can see the heat wrapping the city like a warm, wet blanket.

The very worst place to be was the Vieux Carré. Even at this hour of the night there were people sitting on the stoops, waving palmetto fans and trying not to move as the heat rose off the bricks.

This part of the Quarter was the black section, so everybody noticed the scared-looking white girl making her way to an infamous house. A white girl at this hour in this part of town—people looked knowingly at each other and shook their heads.

Mrs. Thibideaux watched the girl and nodded to her husband. "This ain't no weather to be foolin' around wit' no hoodoo, ain't that right, Jumel?"

Jumel closed his eyes against the heat. "Um," he agreed. "Ask me, never no time to be messin' wit' that woman."

"Lord, Lord," Mrs. Thibideaux sighed, crossing herself, "protect that poor child."

The door to the small cottage on St. Ann Street was blistered and dingy, the green paint bubbling off as if the heat had creeped under the color. When the girl knocked five times, as she had been told to do, some of the loosened paint clung to her fingers.

She didn't expect the woman who answered to be so tall, and so handsome. Old, the girl had expected that—*bon Dieu*, the woman was at least fifty!—but she had expected a face as frightening as the legends, a woman who looked as diabolical as her reputation. It was more than beauty this woman had: it was a great, calm dignity, an assurance of her place and her power, almost an arrogance. Take away the woman's sangfroid, and she would be just another nice-looking quadroon, pretty but unexceptional. As it was, though, she was intimidating and irresistible.

The woman lounged in the door, waving a brilliantly colored fan, a gift, the stories said, from the Chinese emperor. The fan stirred the scarlet scarf wrapped around her hair, and moved the long gold earrings. Her dark, half-closed eyes appraised the girl shivering on the stoop, and when she spoke, her voice was rich as new cream.

"And what brings you out in the heat, *'tite fille*? What business can a young one like you have with Marie Laveau, eh?"

"Madame Marie," the girl whispered in terror, but with great passion, "I want. . . ."

"Blanche. Is that right?"

The girl nodded, astonished.

"I know you, young one. It's not your name, but it's what they call you. Look at that silvery blond hair: who else could you be but Blanche?" She stretched out one languorous hand to lift a strand of it, and the movement opened her blouse. Blanche saw a flash of pale coffee breast moving under the fabric, still youthful, still stirring. The woman was so beautiful. If I looked like that, thought Blanche, would Stephen Marley love me? If he did, I wouldn't have had to come here.

"Come in, 'tite fille. This is no conversation to have out here on the street." Marie moved inside, and Blanche, in a dream, followed.

At least the house was exactly what Blanche expected. Magic was everywhere: in dusty glass jars with ground glass stoppers, in bones and herbs and feathers hanging from the roof beams, in a thousand objects of gold and glass, ivory and iron, strange flowers and flesh dried into leather. Glass wind chimes tinkled from the secluded courtyard. An incense of sandalwood and jasmine and something she couldn't name floated on currents of air and made Blanche feel faint.

As she followed Marie, she saw the two of them reflected endlessly in dark glass and silver mirrors capable of lies.

"Sit," Marie Laveau said, motioning to a small table with two chairs. On the polished surface was a strange deck of cards, not the usual hearts and diamonds that Blanche knew, but intricately drawn pictures. One in particular drew her attention: a man hanging upside down. That's me, Blanche thought, suspended between what I was before I came here and what I'll be when I leave.

Marie Laveau noted Blanche's fascination and smiled. "What is it you want, 'tite fille? A love charm, a gris-gris to bring you the man who makes your body burn at night?"

Blanche looked up astounded.

Marie laughed. "Don't look so surprised. When one so young and so yearning comes to me, it's almost always love that causes the pain."

"It is pain, Madame!" Blanche blurted. "To love someone who doesn't even notice you is torture. I want him to love me. I want him to marry me."

The Voodoo queen waved her hand and looked amused. "How old are you, young one? Fifteen?"

"Sixteen. Last week."

"And how do you know it's love you feel? At that age, love is like the river: it swells and subsides, changes and moves on. The man you want today may not be the one you want tomorrow."

Blanche's eyes narrowed. "Then tomorrow, Madame, I'll come to you again. But for now, this is the man I want."

Marie looked momentarily stunned at Blanche's bravado, then burst into laughter. "You're not as innocently romantic as I had thought, *'tite fille*, but you're practical. This is a rich man, is he?"

"One of the richest in New Orleans."

"And handsome? Ah, of course he is. At your age, you still insist on a rich man being handsome. If a rich man were all you wanted, you could get a dozen without my help. You're young and very pretty. You'll be beautiful soon, when you've aged a bit and can afford to get out of those bayou rags."

"That'll never happen, Madame," Blanche said with bitterness, "My family's white trash, always will be."

"*Là*. That's your family, *'tite fille,* that's not you. No, you, I think"—she ran her hand through Blanche's hair—"are quite different. You're here, yes? And not even scared anymore."

Blanche smiled. It was true.

Marie looked at Blanche for a minute, then gathered the cards and put them aside. In an impulsive movement, she grasped Blanche's hand. Marie's eyes closed as the feeling hit her deep in her solar plexus, a rush of orgasmic energy that always heralded the *power*. She took a deep breath and felt the energy race through her, like exploding stars in her veins.

"What is it you really want, Blanche? Is it love? Or is the power that being the wife of a rich man brings?

Blanche stared at her, confounded. When she decided to speak, however, her voice was firm.

"I know it's useless to lie to you, Madame, even more useless to lie to myself. Yes, it's the power, it's the money, but more than that. I want a respectable life. I may be dirt poor now, I may have to beg from people I hate and who are no better than me but for the fine clothes around their well-fed bodies and the money in their pockets. But my children will be born rich. They'll have loving parents instead of brutes who hate them and beat them. Do I love Stephen Marley? What do I know about love, Madame? When would I have ever seen it, felt it, been able to give it to anyone who wanted it? When would I have been treasured, protected? I want you to make him love me, Madame; I want you to make *me* love *him,* so that I'll know what it feels like."

Still holding her hand, Marie looked into Blanche's eyes for a long time. "Forget the charm," Marie said, "forget the man. You don't need to marry power, you can have it on your own. Don't you know the gifts you have, *'tite fille,* haven't you ever felt the power inside you?"

Blanche felt the energy move, sizzling from Marie's hand into her own, two hot lines of lightning radiating in the dark. She had felt it before, having no name to put to it, but never as overwhelmingly as this.

Marie's eyes were dazzling. Blanche felt enchanted, held captive in the depths there. When Marie spoke in that dark, flowing voice, she felt borne upon it like a drifting boat on the river, directionless, anchored only to the sound.

"Stay with me awhile, Blanche, grow wise in the Voodoo ways. You have the power, I can feel it, still unformed and wild. Learn everything I can teach you and you'll blast the saints with your magic!"

Blanche felt something in her move and expand, pushing outward against her bones as if wanting to burst into a thousand brilliant sparks. Her whole body vibrated with the energy as she clung to Marie's hand.

"Love isn't for women like us," Marie whispered. "Love passes swiftly, but before it goes it drags a woman down, saps her strength. She gives everything and gets nothing in return. Stephen Marley will never satisfy a woman like you, *ma fille;* you are meant for better things. Only the power gives a woman control over her destiny. It never changes, never dies, is always faithful. Your followers will be your children, they will give you the love you need, as they have given me and I have returned to them. Stay with me, Blanche, and choose another life."

The magical cards had fallen to the floor. The colors seemed brighter now, the images alive and moving. Blanche saw her card, the Hanged Man, lying faceup, but across it lay another: a lightning-struck tower, destroyed and transformed.

She reached down to touch it, and gasped as the power flooded through her, raw, vital, waiting to be shaped, power so strong that it blinded her.

But Blanche was not to be blinded to her purpose. "I'll have it, Madame," she gasped softly. "Everything. Stephen Marley, his money, his children, his world. And I'll have my own as well."

She could see only lights in the blackness, but she heard Marie's laughter coil around her like soft, silk rope.

When their daughter didn't come home that night, the Pitres were more curious than worried, and then not much of that. They had produced eight children through momentary, drunken rutting, and were careless of them except as occasional providers. The girl was sixteen, after all, with the body of a woman. She was probably with some man, learning what could eventually turn into a trade, if she was smart.

After a week, they bestirred themselves to call the police. And when time passed and their daughter did turn up again, walking the streets of the French Quarter and the banks of Bayou St. John, they were too terrified of her even to speak to her.

It was just as well. If Blanche was anyone's daughter now, she was Marie Laveau's.

16

New Orleans, 1884

The steamship *Hyperion*, the flagship of the Marley Steamship Lines, was finally home in New Orleans. She moved through the crowded Mississippi lanes making her way to her berth, passing the other steamers and the occasional pleasure boats with the easy grace of a beautiful woman on her own terrain.

Her captain, Stephen Marley, looked over the wharves to the city, feeling the same satisfied excitement he always felt when he came home. He could see the longshoremen ready to swarm all over the *Hyperion* the minute she tied up, and the crowds of visitors waiting for the passengers to disembark.

The cries of the street vendors rose up to the wheelhouse and distracted Stephen. Tall black women, wearing skirts and headdresses as richly colored as the fruits and berries they sold, chanted their songs; old ladies set up little charcoal ovens where they fried hot rice cakes, all the while singing *"Calas! Tout chauds, tout chauds!"* The Snowball Man sold ice shaved fine as the first snowfall, delicately flavored with thick cream syrups. Each vendor had his own distinctive cry, his own stitch in the tapestry that made up New Orleans.

"Damn, I love coming home!" Stephen told his first mate. "Aristide, find me a woman who makes me feel the way this city does and I'll be married in a week. Don't you know any fine Cajun girls back home on Bayou Teche who want a steady husband?"

"You better hold off on that, yes," Aristide advised. "A wife, five or six *bébés,* and you gotta slow down your way of living. Besides, all the ladies seem to like you well enough."

Stephen made a scornful, dismissive noise. "Married women looking for a thrill and waterfront whores looking for a profit. I'm thirty years old. I should have had a son by now and a couple of daughters to make me happy."

"You doing fine: six ships in four years, master of your own line. What for you got to complain, eh?"

Stephen sighed. "I don't know, Aristide. Sometimes I'm not sure whether I'm better off now than before. When I was poor, all my problems could be solved by getting rich. Now I'm rich and I've got the kind of problems money can't solve."

Aristide put a hand on Stephen's shoulder. "*Cher ami,* I'm gonna do you one big favor. You come home with me, you can marry my *cousine* Naomie. Nobody on the bayou cook jambalaya as good as Naomie. She gots a bad temper, she weigh three hundred pounds, and we can't keep shoes on that girl, but she sure could keep you at home, yes! You try slippin' out, Naomie she grab you and wrap herself around you 'til you don't want to go noplace except to bed."

Stephen stared at Aristide for a minute, perplexed.

"Does she use real andouille sausage in the jambalaya?"

At that point, things got very busy in the wheelhouse and there was no more time for talk.

Stephen felt he'd been given a marvelous chance when he first came to New Orleans. He'd shed his old life like a painful skin and started growing a new, stronger one. When he got to know the city, he realized that it was where he wanted to settle. It had a smooth sheen of gentility that pleased him, and a way of life that seduced anyone who stayed for long. There was always something in New Orleans that reached out to newcomers, that made them feel comfortable and welcome, part of the ongoing history of the place. When Stephen felt it, he knew he belonged here.

The city had energy. It was a place where men like Stephen could still make money by hard work and will.

He wanted to build more than a fortune: he wanted to found a great family. When he left England he had given up the ties of blood and position that rooted him so firmly in British soil. He'd hated to leave, but he couldn't stay. His father had fallen hard from grace, losing his property in a long, alcoholic decline. His mother died never having come to terms with that failure. All that was left for him there was a life of genteel poverty among distant, slightly condescending relatives. No matter how hard he worked or how much money he made, he would be fighting the disgrace forever, the family watching smugly for the least slip that would indicate that his father's weakness had carried into another generation. Better to cut those sad connections and let the pain heal with time. He couldn't regain what he had lost, but in America he could start again on his own terms.

He was fourteen when he hired out on a British company ship running the American routes, sixteen when he landed in New Orleans and decided that this was the place he would become a rich man.

New Orleans was good for him financially. Socially, it took more time. Eventually, the old Creole society opened its doors for him—cautiously, to be sure—but Stephen was always a man who knew how to use the slightest opening to his advantage.

Money alone wouldn't have bought him a place among the gently bred Creoles; it was what he did with it that helped him along. He used his growing fortune and influence wisely, contributing to local charities and civic projects. It was Marley money that repaired the crumbling walls around St. Louis Cemetery, and his money that planted the glorious rainbow of flowers in the Place d'Armes.

He had given the money discreetly and anonymously, through his lawyer, which spoke well for his breeding. The people who mattered knew about the contributions within the week, and they lost no time checking his credentials with English friends. The family was impoverished, but one of the very best, and Stephen had been raised and educated with certain standards. He was a gentleman, which counted heavily for him in the South. That he had been poor was no disgrace: money and breeding were two completely different things, and the first could never buy the second. Breeding was all that mattered.

Stephen might have been a little wild, drinking too often in waterfront taverns and carousing with the wrong kind of women, but he was young. Orleanians didn't trust an unmarried gentleman who was too circumspect. The important thing was that he never got into any long-range trouble.

People watched carefully when Stephen finally came to call on one of the local daughters, Miss Cyrie Devaux. Gossip said that he had not formally spoken to her father, but that it was only a matter of time. Stephen and Miss Devaux seemed to be a good match. They had a firm friendship that was a good basis for marriage.

Cyrie would have taken him just as he was. That was the Creole way: good blood meant more than money, and a place could always be found in the family business for a son-in-law. But it had mattered deeply to Stephen that he bring a wife the means to provide her with everything his father couldn't provide for his mother.

It was that obsession that kept Stephen away from New Orleans on longer and more frequent voyages, his ambition burning so hot that it finally beat Cyrie back. By the time Stephen had what he wanted, he had lost Cyrie. Her father, furious at the many delays, refused to have Cyrie wait any longer for a man who hadn't made any binding promises.

Stephen's fondest dream, of family and warmth, seemed to be the only thing out of his control.

The *Hyperion* was safely berthed and Stephen and Aristide walked slowly toward the Marley Lines offices, still talking about life, love, the river, and the sterling qualities of big, beautiful *cousine* Naomie.

"All these years at sea and on the river," Stephen said. "No family, no prospects of marriage. I never had the time. The river's all I've got and now I'm going to have to give it up."

That stopped Aristide cold. "Give it up?" he asked, astonished. "Give up the river? For to do what, *ami*? I can't see you doing anything else."

"Bookkeeping. That's what it comes down to: accounts. I'm having those new ships built so we can expand into the Jamaica, Havana, and New York routes. Maybe into Europe. The lines are getting big, Aristide. It means a lot of work behind a desk now."

Aristide shook his head. "For me, I couldn't do it. My whole life I been on the river, know her like my own wife, yes. It's a hard thing you doing."

Stephen didn't need Aristide to tell him that. "Oh, cheer up, Aristide!" he said. "My misfortune is your good luck. As of right now I'm promoting you. You'll be captain of the *Hyperion*. Congratulations."

"Oh, yeah?" Aristide said, delighted. "Now, that is good news. I always said the *Hyperion*, she the finest riverboat on the Mississippi."

Stephen glanced back at his beauty shining in the water. Three hundred feet long, she was, pure white with towering red smokestacks, her upper decks dripping gingerbread. Her mahogany-and-gilt salon illuminated by a hundred stained-glass transom windows made her one of the most luxurious of the floating palaces. She was his first and best beloved, and he never remembered the sacrifices he had made to buy her, only the pure pleasure he got when he looked at his own name painted on her sides.

"Just . . . just take care of her, Aristide. She's my first-born." He gave a short, embarrassed laugh. "With the way things are going, my ships are probably the only offspring I'll ever have."

Stephen turned to look one more time at the *Hyperion*, so magnificent under the southern sun. He felt something within him change, and thought sadly that whatever life held for him now, it would never be as exciting again.

They entered Stephen's office by a private side door from the street. Stephen had had that door cut so that he could come right from the docks and enjoy a few minutes of silence and a quiet drink of whiskey before the business closed in around him.

"A toast," he told Aristide, setting out a crystal decanter and a pair of glasses. "To the new captain of the *Hyperion*."

But Aristide was distracted. He was peeking out the tiny window in the door to the outer offices.

"Ooo-wee! I think you got business you want to take care of, yes," he said.

Stephen put down the decanter and took a look. "Sweet Jesus!" he breathed.

She was the most beautiful woman he'd ever seen, sitting in the office's ugly wooden chairs with the grace of a queen on a jeweled throne. She was all lavender and silk and clouds of lace, with a lush figure that made him want to rip the silk with both hands. Her silvery blond hair seemed to shine with its own light, caught up in intricate curls that only made it more lucent. All of a sudden, Stephen felt his hands itch to pull out all the hairpins and let it fall.

He'd never had such a sudden, erotic attraction to a woman before.

"Hoo, boy!" Aristide whispered, "I think *cousine* Naomie gonna have a run for her money, yes."

"Do you know her?" Stephen asked, his throat dry.

Aristide squinted a little at the window. "She look familiar. I think I do know her from someplace, but it's the funniest thing . . ." He shook his head. "I think I remember her from someplace bad. I can't remember where."

Stephen was impatient. "Someplace bad? Aristide, look at her. She's no whore! She's obviously a lady."

"No, not that kind of place. Someplace . . ." He made a little sound of frustration. "Someplace scary."

"You must have been drunk at the time."

Aristide shrugged. That was always a possibility.

"It'll come back to me," he said, "but I think this is a dangerous woman, *ami*."

"Any woman that beautiful is dangerous, my friend. The thing to do now is not to keep her waiting, so if you'll excuse me . . ." He gestured toward the side door.

"I'm not fooling you," Aristide said seriously, "I think that woman means trouble. You watch yourself, yes."

Her voice instantly seduced him. It was as light and liquid as champagne, the sound of a young goddess.

"I've come on some distasteful business," she said. "The Marley Lines delivered a shipment to me last week and it arrived badly damaged. I wonder if we might reach some sort of agreement as to what should be done?"

There was something about her eyes, Stephen was thinking. It wasn't the color, although the green was vivid and hypnotic, but it was something else. The way she looked at him spooked him: an intense look, as if she were waiting for some response. Beautiful, yes, she was, but an uncomfortable kind of beauty. Stephen was reminded of a marvelous serpent he saw once. It was the same color as her eyes, a glowing brilliant green, almost phosphorescent. It was tiny, only the size of a pencil, and graceful beyond belief. Stephen had watched it twining its sinuous length along a small branch, unable to look away. It was a green mamba, the most poisonous snake in the world. The death it brought was instantaneous.

He shook his head slightly. Absurd that such a lovely woman should provoke that memory. Better that he should concentrate on business just now.

"Well, there's no agreement to be reached," he said. "If the shipment was damaged, of course the company will replace the objects or compensate you for the value. We've made our reputation on that point."

"That's very civilized of you, Captain Marley," she said. "You'll send someone to appraise the damage, then? I have the shipping receipts with the name and address right here."

Damn! Stephen thought. Why is she looking at me that way? Or am I imagining it?

"We'll send someone in the morning," he told her, reaching out to take the papers. "The gentleman who takes care of the appraisals is . . ."

And then she did something exceedingly strange. Her hand, soft inside its silky glove, lightly stroked his forehead.

He was overcome with a wild perfume, an exotic scent unfamiliar to him, arousing and spellbinding. It floated from her hand, assaulting him with sweet madness.

He could feel the cool, scented glove against the sudden fever of his skin. His mind filled with images that expanded into thoughts that aroused and confused him. It seemed that he was looking at her through a curtain of scented smoke. The silk that he had wanted to tear from her body was indeed gone, and she stood there naked, her delicate hair tumbling over bare breasts, her arms reaching out to him, as if she were a delicious offering to a lascivious god. Or—he grew more confused—was he to be the sacrifice? In his dream, he pushed her on her back against lace pillows, pinning her arms outstretched at her sides while he fed himself on the honeyed milk of her breasts.

Stephen felt as if his muscles were too light to move his body. He was slightly amazed to find that he had the strength to pull her hand down and press his lips into her palm.

She pulled her hand away and the images vanished. Even the memory of them vanished, buried deep in his mind.

She smiled.

Stephen gave a little start. He'd lost his train of thought for a moment. He hoped it wasn't obvious.

" . . . Mr. Elson," Stephen continued, "he'll give us a full appraisal of the damage and we'll take care of it."

She gathered her things. "You've been very kind, Captain. I hope we'll meet again."

"I'm certain we will, ma'am," he said, opening the office door for her.

She left, and Stephen immersed himself in his account books.

All that week, Stephen was left with a vague feeling that there was something he should have remembered, something important, but for the life of him he couldn't think of what it was. This lost memory bothered him, off and on, even through Sunday Mass. One moment he was sitting in the cathedral listening to the priest, and the next minute his mind was completely blank. It annoyed him: he wasn't the kind of man to forget things.

The Mass was ended and parishioners started streaming out into the Sunday sunshine.

"Father Sedona," Stephen said, reaching out to shake the priest's hand, "another fine sermon."

"Aha! Stephen Marley!" The old priest gave him a stern look. "You can't get around me that easily. I haven't noticed you in confession for two months or more."

"Father, I've been too busy to sin," Stephen answered, laughing. He turned his head, distracted, and was pleased to see his beautiful visitor of the other morning, smiling at him from the park.

The old man followed Stephen's look toward Jackson Square and his smile faded as he saw who waited there.

"Excuse me, Father," Stephen said, "I see a friend."

Father Sedona did not release Stephen's hand. "Do you know that woman?"

"Well . . ." Stephen was a little confused at the priest's serious tone. "She's actually a customer of the Marley Lines. We met in my office. Why? Do you know anything about her? I'm afraid I only know her name."

"Blanche Pitre," the priest said, as if it were an obscenity. "Stephen, believe me, she's not for you. She . . ."

He stopped as Blanche walked up to them, turning a dazzling smile on Stephen.

"Captain Marley, how pleasant to see you," she said, holding out her hand to be taken. "And Father Sedona. You know exactly how pleased I am to see *you*."

Sedona looked as if he were struggling for his temper.

"I was just about to take a walk along the levee, Captain," Blanche said, "Would you care to join me?"

"My pleasure," Stephen said. He said good-bye to Father

Sedona and offered his arm to Blanche. As he glanced back, he saw the priest glaring after them.

"Well, that was odd," he said to Blanche.

"What?"

"You and Father Sedona. Don't you two get along? I thought everyone in New Orleans loved him."

"We have a slight difference of religious opinion," she said, "and I'm afraid he takes it more seriously than I do."

The levee was crowded with Sunday-afternoon strollers. Most of the fashionable people of New Orleans came here on Sundays to see, be seen, gossip, and observe. Very few came for the spectacular panorama of the Mississippi River glittering under the sun, the white ships sitting in the water like debutantes awaiting callers. Stephen noticed with a little pride that quite a few heads turned as he and Blanche passed.

"But what about you?" she said to him. "I'm rather surprised you're a Catholic. I thought all Englishmen were Church of England."

"The Marleys have always been obstinate Catholics, all the way back. In fact, several Marleys refused to sign the Act of Succession when Henry the Eighth wanted to make Anne Boleyn queen. We retained the faith, but we certainly lost almost everything else, including quite a few members of the family. We were so stubborn that even the Marleys who were only marginally religious suddenly became more Catholic than the Pope." He considered it. "Actually, I'm not all that religious, but I'm as hardheaded as the rest of my family."

She laughed, then halted. "Oh, is that one of your ships, Captain?" she asked.

They had stopped in front of the *Hyperion*. The next four ships berthed there all bore the Marley insignia on the stacks.

"Indeed it is," he said, inordinately proud of the ships gleaming in the water. "Would you like to go aboard?"

"Very much."

As they ascended the gangplank, two elderly Creole ladies watched them go. Stephen never noticed the ladies' agitation as they whispered and crossed themselves, murmuring soft prayers for Stephen's protection.

It didn't matter. If Blanche Pitre wanted him, the ladies concluded sadly, all the prayer in the world couldn't save him.

The storm that night should have lulled Stephen to sleep. The sounds of wind and thunder, the strange light, the cool air charged with rain and lightning had always soothed him.

He lay cottoned in silence, desperately wanting to sleep. His body felt drugged with exhaustion, but his mind was distracted by thoughts of Blanche's beauty, torturing him with images of how she would look naked and tangled in the rough linen of his bed.

He had finally reached that fine point between waking and sleeping, when nothing is provable as real, when he opened his eyes and saw her standing beside the bed.

He was sure he had imagined her until she put her hand on his head, her perfume bringing the same spin of erotic images that he had felt in the office. And then it seemed perfectly logical that she should be there. He closed his eyes and let her dark scent lull him, a sweet amber tinted with some smokier scent that aroused him. He didn't even have to look to know that he had never had an erection like the one he had now. It was exciting, but it was . . . *strange*. He knew he was awake, but it was like falling into one of those feverish sleeps where dreams come and go, fading in and out of reality.

Her hand trailed down from his face, a cool fire that

tingled slowly over his throat and chest until she found the heart of him.

He tried to touch her, but that drugged, heavy feeling held him. In some of his dreams he had moved like this, trying to run and maddeningly slowed by an implacable force that wouldn't let him escape.

She kissed him, and he couldn't tell which of them was drawing breath in any one moment. He became certain that if one of them stopped breathing, both would die.

He had a brief moment of clarity, a flash on an ancient horror: the succubus, an elegant demon who could drain a man's soul through a diabolical parody of love.

But as her body covered him with heat, it was no illusion: it was real. For the first time in his life, he lay passive while a woman made love to him, doing everything he had dreamed but had never dreamed to ask. With no need to reciprocate, he was free to fully taste every sensation, every nuance; his whole body was alive to what she was doing. He was distantly aware that he would never be able to make love again without remembering this, that everything would pale beside it. He didn't care. This was all there was in the world: her hands moving on his body, her mouth, her thighs locking him inside her, the tips of her breasts leaving tracks of fire wherever they touched him.

His back arched as he erupted and screamed, his breath bursting from his chest into her parted lips. He could feel her warm with it, drinking it as if it were wine. And still she would not stop. She moved and he screamed again, the sensitivity too much to bear and too wonderful to let go.

When it was over he couldn't open his eyes; he couldn't move. He felt that there was a tiny, glowing point of life left in him and if he didn't keep perfectly still, it would go out.

He felt her lips close by his ear.

"You'll come to me," she said. Her voice became slower, softer, and hypnotically soothing. "You'll find what you need in my house. There's a fire to warm you, to calm you, to ease you. You'll be wrapped in lovely dreams that will unfold around you as long as you like. Come to me, Stephen. You must say yes."

How wonderful, he was thinking, how pleasant to be taken care of, to make no decisions, to have no responsibilities. To give it all up.

"Say yes, Stephen," she insisted. "Of your own free will, say yes."

He felt himself stir again, felt the breath deep in his chest. And felt something driven to the back of his mind, some faint note of protest, of warning, drowning in the overpowering heat of the moment.

"Yes," he said.

"So. Now he's yours. Did he remember who you were?" Marie Laveau asked Blanche.

"Not at all. Why would he have remembered a lovesick kitchen maid from four years ago?"

"*Bien*. It's for the best. You can start fresh, if that's what you really want. But it's a mistake, *'tite fille*. You don't love him, you know. You're just clinging to an emotion remembered."

"Four years, *ma mère*, I've done everything you wanted. I've studied hard for you, learned everything you wanted to teach me. But now I want him, just as I did when I first came to you."

Marie shook her head. "It will suffocate you, this society he lives in. Too many restrictions, too many 'shoulds' and 'mustn'ts.' You were never meant to be there among women who fill their idle lives with nonsense. One with your power can't live in two worlds. But have him, *'tite fille*. Until this passion passes—and it *will* pass, I assure you—just don't forget who you are and what your destiny is. You have larger obligations to your people."

"I'll never forget, *ma mère*."

Marie sighed and rested her cloud of graying hair against the chair, the evening light casting her face into shadow. "Despite what they say about me, I can't live forever." She reached out to touch Blanche's hand. "But you, *'tite fille*, that may be an entirely different story."

17

The French Quarter was at its most bewitching in the early evenings, Stephen thought, when the windows glowed warm yellow and the night sky was filtered through violet-colored glass.

He had always taken these evening walks, as much to clear his mind as for the exercise. There was so much to distract him. Street musicians played while little children danced for coins. Magicians pulled silk handkerchiefs and paper flowers out of the river-scented air. Pretty young girls tried to sell him things he couldn't possibly use.

The shop windows stopped him, windows filled with things that gleamed in the jeweled light. Every time he tried to move on, something else would catch his attention: the glimmer of cut crystal, the patina of old wood, the fine sheen of gold. Delicate china baskets were put out for sale, and venerable silver plate. He couldn't just pass by. Something in the color or something in the detail pulled him back for a closer look. Once he saw a retired cavalry sword. It was probably his imagination, but as he peered at the etched blade he thought he saw traces of dried blood. Ironic that the blood should be there even if the body had been dust for years.

Stephen always wondered where these things came from, who had let them go, and why. There was an air of sadness about them, of sacrifice, of families ruined by war and never recovered. Still, he had been dazzled by the shop displays and, unable to resist, had bought them.

Once he had been mesmerized by a crystal chandelier hanging splendidly in a window on Royal Street. It was a masterpiece of workmanship, each drop precisely cut to enhance the light and emphasize the clarity of the crystal. He marveled over it for three days as it hung in the window, then he bought it.

But when he got the thing home he realized it had been a mistake. It was too aristocratic for his house. It had been made for Versailles, not for him, and when he touched one of the almost-invisible prisms, it was like touching water. There was no solid substance to it; it was only something beautiful. It wasn't even useful; the light it gave was too glaring for the room. When the air stirred the prisms, they tinkled like secret, distant laughter.

He had wanted to possess it, and all he could do was look at it.

The shop windows still attracted him, but he was learning to be more practical.

He sat on an iron bench in Jackson Square and let the sights and sounds of the city distract him. He knew that he was trying to delay going home and tried to think for the hundredth time why.

The square was emptying fast now. People were rushing to get home to their families and dinner tables, to be part of the warmth behind those yellow windows. In a few minutes he was alone, still able to hear soft movement as the entertainers packed up for the night, as the last of the faithful trailed out of Vespers at the cathedral.

He closed his eyes and tried to remember Blanche on the first night they were together. He could remember passion, but no tenderness. A vague feeling of having been used, a feeling that was bleeding slowly into his mind these days, came over him again.

What was he doing with her? The doubts, he noticed, only

came when he was not with her; when they were together it was in a molten rush of heat that burned all reason away. But even then, even under the insistent instincts of desire, there was that dark edge, that creeping certainty that what they were doing was wrong—or, at least, what *he* was doing was wrong.

They had nothing in common; they didn't even talk. He was becoming aware that even Blanche was beginning to sense some emptiness there, something that didn't fulfill her. It was as if they were still together only because they were trying to burn themselves out, to drown a passion that never should have been born. There was a desperation about their coupling; it was so violent and so intense that it could blind them to the shallowness of it.

He was aware that, for all her worldliness, Blanche was still very young and couldn't be expected to understand her own feelings. He, on the other hand, should have known better. He had allowed her into his bed when he knew it wasn't right. True, Blanche was living in her own house as a bow to convention, but she was with him on St. Charles Avenue almost every night.

As long as he could berate himself for his irresponsibility, he needn't acknowledge his true thoughts. In the back of his mind there lived the sure and certain knowledge of what he would never admit to himself: that there was something about Blanche—and he had no idea what it was—that terrified him.

But for the moment, until the madness passed, he was helpless to leave her. He had thought about it, made up his mind to end it, had even prepared a speech to her, but he couldn't do it. Every time he began, it ended with Blanche's body twined around him, her heat capturing him just like the first time, and resistance was useless.

He sighed, leaned back against the bench, and looked hopelessly up at the sky.

"Stephen?"

The voice was so unexpected in the quiet square that he jumped.

"Cyrie!" he said, rising to his feet. "How good to see you."

"I *thought* it was you! I was just coming out of the cathedral and saw you; I wasn't sure at first, but then I remembered how you used to love coming here just at twilight, so"—she smiled—"I thought I'd say hello."

"This is the part of New Orleans that always stuck in my mind when I was away. It's strange; you can know every corner of a city, but there's always one part of it that seems more like home than any other. It calls you back every time." He gestured to the bench. "Can you sit a few minutes, or do you have to be someplace?"

She looked uncertain.

"Please," he said, "not for very long."

She sat down. "You don't sound very happy, Stephen."

He ran his hand through his hair hopelessly. "It isn't that I'm unhappy, exactly, it's . . ." He thought about it. "I don't know *what* it is," he said in exasperation.

"Just start talking," she said, "and perhaps you can sort it out. I'll simply listen."

He didn't know where to begin. He couldn't tell her about Blanche, although she undoubtedly knew. Everyone in New Orleans knew everyone else's business. Especially when it came to a scandal, and he was fairly certain that his affair with Blanche was indeed scandal.

"Cyrie, are you sorry that we didn't get married?"

She hesitated, but recovered her composure. "I don't think marriage would have been good between us. I wanted to settle down and you wanted the river. You wanted someone to come home to and I wanted someone to be there. We were at cross purposes."

"I think I've changed. The prospect of a wife, a home, being surrounded by children and people who love you; it's almost irresistible."

"I don't know what to tell you, Stephen. The only answer I have is something that isn't my business."

"Cyrie. Please. Say what you like."

She sighed and thought for a few minutes, as if she were gathering her convictions. When she did speak, it was with the voice of plain honesty.

"If a home and family are what you want, Stephen, do what you've always done: go after them in the most direct way possible. I've never known you to be indecisive before. But it seems that your problem is easily solved. Marry Blanche Pitre. And if for some reason you can't . . ." She took a deep breath. "Get rid of her and start over."

Odd, he thought. She was perfectly calm, and he was the one blushing.

"Although," she said, almost to herself, "I never imagined you to be interested in that sort of thing. You always seemed so sensible."

This mystified him. "That sort of thing?"

"Voodoo. You just didn't strike me as the kind of man who would believe in it."

"Cyrie, what *are* you talking about?"

This time, she blushed. "You mean you don't . . ." She looked away, flustered. "Oh, no. Stephen, really, this isn't any of my business."

"No, tell me." She had already risen half off the bench. He grabbed both her hands and pulled her back down. "What on God's green earth does Voodoo have to do with me?"

She still looked uncomfortable. "Well, that's just it. I don't know, now. I thought you knew about Blanche. Stephen . . .

everyone knows who she is! You can't tell me you haven't heard."

"But you're going to tell me now. Cyrie, I'd like to think we're still friends. If you have any regard for me . . ."

"You know what gossip's like in this town. Last month I ran into some ladies at the market. Of course they made a point of talking about Blanche, not to me of course, but making sure that I was well within earshot. Usually it's just malicious." She stopped and Stephen felt a quick stab of pain. How long had Cyrie been living with the stigma of having been left almost at the altar, only to have his affair with Blanche become the stiletto with which jealous, petty women could prick her? He had never even considered it.

"But this was different," she continued. "They sounded frightened. Some of them, it seemed, had attended the Voodoo dances at Congo Square. And they saw Blanche there."

Stephen laughed. "Is that all? I don't approve of it, but it seems to be a harmless thrill for ladies these days, watching the Voodoos. Blanche is young and curious, I suppose."

"She wasn't *watching,* Stephen. She was leading the rites. When Marie Laveau died a few months ago, she left Blanche as her successor. And Blanche wasn't content to leave the Voodoo worship as it was; much as I disapprove, Voodoo is still a religion and doesn't hurt anyone. But Blanche, they say, wasn't satisfied with that. She wanted more power than the Voodoo gods could give her. No one knows what she did or how she did it, but black magic and devil worship began to seep into the regular rites. There were tales of awful orgies and drunken frenzies, perhaps even human sacrifice to evil spirits that had nothing to do with Voodoo. It got so bad that the old Voodoos, the ones who followed Marie Laveau, dropped out. They were terrified. And the new people who followed Blanche were another breed entirely.

"People have been ruined after they crossed her, some

have died. All the blacks and half the whites in town are scared to death of her. They call her *la Reine Blanche*, the White Queen. The dances at Congo Square are only for tourists. The real rites, they say, are at Bayou St. John and at Marie Laveau's old house on St. Ann. No one knows what they involve, at least no one who isn't one of the initiated."

Stephen sat, stunned. Finally he said, "How long is this supposed to have been going on?"

"I'm not sure. Four months. Five."

About the time Blanche had first come to his bed.

He couldn't say any more. His mind was racing.

"Stephen," Cyrie said, "gossip thrives on itself. But enough people are talking about Blanche that there could be some truth in it, so for your own protection, you had better find out how much."

He still sat there, thinking furiously. Devil worship. Black magic. He knew very little of these things, but he was beginning to know their power. Just because he didn't believe, didn't mean that it didn't work.

"I have to be getting home," Cyrie said, getting to her feet, "I'm sorry, Stephen. I know that these things are hard for you to hear, and perhaps they're only malicious gossip. Blanche is young, beautiful, and she doesn't care what people think; that makes her a target in this town. I know you'll use your own judgment in this."

Something about the rustle of her skirts or the reluctance of her leaving, or perhaps just the almost forgotten softness in her manner stirred something in Stephen, something he desperately didn't want to lose. He was so overcome with it that he rose and impulsively folded his arms around her. She seemed surprised, but she didn't move away.

"I'm so sorry, Cyrie," he said bleakly.

"You have nothing to be sorry for. Things happen the way

they're supposed to happen, whether we like it or not."

They stood like that for a a few minutes until Stephen, aware of her reputation if they were seen and even more aware of his own regrets, pulled away.

"I have to go," Cyrie said, smoothing her skirt self-consciously.

They turned their backs, each dutifully going places they had no desire to be.

18

It was Carnival time, and the city had abandoned itself to the last, lustful pleasures before Lent. Already the parades had started. Stephen sat on the veranda of his house watching the first of them progress down St. Charles.

Crowds gathered along the street, the children in front, and as each elaborate float passed, the children would cry "Throw me something, mister!" The maskers' costumes glittered in the torchlight as they tossed Mardi Gras trinkets and strings of bright beads into the crowd. The cheap glass beads looked like real jewels as they arched in the air over the lights, and at Mardi Gras they were almost as precious. Children screamed and scattered to catch as many as they could.

Nothing is what it seems, Stephen thought, and even the Carnival mood couldn't cheer him.

Was it true? Had Blanche trapped him with black magic? When she made love to him, she sometimes seemed detached: he was just the machine that gave her pleasure or satisfaction or whatever it was she needed. When it was over, she would leave. Just like that. He'd watched her get out of the bed and walk out of the room as if he weren't there.

The memory of it made him wince. It wasn't love. It was a grotesque imitation. Sometimes, he knew, two people will come together simply to feel a connection with another human being, even if just for the moment. That wasn't love, either, not by any measurement, but it was an honest emotion. With Blanche, he didn't believe it was even that. Not now. When they were first together, he had sensed a desperation in Blanche. He thought at first that she was merely uncertain of him and trying to assure herself that he was indeed in love with her. But he grew more aware that it wasn't *his* love she was trying to prove, but her own, as if she were trying to discover something in herself that she *must* have, and that—at last—wasn't there. In some way, Stephen felt that it was less an absence of love than a *failure* of love. Whatever Blanche thought she was going to gain, it hadn't been enough for her, or right for her.

And what about him? Why was he still with her? Was it that his lust detracted him from the loneliness and disappointment of his life? He had thought about ending the affair, and when he wasn't with her the conviction that it was the right thing to do grew stronger. But when she slipped into his bed, her exotic perfume wrapping him in a sensuous dream state, he forgot all about his doubts. Indeed, he forgot everything except the touch of her hands, the feel of her skin under his fingers.

Black magic. She's bewitched you. He couldn't get the phrase out of his mind, where it replayed over and over until it grew into something monstrous.

He thought about her house, the large white clapboard cottage on St. Ann Street, which he had never really seen. He vaguely remembered going there once, right after he met Blanche, but any real memory of it was blocked from his mind. He couldn't recall a single detail of the interior, or of what passed there.

Odd that she had spent so much time in his house, but that he knew nothing of hers.

And that's when the idea came to him. With much less shame than he expected to feel, he decided to blatantly spy on her. He had no idea what he was looking for, what he expected to find, or what he'd say to her, but that didn't matter. The important thing was to *know*.

Black magic. Was it true?

She had told him not to expect her tonight, that she had another engagement.

He took only a moment to throw on his coat against the slightly chill night air, and started on foot toward the French Quarter.

He went through a part of the quarter he hadn't visited in so long, past all the places he'd loved as a young sailor. Green, gold, and purple, the Mardi Gras colors, were everywhere: on banners and bright ribbons hanging from balconies, on flags, on streamers and confetti in shop windows, dripping in glass beads from the hands of delighted maskers. Boisterous streets rang with bawdy music and voluptuous laughter, gradually fading to darker streets whose life was muffled behind silent doors. He turned onto St. Ann Street and walked until he had reached the farthest part, almost to Rampart.

He recognized the house immediately. It stood, like all French Quarter houses, flush to the sidewalk, its front windows secretly shuttered. Its courtyard was hidden by a high, weathered white board fence that connected to the house on either side and ran between Blanche's house and the houses of its neighbors.

He tried the latch on a narrow door cut into the fence, half expecting it to be locked, but at his slight pressure, the door moved silently on oiled hinges.

The small plot of land was neatly cared for, tiny flower beds planted with strange flowers and odd herbs. Stephen recognized two of them: deadly nightshade, distinctive because of its star-shaped purple flowers, and aconite, called wolfsbane, a plant so poisonous that its touch caused illness and death.

Carefully making his way around the plantings, Stephen heard low, excited voices seeping from a partially opened window. He crept up to the window and looked in, thanking God that his excellent vantage point was hidden by foliage. He could see in, but anyone looking out would have trouble seeing him.

He was looking into a wide room, unfurnished except for a high wooden altar set up at one end. Strange symbols, drawn in what looked like chalk, adorned the floor. The only light came from dozens of candles placed all around the floor and in elaborate candle holders set into the walls.

People began to flow into the room, filling it with color and movement. They were predominantly blacks, dressed in flamboyant, fantastic creations of silk, velvet, sequins, and lace in brilliant colors, with gold jewelry setting off the lush darkness of their skin. The few white people among them were more timid in dress and looked insignificant beside the dramatic blacks. All of them were restive, as if holding themselves in an edgy reserve. Even so, they couldn't stand completely still, swaying almost unconsciously to an internal rhythm.

This was torture for Stephen. His cure for nervous energy was movement and action. All he could do now was hide and keep still, and something told him that to do otherwise could mean his life. As the minutes passed, he almost screamed for something to happen.

A muffled drumbeat made him jump out of his skin. Three beats, slow, momentous, definite, that acted on the crowd like a trumpet fanfare. The people parted down two sides of the room, clearing a path from the altar to a place at the other end of the room, which he couldn't see. He assumed there was a door there.

The drums stopped, then began again, a slowly majestic beat, as a woman, cloaked and hooded in red silk, strode to the altar. As she passed, the assembled people deferentially put out their hands to her to be taken. As her tiny hand grasped theirs, they bowed over it, as a subject bows before a queen.

She took her place before the altar, the cloak hiding her face. With one graceful wave of her hand, the drumbeats began again.

This time, the drums swept into a wild cadence of primitive, almost forgotten rhythms. Even Stephen, the unbeliever, crouching there in the night, felt the drums stirring something inside himself, a long-buried primal instinct that wanted to swell to the surface.

Stephen closed his eyes and took a deep, calming breath.

A single scream from a dozen throats snapped his attention back to the room. An extraordinary man had jumped into the midst of the Voodoos. He was coal black, his body shining in the candlelight as if it had been polished. The length of brilliant red cloth he wore around his hips only made him look more naked. He was a tremendous man, over six feet, carrying his size as gracefully as a wild thing would, a force of nature and strength made in man's image. He wore an immense feathered necklace interwoven with gold beads and old bones, and when he walked the whole thing shimmered around his shoulders. The women in the crowd murmured, "Basile . . . Prince Basile . . ." in soft, erotic tones, but he either didn't notice or in his arrogance pretended not to.

At the insistence of the drums, Basile leaped into a wildly pagan dance, every muscle moving under his shining flesh in hypnotic syncopation. It was a dance both sacred and secular, a celebration of the body and its unimaginable delights, unashamed and glorious.

He shivered and leaped, setting the feathers and bones of his necklace flying about his head. As his movements grew more abandoned, sweat polishing his skin to an incandescent light, the Voodoos moaned and moved to touch him as he came near them. He filled his mouth with liquor and sprayed it on them like holy water, and they shook and fell, writhing, to the floor. The whole room was alive with the vital electricity of the Voodoos in their rite of passage.

Basile shivered and circled around the woman in red silk; without touching her, he propelled her closer to the altar, where a beautifully carved chest, pierced with elaborately carved holes in the shapes of fantastic flowers, waited to be opened. She plunged both arms into the chest and lifted a monstrous snake, a huge thing that looked about six feet long. She cooed to it, permitting it to wind itself slowly around her as she closed her eyes in rapture, woman and serpent moving in grace together.

Stephen had heard of this part of the Voodoo rites from his servants, most of whom were Voodoos. The snake was the incarnation of the Voodoo God, the channel by which the Voodoo priestess was brought closer to the spirit world so as to better guide her people. So far, Stephen thought, he hadn't seen anything all that frightening or dangerous: only a group of the devout practicing their religion. True, he didn't know a lot about Voodoo, but none of this looked harmful or evil, and if Blanche was in the crowd, he hadn't seen her. The tales about perverting the true rites with devil-worshiping orgies and black magic were just that: tales told to frighten and excite repressed society women.

He started to slip away, feeling more foolish than he had felt in a long time.

And then everything changed.

The drums stopped. The people fell silent. When Stephen looked back into the room, the snake was gone, presumably back to its box to sleep undisturbed, and Prince Basile was out of Stephen's line of sight.

A young man, covered from neck to ankles in a long white cloak, was being led into the room by two women. From the sluggish way he walked, supported between the women, Stephen could tell that he was drugged. The women led him to the altar and pushed him gently back on it, drawing the cloak back from his body. Its white wings spread over the sides of the altar.

"Do you do this of your own accord?" the priestess in red asked him.

He nodded, and said slowly, "Yes."

The woman opened her own cloak to show her naked body underneath. When she did, Stephen drew in his breath. There was no mistaking that look, those lush curves. It was Blanche. When she pushed aside the concealing hood, her silvery blond hair tumbled over her shoulders.

She was helped onto the altar by the two women, where she straddled the naked, supine form of the young man, holding herself poised just above him. Drugged or not, the man had an enormous erection.

Stephen was too shocked to move. This was definitely not part of the real Voodoo rites. So everything that gossip said was becoming true: Blanche was leading the Voodoos, and she had polluted the ancient religious rites with blasphemy.

As he watched, Blanche lowered herself slowly on the man's erection, throwing back her head in pleasure as she wrapped herself around him. She pinned him there with her body, moving in a raw, primitive rhythm that she had never used with Stephen even in her most abandoned moments. She rocked back and forth, she tossed her head, eyes closed, as her hair swept around her shoulders, across her gently swaying breasts.

The man made no move to touch her, as if he were forbidden. Instead, his hands grasped convulsively at his cloak beneath him, his knuckles becoming as white as the fabric.

The Voodoos moaned, swaying to the rhythm set by Blanche and her lover, their faces and bodies gleaming and hot with sudden fever.

Suddenly, Blanche rose and plunged down onto him again, with a final, incoherent scream that was matched by the man's own guttural moan and the cries of the Voodoos. At the same instant, she raised a golden dagger and plunged it into her lover's throat, slashing sideways. His blood splashed over the altar, staining the white cloak a brilliant, dripping red. His body, still inside Blanche's, heaved in his final spasms, then lay still.

Blanche took a long, deep breath. She motioned for the women to help her off the body.

Stephen was paralyzed. It had happened so fast! His stomach heaved and he leaned over, bent double on the grass.

"Will you come with me, please?" The firm, quiet voice was shocking out here in the night.

Stephen looked up to see Prince Basile looming over him, his face determined. Stephen could tell that this was not a request. He gripped Stephen by the arm, pulling him to his feet.

By the time Basile pushed Stephen into the house, Blanche was alone. He had no idea where the other Voodoos had gone, especially so fast. He felt very feverish, almost hallucinatory. Could this have really happened? he thought. Did I dream it?

But behind Blanche, still on the altar, was the body of the young man. He was covered now with a black cloth, but one of his hands showed slightly from beneath it. Blood flowed sluggishly down one of his fingers, dropping slowly into a spreading pool on the floor.

Stephen wanted to vomit again.

Instead, he was shoved roughly into a straight-backed chair. Basile stood over him, his face calm with the assurance that his strength spoke for him.

Blanche sat daintily on the steps leading up to the altar, just a few feet from the corpse and the pool of blood. With an impatient little face of distaste, she drew her red silk robe closer to her to avoid staining it.

"Why were you out there, Stephen?" she asked conversationally. "Why were you following me?"

He couldn't find the words to answer the question. His eyes kept going back to the still form beneath the black cloth.

Blanche turned her head slightly to look on the altar, then shrugged and looked back at Stephen. "Don't worry about *him*," she said. "He died as he wanted to die, in my service. His sacrifice gave me greater power, and he'll be remembered honorably for it."

"You are *monstrous*," Stephen whispered.

She picked the gold-handled dagger off the floor where it had fallen, still engrimed with blood. She casually wiped it on a corner of the black shroud and set it back down beside her.

Stephen watched, astounded at her casual evil.

"Basile," she said, "I think you can go. Stephen and I need to talk privately."

With a sharp glance at Stephen, Basile reluctantly bowed out of the room.

"Don't think I don't know why you're here." Her voice was conversational, but held a dangerous edge. "I know all about the meeting you had with Cyrie Devaux in Jackson Square."

"How could you know that?"

"It only matters that I know," she said, "and that I know exactly what she told you. You shouldn't listen to gossip,

Stephen; it can be very dangerous."

"But it isn't exactly gossip, is it? Not when it's all true." His first veil of horror was lifting, beginning to reveal anger underneath.

"You have no idea what's true and what isn't, and how dangerous the forces I control really are. Sometimes, even I underestimate them. Now, my advice to you, Stephen, is to forget what you saw. No one will report this man missing or even acknowledge that he was here. And you and I will go on as we always have."

"Bloody hell we will!" he exclaimed, jumping to his feet in rage. "Don't you ever, *ever* come near me again, Blanche. And if you think I'm not going to tell the police about this, you're mad."

She looked unperturbed. "I don't think they'll listen to you but, of course, you're welcome to try. My influence runs deep in this city, deeper than yours. And the fear of me is even stronger."

He sat down again, limply. "Why, Blanche?" he said tiredly. "I don't love you. You don't love me. You never did. Why spin this out?"

A strange look crossed her face. "I did love you. Long ago. Longer than you know." She looked, just for a moment, softer, childlike. "But I was very young then, and thought love meant something. I thought that it would transform me, save me from . . ."—she seemed not to be talking to him—"from my own life." Her eyes were very far away, her face veiled with a wistful longing that had receded so far from her grasp that she knew it was useless to grieve for its loss.

In the sad silence, his cold voice was like a harsh slap. "I don't believe you."

Her face became stone again, and the woman she could have been died inside the woman she had become. "It isn't important that you do. I know you've been trying to get away from me, Stephen, but I tell you now: you never will. Not as long as I want you. You're *mine,* and you can't imagine the price I paid for you. You may have acquired a temporary distaste for my"—she waved her hand toward the corpse—"methods, but eventually my hold over you will be as strong as it ever was."

"I can't begin to tell you how wrong you are," he said coldly.

"Indeed?" She stood up slowly and moved toward him, pressing against him, running her hands lightly over him in all the ways he was powerless to resist. He could smell her perfume, feel her heat burn him, as she stretched sinuously out of the red silk robe, her skin reflecting the candlelight.

When she felt his involuntary reaction, she laughed, and he almost wept to think that he was reduced to this, that she was right about her hold over him.

"You'll never leave me, Stephen," she said with a soft menace. "And can you guess why not?"

She pulled his head down to her face, her lips lightly grazing his ear as she whispered.

He drew back sharply, his mind gone cold with denial.

She only smiled.

"No." His voice faded as the disbelief turned to horror. "That can't happen, Blanche. It's not true!"

"Oh, it's quite true," she said, and her smile grew demonic.

He lost control then. "Never! I'll kill you first, Blanche!" he screamed, pushing her away. She staggered against the altar. Trying to balance herself, she pulled the black covering off the corpse. Stephen looked on in horror to see the young man's body so nakedly exposed, drained white, more dead than anything he had ever seen in his life, the throat still gaping with a red-crusted gash. The body rolled slowly off the altar, its head hanging at a ghastly angle, and smashed faceup on the floor.

Its blank eyes opened, staring at Stephen.

I have to get out of here! Stephen thought wildly. In his confusion, he turned exactly opposite the door, back toward where Blanche had fallen. She was trying to stand, seeming slightly dazed.

Before he could move, Blanche caught him completely by surprise, springing at his throat with fingers like claws.

He couldn't pry her hands loose. He kicked, bucked, twisted his body and pounded at her, dragging her all over the room, but she was unshakable. The most gruesome thing about it was that she was looking at him exactly the way a child looks at a dying beetle: with an air of detached concentration.

"I can't let you kill me, Stephen," she said. "And I can't let you interfere with me."

He felt his chest convulse as his lungs struggled to keep him alive. Blanche's face disappeared behind an explosion of lights as she gradually closed the arteries in his neck.

They were close to the altar now, slipping and falling in the sticky, slippery pools of blood. The livid face of the corpse was only inches from his, its eyes staring hideously into his own. Stephen felt something under him, something sharp. The gold-handled dagger. He tried desperately to stay conscious as his hand closed around it.

He brought it up behind her back and plunged it in.

She released her hold on his throat.

Blanche's eyes opened wide in surprise; she looked at him with disbelief.

"Oh, Stephen," she sighed, "you have no idea what you've done." And she whispered in his ear again. Then blood started to bubble from her mouth, at first a frothy pink foam, then exploding from her punctured lung in a fine red spray that covered Stephen's face and throat. In only a few seconds she was dead, suffocated.

Stephen couldn't move, even to push her off him. He expected Basile to burst through the door at any second and finish him off. Surely, killing the Queen of the Voodoos rated a long, excruciating punishment.

He took a deep breath, then freed himself from Blanche's dead weight. He staggered to his knees, then managed to stand upright, the dizziness and sickness clearing slightly from his mind.

He looked slowly at the pair of bodies on the floor: the dead young man and his murderer, Blanche, as beautiful as she had ever been in life.

Her last words dropped like a black curtain over his heart.

Panic took him then, and he burst out of the room, out of the door, out into the cleansing night, not knowing who or what, if anything, followed him.

The Louisiana swamps are as close as the modern world gets to primordial darkness. In some places, they swallow the light, the air, and transform them into something else, an entity of dark secrets. And, at night, man's oldest magic revives there.

The only light came from a small fire as a tall, powerful black man stood before a crude altar: a board placed on a pair of sawhorses. The man and the altar were encircled by a ring of burning sulfur. Outside the ring, with their backs to the altar, stood nine of Blanche's most fanatical followers.

Blanche herself lay upon the altar.

Basile was frightened, but not of the night and not of what he was going to do. He was only afraid of failure.

What had to be done here in the fertile darkness was an old and profane ritual, and to witness it, even by accident, meant death. To have accepted the task and to fail meant much, much worse.

The rest of Blanche's people waited out of sight, in another place not far away. They swayed and muttered in low tones to the muffled beat of the drums, in a soft, hypnotic rhythm that repeated over and over, sending the gathered energy of their wills into the burning sulfur ring.

Very soon, they would have an answer. They would know that justice had been served. They could not know what form it would take, but la Reine Blanche would have her vengeance.

PART
FIVE

†

19

The Kiss of the Moon:
Andrew

The Reverend Mother Pauline was a good woman to know when you had a bad problem.

It was Angela's idea for Andrew to meet Pauline. Since his original curse had stemmed from bad magic, perhaps a faithful practitioner of the real religion could find a way to break it. Mother Pauline was the reigning Voodoo Queen. She commanded an awed respect, not like *la Reine Blanche* because of her evil, but because Pauline was a powerful Voodoo woman with a good heart and good counsel to give her people. Angela had met Pauline in the course of her work, when she wanted to learn more about Voodoo as it was practiced in New Orleans.

Mother Pauline was a tall, dignified woman in middle age, her skin the color of shadows. Voodoo was part of her heritage as a black woman, and she was glad to keep the old faith.

"How could I be anything other than a Voodoo?" Pauline had asked Angela once. "It's the old religion of Africa, of my people."

"But, Pauline," Angela pointed out, "you don't practice pure African Voodoo, or even Haitian."

"You're right, there's a big difference!" Pauline slammed her ivory-headed cane on the floor. This startled Angela until she discovered that Pauline did this merely as punctuation. "Voodoo in New Orleans is an evolution, my dear, an evolution. When New Orleans was young, blacks arrived from everywhere: slaves from all parts of Africa, free people of color escaping the political turmoil in Haiti, even blacks from Europe. All brought different ways, and in New Orleans they blended. They melded into the same religion but with many different practices, like Protestantism, you understand?" Pauline laughed. "They adapted their religion to the new situation. Oh, my people are nothing if not adaptable, my dear! Look at all that black people have been through and deny that!" Again, the stick hit the floor.

"When the Christians forced them to give up their many gods, instead of fighting, my people simply adapted them to the Christian saints and worshiped the old gods and the new, with both names. So the Christians were satisfied, and my people didn't have to abandon the old ways. It was very beneficial."

Angela laughed. "And the missionaries were only too happy to build schools and hospitals for their 'new converts,' right?"

Pauline shrugged and smiled. "Everyone was happy with the arrangement. Now me, I practice the old ways; part science, part faith, part magic. I work with the spirits, I heal by the laying on of hands and by herbalism. I was born with the power, the seventh daughter of a seventh daughter."

Pauline had taken a shine to Angela. "You have faith, my dear," she told her. "I can sense it." Angela professed to have not much faith in any religion, and said as much. "Oh, no, dear," Pauline said positively, "you believe in the powers of truth and of love. That's a religion of sorts." And Angela had had to admit that it was.

Mother Pauline lived in an ancient, charming house on Rampart Street. "A holdover from slave times," she said, "when 'quadroon' women were set up as mistresses in these houses by wealthy white men. A shameful practice but, my dear, part of our sad history and nothing can be done about that. If a black woman could better her station in those days . . . well, a woman does what she has to do to survive and that's gospel truth. Me, I sometimes think about the secret tears shed in this little house and I sigh."

On this visit, with Andrew reluctantly by her side, Angela approached Pauline's house with apprehension. She felt that she was going to be told what she didn't want to hear: the truth.

"I suppose I'm nervous because I'm out of my element here," Andrew told her. He wasn't wearing his clerical collar, but he felt like it.

"You're more in your element than you realize," Angela said, ringing the bell. "Mother Pauline is the most religious woman I know. You both have idealism in common."

Mother Pauline's grandson, a boy of fifteen or so, opened the door. His face brightened when he saw who was there. "Angela!" he said. "Nice to see you again. Grandma's waiting for you out in the garden."

Angela took his hand briefly. "Antoine, I swear, every time I see you, you just get better looking." Antoine fidgeted a little, but looked immensely pleased. He led them into a large, airy courtyard, then left.

Pauline sat at an iron lacework table set with a pastel cloth, fresh daffodils, and a huge, frosted pitcher of fruit punch. She rose and gave Angela a hug. "My dear," she said with affection, "I'm so glad you came to me in time of trouble."

She drew back and looked at Andrew, and her face, still welcoming, became touched by sadness. She took both his hands in hers. "You must be strong, loup-garou," she told him softly, but positively. "Everything dies or everything changes, even a curse."

Andrew looked quickly at Angela. He had no idea she'd told Pauline his problem. Her mystified look told him that she hadn't said a word.

"Don't be surprised," Pauline said to Andrew as they all settled at the table. "You're merely the proof of an old Voodoo legend, my dear. For generations, we all knew that *la Reine Blanche* had left one of her darkest curses, but we never knew in which family. So we waited, sure that someone so cursed would make his or her way to us for help, and dreading the day it actually happened."

Pauline sighed and shook her head. "And now you're here. In such sorrowful circumstances. The Voodoos pity you, my dear, but there's so little we can do."

Andrew felt a steel band tighten around his chest. "I had hoped that you wouldn't say that, Pauline."

She held up one of her long fingers. "I didn't say that there was nothing to be done. But the advice I give you, you might not want to hear."

"Tell me," he said.

"First, let me tell you about the White Queen. How much do you really know?"

Andrew shrugged. "I know she was my great-grandfather's mistress. That she's responsible for this curse, and that Stephen Marley killed her."

"Ah, you see?" Pauline said. "But there's the problem, my dear." She banged her stick on the paving stones. "*La Reine Blanche* never died."

Only Angela looked stunned at this news.

"I've *seen* her, talked to her," Andrew said. "At first, she seemed real, then she just . . . faded . . . like a ghost. What's the truth here, Pauline? Do you know?"

"You have to understand, my dear, that the Voodoo that Blanche Pitre practiced has never been seen before or since she introduced it, a profane religion that demanded the souls of its followers, more black magic and devil worship than Voodoo. Personally, I think she called it Voodoo just to attract followers, so they would feel more comfortable at first, until they were so deep into it that there was no way out.

"People say that she sold her soul for power, but that's overly dramatic. What she was doing was calling into play *real* forces and powers, powers over which she had only the most tenuous control. Unlike our Voodoo *loa*, Blanche's spirits would serve her only because she forced them to, and if she made the slightest miscalculation they could turn on her at any minute. Eventually, they did. What you're seeing when she appears to you is her body, that's true, but it's a physical body subject to occult physical laws of which we know very little. The natural law that we know doesn't apply here. Her own hate powers her body, and the body keeps the hate alive. Break that cycle and you've broken her power."

There was a long silence. Angela was mystified, but Andrew understood all too clearly. "You're saying," he said slowly, "that I have to find her, and kill her."

"Exactly."

"I'm still confused," Angela said. "How can she be dead and alive? Are you talking about a zombie?"

"Much more than that, my dear. Remember, this was the work of evil. A zombie is the product of poisons, chemicals; the body of a zombie is never really dead, only in deep suspension. And there's no real magic to a zombie; only a certain chemical competence on the part of the Voodoo who is misguided enough to create one.

"But Blanche was *dead*, my dear, unquestionably dead. Her followers took her out in the swamp and performed the darkest of rituals over her body. And weeks later, the beautiful *Reine Blanche* was seen at Bayou St. John, sitting on a gilded throne and presiding over the dance. Ten years

later, twenty . . . people still claimed to have seen her. And
any nonbelievers who *did* see her, even by accident, had
something catastrophic happen to them later. Someone close
to them died, someone got sick, there was a sudden loss
of property, even sanity. This sort of thing happens when
you're dealing with bad magic: the evil forces are like a
cloud of smoke, and if you pass too close, even innocently,
some of it clings to you. That's why I tell my people to stay
well away from those practicing black magic. No good can
come of it."

Andrew passed a hopeless hand over his eyes and leaned
forward, resting his head in his hands briefly and hopelessly.
"Where is she now, Pauline? Where do I find her?"

Pauline made a helpless gesture. "Nobody knows. She
appears, disappears, fades in and out of sight. She obviously
has some control—or *something* has control—over her physical body in a way we don't understand. Perhaps what people
see isn't her physical body at all, but sort of a . . ." Pauline
hesitated. "Oh, it's like a hologram, a projection. But that
body has to exist somewhere, in some form: the bad spirits
are drawing energy from it, like a vampire draws blood, and
giving back just enough to let the body renew itself and its
energy. It's a bad cycle.

"And, my dear"—she took Andrew's hands in her warm,
reassuring hands—"I don't think you could kill her even if
you *could* find her."

"You mean, she might not be able to die?"

Pauline shook her head. "No, I mean *you* couldn't do it. If
you could kill with a clear conscience, why would your curse
cause you such anguish? How can you commit a premedi-
tated murder, even of someone like *la Reine Blanche*, and
live with yourself afterward? When you kill as a loup-garou,
it's entirely different from killing someone in your human
form. A human being isn't ordained to kill; a loup-garou is."

"Ordained to kill?" Andrew drew back a little in surprise. "What does that mean?"

"You must learn the true nature of the loup-garou, my dear. And I can't teach it to you. All I can explain to you is that we human beings see life in such a limited way: we're born, we live, we die. But there's a larger scope of things that we never see. One of my sisters is a wise woman, a Witch. She taught me about the Great Wheel, that turning of cycles: birth, life, death . . . and rebirth. The rebirth, the renewal of life, is the key. This life is only a small step in our larger lives; we die, but we're constantly reborn. And every time we live again, we've learned to be better people and to give more to the world. We've come one step closer to breaking out of our self-centeredness.

"The loup-garou is an instrument of destiny, my dear. A harsh one, to be sure, but a tool of the gods must necessarily be of hard metal. For me to tell you any more than that would be foolish; those are lessons that others must teach you. But as far as *la Reine Blanche*, keep in mind that your destinies are closely linked. What can kill you can kill her, and though very little in this world can hurt either of you, you can destroy each other. But I don't think you can do it, my dear; you have a good heart and you have compassion, and that's the one thing a loup-garou cannot afford."

Pauline touched a small silver bell that stood on the table. Almost immediately, a young girl came out of the house. She couldn't have been much more than sixteen or so, but her air of superb confidence made her seem much older. She looked quite frankly into Andrew's eyes and he had the uncomfortable feeling that she could see secrets he never knew he had.

"There's someplace I want you to go," Pauline told him. "Don't take anyone or anything with you, just go there and wait. My little Mae,"—with her hand she indicated the beautiful young girl—"will guide you there and tell you what you need to know.

"Just remember that the loup-garou has always been a part of Louisiana history, and there are good reasons why. You must find a way to accept it and live with it, and if you're going to start that journey, you must begin at Bayou Goula."

20

He could feel Bayou Goula before he could see it. He felt the pull, the power, as if he were magnetized toward it. God knew he should have been nervous, but he felt some strange, excited energy at the pit of his stomach, flowing into his nerves.

Maybe part of it was Mae. He wasn't sure what her connection with Mother Pauline was, whether she was her daughter or a friend or a follower, but the girl definitely had Pauline's wisdom. And she had something more: a capacity for comfort. Just her presence was reassuring.

"Bayou Goula is the ancestral ground of the loups-garous," she explained to Andrew. "No one knows exactly why, but from way back before slave times it was known that the loups-garous gathered here to dance under the full moon."

"Dance?" Andrew said, mystified at the use of the term.

She laughed. "You got a lot to learn, Father! But don't you be nervous. You probably think you're all alone, but there are lots of loups-garous. I brought another one out here myself just a few months ago."

"Have you seen him since?" Andrew said with shaky humor.

She laughed knowingly. "Let's just say he's a lot happier for it."

Mae sighed and looked around. The sky was just beginning to fade, although the moon hadn't yet risen. "Well, I have to go now. But don't you worry about a thing. This is just where you're supposed to be and nothing bad's gonna happen to you."

She reached up and gave him a kiss on the cheek. Nothing overtly sexual, but lingering enough and with just enough body language to let him understand that the girl was an inordinate tease. He knew she wasn't serious, and so did she, but it was obvious that she enjoyed herself all the same.

"Now you be a good boy out here, you hear?" she said, and with a wave and a wiggle she was gone.

Andrew breathed deeply and sat down on the cool grass. The sky was getting darker, blooming into a luminous dark blue as the sun disappeared completely. Andrew didn't feel the way he thought he would. Instead, he was pumped with a weird energy and optimism. He began to feel more comfortable. He leaned against a willow trunk and started to relax for the first time in months, letting the moon pour its light over him. For some reason it calmed him. He had no idea why it should: moonlight, lately, had meant only trouble.

Movement across the clearing distracted him. Instinctively, he moved slowly and quietly back, behind the tree.

A big bear of a man in a tie-dyed T-shirt and well-worn jeans stepped into the clearing. He looked appreciatively around the bayou with a pleased expression, whistling a tune as if he were in his own backyard. He gave every indication of a man happy and content to be alive and in exactly this place at exactly this moment.

The man stripped off his clothes. He folded the clothes neatly and leaned over to tuck them into a canvas bag, his long ponytail of dark hair falling over his shoulder. He reached back and unbound his hair, not bothering to shake it out, before he hung the bag from a nearby tree limb.

Andrew eyed the man with a slight competitive envy. He was in absolutely superb shape, like a bodybuilder, but slimmer, with every muscle perfectly delineated.

The man stood absolutely straight. He threw back his

head, spread his arms, and closed his eyes like a sunbather gathering streams of sunlight.

After a few minutes, he gasped and doubled over. Andrew could hear his explosion of breath clearly, even from across the clearing. The man fell to his knees.

The light was clear enough so that Andrew could see the man's hand, the tanned skin darkening with hair, the nails shooting out into claws.

Andrew was so stunned that he couldn't move as he watched the familiar transformation. But though the mechanics seemed to be the same, the attitude was entirely different.

The man seemed to enjoy the pain, mixing the panting gasps with satisfied laughter. Andrew could actually see the spasms riding his body as the change took him but the man smiled through each wave. Andrew saw—and couldn't believe he saw it—that the man had an enormous erection.

When the transformation was complete, the man let out a long, contented sigh, followed by a short laugh. He ran his hands contentedly over his changed body.

"Sweet Jesus," Andrew muttered softly, unable to stop himself.

The loup-garou froze; his head came up and he turned slowly toward the willow where Andrew was hidden.

Andrew knew. No one but a loup-garou, with his supernatural senses, could have heard such a soft sound from such a distance. That one little slip was going to be the death of him, literally.

The loup-garou crouched, charged, and stood towering over Andrew in almost less time than it took to think about it. Andrew knew this game: the werewolf would toy with him before he ripped him apart. If this loup-garou was bored, or merciful, the death might be quick. Otherwise . . .

The werewolf stood there for a few heartbeats, his teeth

bared and slavering. Andrew tried to suppress his fear, knowing full well that this was what the werewolf wanted, that the scent of it would only make things worse.

He began to whisper his last confession.

And suddenly the loup-garou backed off. He tilted his head, perplexed, looked straight into Andrew's eyes and laughed. Laughed!

He shook his enormous head as he crouched easily and comfortably on the ground, in perfect relaxation. His black hair, now grown almost to his buttocks, billowed around him and swept over the evening grass.

"Ooo-*wee*, I guess I nearly made a bad mistake, yes," the loup-garou said in a lilting Cajun cadence.

Andrew sat down suddenly, too, not from relaxation but from total surprise.

"Here I'm thinkin' I got me the fool of all time to be sneakin' around out here on Bayou Goula at night, and you turn out to be a brother loup-garou." The werewolf laughed again. "So why you out here, brother? No loup-garou comes out to Bayou Goula just to stand around and watch, no."

The first time Andrew opened his mouth, nothing came out. He tried again. "I don't know. I'm not at all sure why I'm out here. Someone sent me. Mother Pauline."

"Oh-h-h, yeah. The Voodoo queen," the loup-garou said. "She must have sent you out with Mae, right? But now I'm the one who's confused. You already a loup-garou, I can tell. You don't need no spells to make you one, which is why Mae brought me here the first time. So . . . it must be something else. You know what I think? I think you got a heavy problem, my friend. But there's nothing a loup-garou can't work out with another one, so why don't you just tell me all about it, eh?"

"Being a loup-garou *is* my problem."

The werewolf looked at Andrew knowingly. "Oh, so that's

the way it is with you. You not a loup-garou by choice. Now, that is sad, *cher ami*, very sad. Now I know why Pauline sent you out here. Somebody put the curse of the loup-garou on you, right?"

Andrew nodded.

The werewolf shook his head. "That's the worst thing I can think of, *ami*. I'm sorry for you, sorrier than you know. I wish there was something I could do for you, but all I can do is tell you what Pauline sent you out here to learn. So let me find out what that is."

The loup-garou quickly took both Andrew's hands in his, closing his eyes. He took several deep breaths, then was very still. Only shadows flitting across his face showed any movement. After a few moments, he nodded his head, then opened his eyes.

"I want to tell you about the life of a true loup-garou, one born to the gift. We're part of destiny, my friend, part of the turning of the great wheel. Birth, death, rebirth. The loup-garou doesn't kill just for the hell of it; sometimes we kill for very specific reasons. We kill to live, but we also kill for justice. When human justice fails, the loup-garou succeeds. We learn to control ourselves and choose our victims, so that when we kill, we might as well do some good. This is the difference between me and you, *cher ami*; that I can accept the freedom and the power of the loup-garou's life because I've accepted the responsibility that goes with it, that obligation to dedicate my kills to the greater goal of justice. You kill only from a hunger you can't control, and there's no other purpose to it.

"You saw how I could tell what you are. I think I can tell *who* you are, too: you're one of the Marley family, yes?"

Andrew was astonished. "Yes, but . . . ."

"But how did I know that? Don't *think*, my friend . . . *feel*. Just let your mind go and listen to what it tells you, not what you want it to say. You have what we all have, that psychic power of the loup-garou that lets us look into the human conscience. I know about your family because every loup-garou in Louisiana knows that sad story: the most precious gift of lycanthropy perverted into a curse. But I know about you because I'm part of your mind. We're all linked, we loups-garous, every one of us, no matter where we are. We're *family*. I know your name, I know you're a priest, and I know your life is a waking nightmare, a torment that burns you until your soul has no more tears to pour out."

Andrew turned his face away.

"Accept the power, Andrew. There's no other help for you. You're going to be what you are for the rest of your life, and the rest of your life is going to be very long, maybe as much as nine hundred years."

Andrew looked at the loup-garou in horror.

"Ah, yes. Another thing you didn't know. But it's true; a long life is the gift that the Moon Goddess Hecate gives her lovers."

"I can't imagine living another year like this," Andrew said painfully. "To tell you the truth, I don't know if I will."

The loup-garou sat back on his heels a little and regarded Andrew analytically. "Oh yes, you'll live," he said positively. "You won't do what your father did. And you know why? Because you're a true loup-garou. You're meant for it. Think back: When you were a child, didn't you love the night? Didn't you sneak outside and run under the moon before you went to sleep? And more to the point: don't you have a keen sense of outrage when you see human justice fail, when criminals slip through loopholes designed to protect the innocent? That's where the loup-garou comes in, *cher ami*. We're Hecate's children, and Hecate is also the goddess of justice and revealer of secrets. That's why we have that power to ferret the truth from men's minds. We discover the truth and we correct injustice. Always have."

"Call it what you will. It's still murder. And I can't live with it."

The loup-garou shook his head. "Why do you think we're alone here, brother? Why aren't there hoppin'-mad werewolf hunters and shotguns filled with silver? It's because we're *supposed* to be here. The loup-garou is part of the great wheel, part of justice, part of the process of death and rebirth. We dispatch those people who are doing wrong, and when they come back in other souls, they've learned better."

"How can I believe that?" Andrew said. "I'm a priest. A Christian. It goes against everything I was raised to hold true."

"But it confirms everything you've known in your body since you were a child."

The two of them sat quietly for a moment. The loup-garou knew that the truth was rising hard in Andrew, and that, just as insistently, he was going to try to push it down.

The loup-garou looked around the bayou once more. "Used to be, in old times, a hundred werewolves came here to dance under the moon. Male, female, Cajuns, Creoles, Americans. Bayou Goula always been our sacred ground. They all met right here, dancing for joy, making love to increase their strength, transforming and running wild and pure under the light. The most beautiful people you ever did see, *cher ami*, all of them werewolves, all with the power, all with the sense of Hecate's justice strong in them. Now the old ways die and not so many of us come. But we're still here, brother, still part of the legends of Louisiana.

"And you," he said, taking Andrew's hand again, "you're part of it, no matter how you fight it. You're the moon's own child now. Like calls to like, *ami*, and we recognize another werewolf, even if you don't recognize yourself. And if it comes to pass that you break your curse and you never transform again, all your life you'll feel like there's something missing, like you've lost something precious, a chance that never came to fullness. When the full moon rises, your body gonna burn with longing and your eyes sting with quick tears and you won't remember why. A great sadness will well up in you that you can't name and that stays with you a long time. And you won't even know that you cry for what you've lost."

The loup-garou rose and suddenly swept Andrew up in his massive arms. He brought his fiery breath close to Andrew's lips and kissed him deeply. Just as quickly, he released him and set him on his feet.

The loup-garou laughed his booming wolf's laugh. "Now you'll never forget Achille the loup-garou," he said, touching a claw to his own chest. "Don't you fight no more, *cher ami*," he said kindly. "You believe you're a man of God, of compassion. But you know that from the beginning you had the kiss of the moon on you, and it gonna stay with you forever."

Achille turned away and stared out into the night. Following his look, Andrew could see the trees move, changing with strange shapes and colors as the moonlight grew older, brighter.

"Come with me now, brother," Achille said seductively. "Run with me, feel your strength, your power. Take control of it instead of letting it control you. Feel your body do what it was meant to do; let the moon make love to you."

Andrew started to stretch out his hand to Achille, but suddenly drew back.

Achille laughed softly. "No good to fight it, *ami*. Better that you come with me and accept what you are. Your God don't know you anymore, but the children of the moon are your people."

In confusion and despair, Andrew fell to his knees and buried his head in his hands. He slowly became aware of soft voices, of tender caresses, voluptuous touches edged with silken pain, of crystalline claws mingled with soft fur. He raised his head and found himself ringed by a dozen werewolves, their glowing eyes hypnotizing him, their beauty stirring him.

"You've come to make me do murder!" he screamed in panic. But the conviction in his voice was uncertain and weak.

"No . . . no . . . ," they all murmured.

"You one of us," Achille said. "And you don't even know what it means. Let us show you; be our true brother. Come with us."

"No need to be afraid," one of the women said. Her voice was a silver bell muffled in dark velvet. "How could we hurt you? It's you who hurts us, Andrew. Let us show you how to live in peace with yourself." She was not yet changed, and her eyes were dark with passion, her hair the color of gold flames. Zizi. Her bare breasts brushed his cheek as she knelt toward him. One graceful hand trailed over his face, and Andrew, obeying an impulse he didn't understand, pressed the hand to his lips, took the long fingers into his open mouth, and breathed in the female scent of her. He had never felt so aroused, and so comforted.

He felt her delicate nails begin their change into claws.

Do it, something inside him said, let go. Accept what is offered. Save your own life.

And from deeper, another sound: Never. Don't give in.

But he wanted it. More than anything he had ever wanted. He began to let go, to allow the power to flow into him, streaming from the moon into his blood.

When his transformation began, it was completely different. The pain came like a slow, erotic movement from the base of his spine, through his genitals, up toward his belly. He felt strong hands, half-human, half-werewolf, caress him in the most intimate of ways. Savage bites, pain and pleasure intermixed, fell harmlessly all over him.

He had never been in control of his transformation before, and the power was as seductive as the rest of it. He felt the long, slow prelude that would lead to a monumental burst of passion and power.

Again, the voice: stop now, or you'll never go back again.

The voice grew stronger, screaming in his mind, blocking out anything else.

With a tremendous effort of will, he broke away from the loups-garous, screaming his denial of the power, and the transformation instantly left him.

As he ran from the clearing, he looked back just once to see Zizi, tears staining her changed face as she watched him go. He felt that, of all he was leaving behind, she would have been the most precious to him.

He saw all of them them change and embrace, drinking in the power of the moon and of each other, and was not surprised to see Georgiana there, reaching for Zizi to offer solace. He now understood what Georgiana had done so that she could live with herself and her curse, and he couldn't blame her for it.

Georgiana looked toward Andrew, then turned away sadly.

He was only a few yards away, but was as lost to them as one who had wandered to eternal distances. But before he left, in a confusion and a desire and a grief he couldn't understand, he watched the loups-garous dance on Bayou Goula.

21

Andrew couldn't put Bishop Acker off any longer. He should have been assigned to a regular parish by now, but the bishop had been very understanding since Johanna's death, giving Andrew time to put the family affairs in order.

Bishop Acker was relieved to see him. "Andrew, we have to think of a good place for you," he said. "You'll be glad to hear that I've had several requests for your services as curate. Father Moore wants you for St. Timothy's, and frankly, I agree. You came out of that parish and you understand how it works."

Andrew shivered at the thought. Ministering to people who knew him, or *thought* they knew him, was just too hypocritical. Damn! The whole thing was wrong: his even being here about to accept an assignment was a mistake. He thought he could handle it, thought that what Walter wrote was true, that his faith would save him. Now he wasn't sure about anything.

He was silent for so long that the bishop was puzzled. "Is there some problem with St. Timothy's?"

"I can't do it, Father," he said slowly. "I wouldn't be a good priest, not just for St. Timothy's . . . for anyone. Not even for myself."

"Andrew, what is this?" the bishop asked kindly, "I know some terrible things have happened to you recently. Your mother's situation saddened us all. But that's the sort of thing that makes you strong, that teaches you."

When Andrew started to speak, the words weren't what

he'd planned. They just burst forth from someplace in his soul that wouldn't contain them any longer. He'd meant to tell the bishop the truth of his situation and take whatever consequences came of it, but when he heard what he was actually saying, he sensed that his words were deeper truth than he had known was in him. He didn't have to confess his lycanthropy. It was only the manifestation of a deeper problem.

"If I'd been a good priest," he said with intensity, "all this would never have happened to me. But I've failed my faith in some fundamental way; there's some crippling flaw that's been there from the beginning."

The bishop had never expected a confession like this. He had heard them from other priests, but this one had always seemed above that self-doubt. He kept his voice level and quiet, not wanting to intrude too much on what was obviously an outpouring from the heart. "And what makes you think that?"

Andrew took a deep breath, trying to find the words he'd hidden for so long.

"I'm an arrogant man, Father," he said, "and I've never come to terms with that. It was the intellectual cocoon of the church I loved, the study of philosophy and theology, the discussions, the debates, the kind of atmosphere I found in the seminary. But as the time came for me to leave that cocoon, I realized that I was going to have to deal with people, not ideas, and I wasn't prepared for it. I was afraid they'd all find out what a fraud I am. Me, with my sheltered rich boy's life; what did I ever know about problems? If I had one, someone would take care of it. And suddenly I'm expected to tell everyone else how to deal with their troubles? Father, who am I to judge anyone?"

"We *don't* judge. It's for God to judge, the priest is only the intermediary. Andrew, you don't need omniscient wisdom. All you need is compassion."

"Once, when I was about thirteen," Andrew said, "I started locking myself in my room every night with a dirty magazine. Maybe it wasn't my first brush with guilty pleasures but it was sure as hell the finest. Then I became convinced my soul was damned forever. I was concerned about it, but not concerned enough to stop *doing* it. Going to confession was out of the question because I was sure that Father Moore would know who I was and would never look at me the same way again. I just knew that I was in mortal sin, and I couldn't take communion unless I'd been to confession, so I made excuses not to take communion. Eventually, the whole thing was killing me so much that I just had to get out from under it. So a week later, I found myself in the confessional, sweating bullets.

"I had this whole long list of minor sins I'd made up just to avoid getting to the real one. I figured I'd slip the masturbation thing into the middle and he'd slide right past it. I actually thought that this was an original idea. It seemed to work, though; Father Moore absolved me and assigned me a penance and I was home free.

"But just as I was about to slide out the door for a clean getaway, I heard him say very clearly, 'It's normal, you know. People your age are just curious and you're going through a lot of changes. The thing is not to get so guilty that you let it keep you away from God. I want you to try and control yourself, but remember: you'll get over it.' "

Andrew sighed. "Okay. So it wasn't exactly canon law, but I left there immensely relieved. Father Moore did it so well, and I still don't understand *how* he did it. We're all good people, Father, convinced that our unthinking little sins are going to do us in. Father Moore put things in perspective and let us believe that we're better people than we give ourselves credit for. He understood trouble. He understood the simple, everyday confusion involved in just trying to live from moment to moment. And he understood pain. I never did."

The bishop leaned back a little and regarded Andrew. "Well, you certainly understand it now, don't you? Your father's suicide, your mother's illness and death. You can't tell me that you haven't learned something from having survived all that."

"I suppose I have. But I desperately want to be the kind of priest Father Moore is, and I see now that I'll never make it."

"No. You probably won't. However, you could be a better one, or maybe just a *different* one. This is like any other job, Andrew; we bring to it what resources we have available. Father Moore gave you what you needed because he's the kind of man he is. For all you know, someone's waiting for what only you can give.

"You're a good man, Andrew. If you weren't, this issue of ethics wouldn't bother you so much. I've known you for a long time, and I know that if God lives in any man, He lives in you. You don't see it now, but it's there, an indelible mark on your soul. God has left his fingerprint on you, and no matter how the world buffets you about, you can always locate that mark and know you're safe. You have more strength than you know. You just have to learn to draw on it.

Andrew was completely flabbergasted. When he could speak, it was only a whisper. "I don't know how to start."

"Of course you do," the bishop reassured him, "and I know just the assignment for you. Someplace where, I guarantee you, everyone's worse off than you. If you want to learn about real life, this is where it grabs you by the hair and drags you through the refiner's fire. You can do some good there."

*   *   *

St. Matthew's wasn't a church, it was a glorified soup kitchen and homeless shelter. It had more transients than parishioners, and all that kept it running was a handful of volunteers. They certainly didn't have any money, and what they had went toward feeding the hordes of homeless that settled into the pews to catch a little sleep in safety. Andrew had never seen anyone sleep like these people; they were always in such extreme stages of exhaustion that when they slept they were almost comatose. Some of them were drugged or strung out or drunk, but even the ones who weren't slept the sleep of Judgment Day.

Ironically, the church building itself was magnificent, a splendid ecclesiastical palace built when ostentation was cheerfully indulged by a wealthy turn-of-the-century congregation. With the lack of funds over the years, it was getting shabby, but it aged in the same way that New Orleans did, with infinite grace and dignity.

A few months after Andrew had taken over St. Matthew's, Simon came to visit. "I don't believe this place," Simon said, sitting in a front pew with Andrew and looking around. "It reminds me of a crumbling Venetian *palazzo*."

"Angela says that it's a shadow of its former self," Andrew said.

"Remnants of beauty are better than none at all, I suppose. How many churches these days boast an elaborate frescoed ceiling, even if it *is* peeling off in stages?"

Andrew looked up, appraising the work. "A lot of my parishioners like to study it before they fall asleep. I hope it imparts a little subliminal piety."

"And what will you do here?" Simon asked.

"What I can. What needs to be done. I'm the only priest here, since nobody wants this job and the diocese can't afford to pour much money and manpower into it. There's just me and the combination janitor/handyman and a dwind-ling flock of volunteers. Half the time, I end up borrowing altar boys from the Catholics down the street—never let either of our bishops hear about *that*, will you? The parish-ioners are the elderly remnants of the old families; they do what work they can, but I can't possibly expect them to do much. They're great in the soup kitchen, though. The ladies have been raised with certain standards of hospitality and they dish up the food with so much panache that the homeless think they're dining at Antoine's."

"Can they cook?"

"Are you kidding? They just send their own cooks over sometimes. But Angela takes care of that, usually."

"Angela!" Simon laughed. "Can *she* cook?"

Andrew shrugged. "Well, she makes popcorn fairly well. But she shanghais her students. A couple of days' duty here can add up a few needed grade points. She says its good for their moral fiber."

Simon relaxed a little in the upright Gothic pew. "You're happy with all this?"

"I think so. Yes. Yes, I am. And afraid. But, Simon, if I let that fear stop me, that means I've given in, that I've let the curse really destroy me." He touched the crucifix shining against his chest. "I don't quite know what's going to hap-pen. But I'm managing. I can't just take from life anymore, Simon. I've got to start learning to give something back."

Simon glanced around at the back pews, already starting to shelter the first few souls. "If that's what you need to learn, I think you've been enrolled in the right school."

A tiny old woman with a walker made her way to Andrew. "Father Marley?" she said tentatively. "I hate to interrupt you, but I found another of those posters you want. I haven-en't seen this one before. I think it's new." She held out a water-stained piece of paper.

It was a "missing" poster, the pitiful homemade kind posted by friends or relatives of lost people, a crudely lettered sign with a black-and-white photo of a young man photocopied on it. Andrew carefully scrutinized the face.

"Thank you, Mrs. Janpier. I haven't seen it, either; it must be a new one."

"I'll say a prayer and light a candle for the family."

"Please do that."

Mrs. Janpier shuffled toward one of the statues with banks of votive candles at its feet.

Andrew studied the poster and his face grew hard, his eyes stony.

"What is this?" Simon asked.

"Sometimes the church sends money to the families of missing people," he said, not looking at Simon.

"Since when has this parish got the money to do that?"

"We can always find a little."

"Bullshit. You're drawing on your own funds to support this crumbling parish, aren't you? And you're not telling the bishop." He took the poster and scanned it. The lost man was last seen drinking with friends in the Grand Mallet, a roadhouse known for its spicy food and spicier zydeco music.

Simon felt the sorrow of sudden realization. "The loup-garou. It killed him, didn't it? You're collecting these posters, hoping you can locate the families of the victims."

"So far, this is the first one I've found," Andrew said reluctantly. Then more briskly, "Look, Simon, I hate to rush you, but I have a lot to do this afternoon."

"What do you think you're buying with this, Andrew?"

"I'm not buying anything. I'm trying to bring a little consolation to these people and all I can offer is money. I can't make up for what I did, but I can do *something*."

"You don't have to pay for what it does."

"Don't call him 'it.' 'It' doesn't do anything. I do. It's *me* who kills those people, and I have to accept the responsibility."

Simon sighed heavily. "I've tried to make you understand that you *aren't* responsible. You aren't a killer."

"You're so wrong," Andrew said patiently. This was the first time Simon had ever heard Andrew discuss the loup-garou in this calm tone of voice. "I try to fight it, but that murderous instinct is there. Not in the loup-garou, in *me*. It's strange, Simon; you tell me that I don't have to answer for what the werewolf does, but what if it's the other way around? What if he can't be responsible for what I do, what I feel? What if he had a set of ethics, a code of responsibility for his acts, and he couldn't exercise that freedom of choice because I'm the one who holds him back? I think that, in some way, he reaches out to me to master my own weakness, and if I could, if I could only have more forgiveness, more charity, the werewolf couldn't exist. At least, he couldn't exist as he does now, a mindless killer." Andrew's eyes grew distant. "Sometimes I think he doesn't *want* to exist. I really think he wants to die rather than live contrary to his own set of principles."

This last part chilled Simon's blood. "Andrew," he said carefully, "you don't want to die."

Andrew shook his head. "No. I don't want to die."

Simon realized that there was something Andrew wasn't saying, and that he would never say. Like Walter, Andrew would someday reach his breaking point, and he knew it.

"I want *someone* to die," Andrew said strangely. "The woman who placed this curse. If I could turn back time and kill her, I would, without a blink of regret. I think about my father and Georgiana and all the lives we've taken and the lives we've ruined, and I can feel my own hands around her throat. Not the *werewolf's* hands, my own. At times, I have this ghastly vision, horribly clear in every detail. I can hear the heartbeat slowing, the breath choking, I can feel the heat of blood between my fingers. And I'm glad of it, so very glad. I can hear my own voice, far away, laughing in the madness of murder."

Simon said nothing, but the chill never warmed.

"And until I can rid myself of that vision and that desire, Simon, I'm responsible. For what I do when I'm changed, for who I am both now and under the moon. So I'll keep fighting it, with money, with time, with constant prayer, with whatever I can manage. Please, Simon, let me do what I have to do in peace. Whom can it hurt?"

Simon knew, but said nothing.

22

Andrew had never had such a difficult time saying Mass. He had the sweats, his voice cracked. He couldn't seem to control his hands: as he was about to administer the Host, he dropped it. The altar boy caught it on the paten, so no harm was done. It was simply assumed that Father Marley had caught that flu that was going around.

Andrew couldn't keep his mind on what he was doing. The night and Bayou Goula, Achille and Zizi kept flying in and out of his mind like dark sails against a turbulent sea. Achille's words, particularly, kept coming back to him: You'll always be a true loup-garou.

But words are only words. Andrew's torment was the feeling that swept over him that night, the total surrender to the power of the loup-garou, a surrender so complete that he was ready to abandon everything that he thought had been important in his life. And he knew that, at that precise moment, he would have given it gladly and his soul would have been lost.

He was desperate to believe that his sudden drawing back was the right thing to do, that it was a confirmation of everything he had always known his life should be.

What haunted him was how much it had hurt.

Even now, as he was going through the old, familiar rituals that had once given him so much comfort, he realized that he couldn't do them again. He couldn't live in two worlds, worshiping two gods. He would finish this Mass and that would be it. When he elevated the Host, the sacrifice he offered would be his own.

He was further unnerved by the black teenage boy in the back pew who stared at him all through Mass. Every time Andrew turned to the congregation, there he was, his eyes measuring, calculating. He didn't take part in the service at all, not even bothering to stand or kneel or pick up the prayer book, just sitting quietly and doing that damnable staring. Andrew knew the face, or thought he knew it, but couldn't place it.

After Mass, the boy was the first in line as Andrew stood at the door saying good-bye to the communicants.

"I'll wait inside for you, in the confession box, after everybody's gone," he told Andrew quietly. "I know something you want to know."

Ten minutes later, the boy was sitting in the confessional with the door open, carelessly swinging his legs as if he were sitting in the sun on the levee.

"Do you want to make your confession?" Andrew asked him.

The boy shook his head. "I got to tell you something. Something private."

"Wouldn't this be better in my office?"

"This be fine," the boy said, looking around the box. "Why don't you get in the other side?"

Feeling oddly light-headed, Andrew slipped into the priest's side of the confessional and opened the connecting panel. "Okay. Let's hear it."

"I know who you looking for," said the boy's disembodied voice, "and I know how you can get what you want."

"What makes you think I'm looking for anyone?"

The boy's voice turned impatient. "Hey, I come here to *help* you, loup-garou. So you be straight with me."

Andrew's back stiffened. His mind went completely blank and then he remembered the boy. Mother Pauline's grandson, Antoine.

"Now you listen, loup-garou, because I can't come here again. My grandma would wear me out good if she found out that I even *know* the stuff I'm about to tell you. Now, you go to St. Louis Cemetery Number One, down by the projects, you know which one that is?"

"Yes."

"Go in the evening, just before dark, and you wait. Stand by the tomb of Marie Laveau, you'll know it when you see it. Pretty soon, there'll come a woman, and you talk to her."

"And tell her what?"

The boy laughed briefly. "Loup-garou, you ain't gonna have to tell her a *thing*, believe me."

Now it was Andrew who was impatient. "Look, I appreciate you telling me this, but don't play games. If you know about me, you know I'm looking for *la Reine Blanche*. Can this woman help me find her? Who is she?"

The boy's voice grew seriously quiet. "I'll be straight with you, I don't know exactly who she is. She's a Voodoo, but she's not a Voodoo like my grandma. Pauline's a good woman with a good heart. This woman's got a heart blacker'n a swamp night. I don't know what she can tell you, but one thing's sure: Pauline don't know the things this woman knows. Grandma doesn't understand evil like this, she ain't got it in her. I only know about this woman because I hear people talk, and believe me, they don't talk loud and they don't talk much. So you go to St. Louis and you be as careful as you can be. Here, I got something for you."

The boy pushed a small red cloth bag tied with gold cord through the wide space in the confessional grille. It had a sharp, sweet scent.

"That's a conjure bag to protect you from evil. You carry it with you, especially out to the cemetery."

"Thanks, but I have a crucifix."

Antoine snorted again. "Yeah, and it gonna do you a lotta good. Look here, loup-garou, you not dealing with your sweet, do-good saints here. You smacking right up against the oldest kind of badness. So my advice to you is to take protection wherever you can get it."

Andrew held the red bag tightly in his hand. He did indeed feel some kind of protective energy radiating from it.

"I'll carry it. Thanks. But what's your stake in all this, Antoine? What do you get?"

"I get you to leave my grandma out of this whole thing. She'll put herself in a bad spot to help you, that's the kind of woman she is. And she don't know what she'd be up against; it would kill her to fight it. I feel sorry for you, loup-garou, but don't come back around again. You nothing but trouble."

"I'm sorry," Andrew said, but he'd already heard the other door close.

23

The tomb of Marie Laveau had been a shrine ever since she died. Half the old cemeteries in New Orleans claim to have the *real* tomb of the *real* Marie Laveau, but believers still come to the oldest, the one in St. Louis Number One. For decades, they've left food or gris-gris as an offering to Marie, "paying off" for favors granted, for sharing her powers even after death. To outsiders, it was simply a typical New Orleans burial: a white stone oblong rising three tiers up, tall enough to hold three coffins in its cool protection. It was in the top tier that Marie Laveau's bones lay, still commanding respect and awe after more than a century. The simple carved slab forming the top door of the tomb was marked all over with chalked crosses and arcane symbols, full of meaning for the faithful, curiosities to everyone else.

The waiting was like coarse sandpaper over Angela's nerves. She leaned her head against the cool marble slab of the tomb. There was a good-sized crack running between the edge of the slab and the wall of the tomb, where believers sometimes dropped silver coins, more offerings to Marie for her magic.

Angela slowly inclined her head to the slab, her lips close to the crack. "Marie?" she whispered, so softly that no one outside the cool darkness could hear. "Can you give me what I want? Can you lift a curse? Can you restore a lover? What can I give you, Madame Marie, if you'll do all that?" Angela put her ear to the crack.

A sigh, deep and resonant, moved inside the dark. Air currents, Angela thought, circling restlessly in the evening, whistling gently over the dreamless shapes of the dead.

Andrew drew close behind her, circling her body with his arms, his lips briefly brushing the back of her neck. "I suppose it's useless to ask you again to go home?" he said.

She covered his hand with hers. "You know it is. I'm here for the hard times, babe. I told you that."

"I just don't want to worry about you, Angela."

"Don't. Remember, I'm armed and dangerous tonight." She tried to make light of it, but the pistol loaded with silver bullets rested heavily in her pocket, the weight of it like a rattlesnake coiled against her body. It hadn't been her idea to bring it, and the only way to deal with the horrible implications of its being there at all was to joke about it.

He turned her to face him and looked seriously into her eyes. "Don't even hesitate, Angela. Don't waste a single second thinking about it."

They had covered this ground earlier, Angela's tears washing ineffectively over Andrew's stony determination. It would end for him tonight, one way or the other. If the unthinkable happened, she was to pull the trigger, then go straight home to Simon, who would be her alibi.

Angela glanced at Georgiana, sitting a few yards away on a stone bench. In just this short space of time, she had fallen under Geo's spell the same way that people had been doing since Geo was young. But the joy of life that drew people to Geo had changed over the years, and the slight touch of sadness, or perhaps just resignation, had given Geo a powerful air of mystery that mesmerized those around her. One felt that Geo had been told great truths, had discovered great secrets out of her adversity, and that she nurtured them within herself. Angela felt that Geo could solve her problems as she had solved her own, if Angela could only bring herself to ask.

And what if she had to pull the trigger twice? How could she do it? How could she lose both of them?

She rested her cheek again against the marble slab. Madame Marie, she pleaded, make everything come out all right. Use all the magic you have. She listened absentmindedly to the air currents inside the vault.

Air currents? Angela's brows furrowed a little. How can air be moving in a tomb that's been sealed for almost ninety years? There wasn't even any wind outside the tomb. Angela squinted into the crack in the slab.

A glint of silver caught the wisp of light coming from the crack. Not metallic silver. Silvery strands, almost like . . .

Angela drew back from the tomb as if she'd been slapped. "She's here!" she said hoarsely.

She spun around and looked at Andrew and Georgiana. "She's *here!*" Angela said urgently.

"Who? Where?" Andrew said in confusion.

"Blanche! She's here! In Marie Laveau's tomb. This is where the Voodoos hid her, in here, where no one would dare look!"

Georgiana froze. Andrew rushed to the tomb, running his hands over the slab.

"Look!" Angela said impatiently. "Shine that flashlight in there. You know what she looks like. Is that her?"

Andrew aimed the light beam into the crack. "I can't tell," he said, frustrated.

"Open it." Georgiana's soft voice was unnaturally calm.

"We can't do that!" Angela gasped. "You can't defile a tomb!" Even Andrew looked doubtful.

Without a word, Georgiana picked up a medium-sized bronze flower urn from one of the tombs. It was solid and heavy, but Georgiana's residual loup-garou strength allowed her to swing it effortlessly against the cracked marble.

The weakened slab shattered and settled in several pieces at their feet. Angela gasped and buried her face in Andrew's shoulder.

She was as beautiful, and as perfect, as the day she died. Blanche Pitre, against all known laws of nature, had been flawlessly preserved in Marie Laveau's tomb. Andrew pushed Angela gently away, and moved closer, his attention riveted on the body.

"I don't believe this," he told Georgiana. "Look at her! She looks exactly as I saw her that first night." He reached out tentatively and touched Blanche's cheek.

Her eyes opened. He jerked back, terrified.

Georgiana screamed, muffling the sound behind her hands. Andrew looked up from the awful sight of Blanche's staring eyes to see Geo, her own eyes fixed on a spot behind the tomb.

Just beyond the tomb rose a vague, faint cloud, dark as the clouds that run before storms, moving quickly, taking form. It changed from green to black to gray, like the veins of some insubstantial marble, a cloud that concealed.

Angela noted that the wind had risen, but failed to stir the cloud.

From the ugly swirls of it emerged a graceful hand, its long fingers seeming to part the vaporous veil. The cloud moved over the tomb, down over the body, enveloping it, then dissipating slowly, becoming absorbed into the unmoving form.

The three of them watched in dreadful fascination as the body on the slab began to move. It jerked slightly, as if unused to movement, then stretched languidly like a woman waking from a peaceful sleep. A slight moan came from the red, parted lips. Blanche's hands grasped the edge of the tomb as she pulled herself out of it, seeming to float lightly to the ground until she stood upright before the vault in which she'd slept so long.

She was as beautiful as the Marley werewolves had described her, her face perfect in its calm clarity. She looked like a woman who had lived her entire life in placid retreat. Blanche looked serenely around her, taking in the three observers and settling her open gaze on Andrew.

She smiled sweetly. "You found my body," she said. "How clever of you. And people have been searching for years and years."

Andrew couldn't move. There was an innocence about her as she stood so still, as if this woman was the complete opposite of the woman who had appeared to him on the night of his transformation, a magical fairy, good twin to the evil one that he knew. It took him totally by surprise that he was moved to compassion. She must have looked like this when she first met his great-grandfather, when she was in truth an innocent girl whose only weakness was love and who was drawn into terrible things because of it. If the Marleys had paid a high price, he realized, she must have paid a higher one.

Surely, he thought, this woman must have another side to her.

"Blanche," he said softly, as she moved slowly toward him, "please, end this. End it for me, for yourself. How can you live in this half world, not dead, not alive, never knowing the hope of heaven? This can't be what you wanted. You can still find peace."

She looked at him curiously. "My time for that has passed."

He shook his head. "Not if you truly want it. Blanche, it must be over tonight. Haven't we all paid enough, you as well as my family? I know what Stephen did to you. I know he murdered you, and that you sold your soul to come back. But I promise you it isn't too late: you may have forgotten God but he will never forget you. All you have to do is let go of all this."

"You believe that? About Stephen?" She said with a strange detachment. "You think that I suffered all this time just for my own death?"

"He did a horrible thing. I can't excuse it. But it was one life, Blanche, *one life*! He's paid for it, I assure you, in this world and the next. But how many other lives have you sacrificed? How many innocent people have died because of what you've done? You just can't continue with this! Think of your own soul, Blanche!"

Her face changed with such rapidity that he cringed away from it as if from a physical blow. Here was the Blanche he knew, her eyes overfilled with murderous intent, her face malevolent, the perfect bloom of evil.

"*One* life?" she said savagely. "Stephen Marley is responsible for more than one life, priest. You talk about the death of innocents. . . . What's the position of your loving God on killing children? Does he love and forgive murderers of the helpless?"

She leaned closer to Andrew, the fury in her face almost scorching him.

"Stephen Marley didn't just kill me, *he murdered my child*!"

Georgiana moaned softly as she realized what Blanche meant.

"With all your mind probing, you never found that out, did you?" Blanche said to Georgiana. "Stephen knew what he was doing. He knew I was pregnant: I had just told him. And he knew it was his child."

Georgiana sagged against the marble tomb, unable to look at Blanche. Andrew stood completely motionless.

"It made no difference to him, but it would have made all the difference to me. It would have changed my life. . . ." Blanche's voice was pathetically wistful. "I *know* it would have. Children change everything. But for Stephen our child was only a nightmare, an unwanted chain that would bind him to me. And he couldn't stand the thought of it." Her voice was rising again to a painful edge. "And so he killed me, and he killed our child. Stephen took away the only thing I had that was pure and good, my only chance to understand what love was. I could live again, in this 'half world' as you call it. But not my baby. That was my real sacrifice, though I didn't realize it at the time. It was the price I paid, and it was much too high."

There was only the soft sound of Georgiana sobbing against the tomb, her tears staining the old stone. Angela wanted to comfort her, but found that she couldn't move: she wasn't sure whether it was Geo who touched her more, or Blanche.

"Any children Stephen Marley had, he should have had with me! My child died, my soul died with it; any thread I could have grasped to pull myself out of that life was broken when I saw the look of horror in his eyes when I told him I was pregnant.

"But he went on with his life! He married, he had babies, he had everything he ever wanted. Why should his children lead glorious, successful, satisfying lives when my child lies still inside me, never to be born, to have no life at all? Wasn't it a Marley, the first of a new generation, the same as all of you? I couldn't give my child its life back, but I could take yours. I could make all of you feel my torture, my grief, my loss. There will never be enough Marleys to suffer enough lifetimes for what you've done to me. It will never end. Never. Not until the last of you dies in agony and guilt."

She brought her face closer to Andrew, the stench of her death-filled breath stinging him. "And I tell you, priest, you *are* the last of your line. In your heart, you know it. The only hope for you is for me to take pity on you, and you realize that will never happen. Stephen Marley took no pity on me. Or on our child."

Georgiana raised her head, her face ravaged. "I have pity for you, Blanche. You cannot imagine what I feel for you."

Blanche turned on her in rage. "*I don't want your sympathy!* I don't want your tears. I want your suffering, and your anguish. I want your *life*! What you'll never understand is how much I hate all of you, the constant resentment I bear you, that grows every minute, every year, every decade. And it will go on and on, until all of you are dead."

Her eyes turned to Andrew. "But if you want to end your family's torture, priest, I'll tell you what you can do. Kill me. Really, finally kill me. Do what Stephen couldn't finish. Do it right now and end your curse."

She touched his face lightly, her changing, persuasive voice like a light feather over his mind. "You know you can do it, priest. Haven't you been thinking of it, dreaming of it? You wake in the night longing to do it and you tell yourself in the morning that you never had such thoughts, that a priest of God could never entertain the slightest notion of murder. And yet . . . it's in your heart, constantly, the furious anger that knows no reason."

She knew by the look on his face that she was right, she had divined his secret, guilty thoughts and presented them to him as trophies. All he had to do was reach out his hand . . .

She also knew that he could never do it.

He was paralyzed by his principles, by his unwavering vows as a priest, and by the compassion in his own character.

She knew that this was his greatest strength, and she had turned it into his greatest weakness.

"You never know who'll be next, do you?" Blanche said. With a flash of movement, she grabbed Angela by the hair, and pulled her face toward her own. "For instance, this one would make a pretty loup-garou, don't you think? And what lovely children you'll have, the two of you, provided you can keep from killing them."

The suddenness and shock of the move immobilized Angela. The pain blanked out her mind for a few seconds, but when she saw the stricken look on Andrew's face, her rage overwhelmed her fear and any remnant of sympathy she might have held for Blanche. She reached up, intending to break all of Blanche's fingers, but found the hand tangled in her hair to be like tempered steel.

Blanche simply laughed.

Georgiana, who had been edging closer to Angela, Andrew, and Blanche all this time, reached quietly into Angela's pocket and withdrew the pistol.

She pointed it steadily at Blanche's brains. "Remember, Blanche," Geo said with iron calm, "the ties between a werewolf and its creator. What can kill us can kill you. Maybe nothing else can touch you, but you're exactly as vulnerable as we are to silver.

"You say you don't want my sympathy? Fine. I don't grieve for you then, Blanche, but I grieve for your child. Not just because it died, but because if it had lived you wouldn't have loved it any more than you loved Stephen. He knew that. And he knew the kind of life you would have given it, because you knew no other. He killed you both rather than see an innocent baby led down the same road you took."

Blanche stood stunned, unmoving. Then she spoke very softly, her voice turning darker and nastier. "How was it,

Georgiana?" she said with slow deliberation. "Your husband *was* beautiful to look at; was he tasty as well? Was his flesh sweet, his blood warm and strong?"

Such absolute cruelty stunned Andrew. He glanced at Georgiana and saw that though she stood firm beside him and her hand never wavered, her shaking lips and the sudden haunted look in her eyes tore at him.

Georgiana should have been a wife, a mother, should have had grandchildren who adored her and her sunny good humor; at the end of her life, surrounded by her family, she should have had the peace of God. Instead, she was forced to adapt to an unnatural life and a single, stunning memory that would torment her forever.

He thought of Walter's life and how it had been transformed into horror all at once. He thought of his own future, so bleak that he was willing to die rather than live through it. When he thought of all these things, his rage swept him away on an uncontrollable cataract of unreasoning fury.

He stepped back and lifted his face to the half-moon. For the first time, he appreciated the power of it, the serenity of acceptance. A half-moon, he thought, my own sign, half-man, half-beast. But can I make of myself a perfect whole? Everything Achille and the loups-garous taught him on Bayou Goula returned to him, and now made sense. The kill was for justice, the kind of justice that man can never know, that only the gods can bestow. Justice belonged to the gods, and the loup-garou was their instrument.

He heard Achille's words: Listen to your body, listen to your soul.

He opened his mind then, concentrating on nothing, only on what the moon had to tell him. Hecate, he thought, goddess of justice, of the dark of the moon, mother of werewolves. Take me. I want it, I accept it. Aren't I one of your own children? Make me your lover.

The moon grew brighter, larger, spilling a single silver beam around him like a crystal cocoon, within which he would transform not only in body, but this time in soul.

When the transformation began, it was not like before. He hardly realized the change in his body but for the waves of contentment and power flowing through it. He knew that he was about to do what he was meant to do, a fulfillment of the judgment of a higher power than himself, and as he changed, he welcomed the sensations almost as a religious revelation. It coiled around him, satin tipped with steel, the edge of pain blunted by the sensual pleasure of it. The final moment of transformation burst over him in a long, seemingly endless spasm of sexual power. This was what Achille had, what all the loups-garous had, and why they cherished it. Not simply for the physical sensations, but for the absolute correctness of it, the firm sense of purpose. Never in his life had he been so sure that what he was about to do was right.

Fully transformed, but still half in his dream state, he purposefully reached for Blanche, knocking Angela firmly but gently aside. Blanche's long, enraged scream trailed like a banshee wail upward in the night air. She clawed and hammered him, she tried to gouge his eyes. She fought him with the accumulated strength of evil, the strength that flows from a source not within the soul of man, but from the soul of hell.

For the first time, the contest was equal for the werewolf, the stakes high, the outcome uncertain. But his sense of purpose, his sure knowledge that it wasn't simply his own will guiding him, stood him firmly and powerfully.

Blanche clung to his body, her hand clawing his hair, her teeth tearing at the flesh of his throat. From inside himself he drew a great burst of strength. Crying "No more!" he shook her off. She landed on her feet, only yards separating them. She looked into his eyes, and what she saw there terrified her. He took a deep breath, and with one purposeful sweep of his arm and outstretched claws, he decapitated her.

Blanche's head rolled on to her shoulders, tumbled down over her breasts, fell at the feet of her still-standing body. Her blood fountained into the air and turned to jeweled dust; her body fell, then withered, dried, the flesh falling away, turning to dust, catching flight on Hecate's wind to leave only the bones like hard ivory reeds, dropping to stillness on the evening grass.

He saw Angela, her face buried against Georgiana's, encircled in Geo's nurturing embrace; and he saw Georgiana, her own face reflecting cold joy in his triumph.

And then the agony took him, so unexpectedly that even his mind was stunned into silence. As he had done so many times, he dropped to his knees, mastered by pain, but this time unable to comprehend what was happening to him. He had accepted the power, he had taken it, had put aside his conscience and done what had to be done. Now, why the pain? Why the sudden reversal and the sense of overwhelming, impending loss?

He was surprised at his own tears, even more surprised to hear the voice that seemed to come from the very night itself: pure, lyrical, and not to be questioned. "Hecate," he whispered.

"Not for you, Andrew," she told him. "My children love me of their own free will. You made your choice from desperation; you are not mine to keep. But remember that you will always be mine to love, and I will protect you. Return to your God, Andrew, and be happy and fruitful in this life."

He knew that by accepting the power, he was relinquishing it, that Hecate had given it to him only temporarily to do what must be done to serve justice. But it was exactly as Achille had told him: he would remember the power, the knowledge of pure justice, the strength of righteous anger. He would long for it, his body would burn for what he had given up. And though he had been given his freedom, it would never make up for the bonds of brotherhood.

Crouched in the grass, on his knees, he cried exactly as he had cried the night of his first transformation; he still grieved for what he had lost, but what was lost was not the same.

Georgiana and Angela knelt beside him, both quietly waiting for his despair to pass. Georgiana reached out softly to stroke his hair.

Her touch seemed to bring him back to them. He lifted his head and took her hand. "We're free, Georgiana," he said. "We can start our lives over."

But Georgiana shook her head ruefully. "I was always free, Andrew. I made my own freedom when I accepted the gift of the moon. I accepted it wholeheartedly and without question, at a point in my life where I had thought I'd lost everything. When I felt the moon take me, as you did tonight, the curse ceased to be a curse. It became a blessing. The loup-garou's life isn't what I planned so long ago, but it's become the most fulfilling life for me.

"I'm happy for you, Andrew," she said, "and I love you. I think that what I needed most of all, and why I was brought back here, was to heal my life, to be reconciled with my family and mend those broken ties. I have close friends in New England, all werewolves, all dedicated to Hecate, and I love them. But it's not the same as these ties of family. I have a life in Boston, and a lover in Rome whom I see often enough. And now that I have you and Angela, I have my family back, too."

Shaken and bruised, whole people again with whole lives, they left the cemetery. They never once glanced back at the sad remains of *la Reine Blanche*, now no more than a memory shifting in changing winds.

*   *   *

The cemetery was quiet after they left. A boy, just on the edge of ambitious manhood, crept from behind the tombs where he had concealed himself all this time. He stared, slightly frightened but determined, at the bones of *la Reine Blanche*. Reverently, he touched the shimmering dust. It seemed to leap at his fingers all on its own power, sticking to his skin as if recalling its own recent life.

Something caught his eye among the few delicate bones, something shiny and dark. He leaned closer. It was a lump of blackest obsidian, a stone born in flames, shining there in the dust and bones as if lit from within.

It was exactly the size and shape of a small woman's heart.

He stared into the depths, afraid to touch it. It glowed with the fire of life, and of unimaginable power.

Something told him to take it, a voice that seemed to come from all directions, yet from the inmost parts of his mind.

He knew that voice.

He gathered a few of the bones, a pocketful of the glittering dust, and hid the black obsidian heart next to his own pounding one.

It would be his alone, his own special secret. He vowed never to tell anyone that he had it, not even his grandmother.

Epilogue

Andrew Stephen Marley

And so I broke the Marley curse and became a free man. I married Angela in the full majesty and binding power of the Church, but as we looked at each other before the altar, about to say our vows, we knew that our real bond had been forged in that graveyard in a night of murder and blood, and of invincible trust.

When I looked into the face of my daughter, my newly born first child, I saw no trace of the Marley stain, no taint of madness to mar what was going to be as perfect a life as I could give her.

As for my own life, it has been as I pictured it so long ago, when I was twenty-two and arrogant in my sureness of the future. I say Mass, I watch Angela, pregnant for the second time, in the front pew shushing our daughter, I'm surrounded by loving parishioners after Mass and adoring little children in Sunday school.

Georgiana returned to her home in Boston after a tryst with her mysterious lover in Rome, about whom she never speaks. We still see her at Christmas and other times, just like a normal family, although we've had to explain to other family members that she's a distant blood relation. Simon fell in love with her, and sometimes travels to Boston to be with her, but knowing what her life is like when he isn't there is a torment for him. He tries not to think about what she does under the moon. I think that Georgiana is finally happy, in her way, and that her affection for my children will atone a little for the children she was—and still is, I'm afraid—too terrified to have. I wish that Georgiana would marry again and finally lay the ghost of her first husband to rest, but it just seems impossible for her.

My life is solid, settled. I'm content with it.

But still that dark goddess haunts me.

Not of her doing but of mine, she comes to me on soft, fragrant nights when the moon is full. And I become sure, as my ears strain to listen, that I can hear the voices of the loups-garous on Bayou Goula, and especially one voice; remember one pair of deep amber eyes, one sheen of gold hair as Zizi bent to touch me and opened the most closed compartment of my heart.

Although I've never done it again, I can still feel the sting of the tears I cried in the cemetery, when I felt the dark goddess, my lover, my eternal heart, retreat back into the night, as her generosity of returning me to myself tore away part of my soul.

Achille was right. The kiss of the moon will stay with me forever.

THE WEREWOLF'S KISS

THE VOODOO MOON TRILOGY
Book 1

by Cheri Scotch
ISBN: 0-7434-7455-4

The world of the Louisiana werewolves... Sensual and seductive, it holds secrets that only the initiated may share. Sylvie Marley is drawn to the moonlit bayous, to her lover, Lucien, and to a choice between the debutante's life she knows and the werewolf's life she craves.

But for Sylvie there is a hidden danger: A madman must have her power—the power she is unaware she possesses—to satisfy his desire, to make himself King of the Voodoos. All he needs is Sylvie's total surrender—and one act of ritual murder....

"Draws the reader seductively into its embrace... Keep your eye on Cheri Scotch...the new reigning queen of chilling, erotic horror."—**Ray Garton**, author of *Dark Channel*

COMING JANUARY 2004

THE
WEREWOLF'S SIN

THE VOODOO MOON TRILOGY
Book 3

by Cheri Scotch
ISBN: 0-7434-7981-5

THE CONCLUSION OF
THE "VOODOO MOON TRILOGY"!

Sylvie Drago surrendered to a secret and sensual world no mortal woman could imagine. With her faithful lover Lucien, she discovered the beautiful, haunted world of the werewolf—a timeless realm of passion hidden in the shadows of the Louisiana bayou...

But the promise of eternal desire has been broken. Lycaon, the first werewolf, has returned from the past to control the loup-garous' destiny...a centuries-old evil that reaches out to possess their fold. Only the power of undying love can stop it. But when the full moon rises, it will be too late....